Casanova's Chinese Restaurant

ANTHONY POWELL was born in London in 1905. Son of a soldier, he comes from a family of mostly soldiers or sailors which moved from Wales about a hundred and fifty years ago. He was educated at Eton and Balliol College, Oxford, of which he is now an Honorary Fellow.

From 1926 he worked for about nine years at Duckworths, the publishers, then as scriptwriter for Warner Brothers in England. During the Second World War he served in the Welch Regiment and Intelligence Corps, acting as liaison officer with the Polish, Belgian, Czechoslovak, Free French and Luxembourg forces, and was promoted major.

Before and after the war he wrote reviews and literary columns for various newspapers, including the *Daily Telegraph* and the *Spectator*. From 1948–52 he worked on the *Times Literary Supplement*, and was literary editor of *Punch*, 1952–8.

Between 1931 and 1949, Anthony Powell published five novels, a biography, *John Aubrey and His Friends*, and a selection from Aubrey's works. The first volume of his twelve-volume novel, *A Dance to the Music of Time*, was published in 1951, and the concluding volume, *Hearing Secret Harmonies*, appeared in 1975. In 1976 he published the first volume of his memoirs, *To Keep the Ball Rolling*, under the title *Infants of the Spring*.

In 1934 he married Lady Violet Pakenham, daughter of the fifth Earl of Longford. They have two sons, and live in Somerset.

Anthony Powell was made a Companion of Honour in 1988.

Books by Anthony Powell

Novels
Afternoon Men
Venusberg
From a View to a Death
Agents and Patients
What's Become of Waring

A Dance to the Music of Time
A Question of Upbringing
A Buyer's Market
The Acceptance World
At Lady Molly's
Casanova's Chinese Restaurant
The Kindly Ones
The Valley of Bones
The Soldier's Art
The Military Philosophers
Books Do Furnish a Room
Temporary Kings
Hearing Secret Harmonies

To Keep the Ball Rolling (Memoirs)
Volume I: Infants of the Spring

General
John Aubrey and His Friends

Plays
The Garden God *and* The Rest I'll Whistle

Anthony Powell

Casanova's Chinese Restaurant

A Novel

Flamingo
Published by Fontana Paperbacks
by agreement with Heinemann

First published by
William Heinemann Ltd 1960
First issued in Fontana Paperbacks 1970
Eighth impression March 1983

This Flamingo edition first published
in 1984 by Fontana Paperbacks,
8 Grafton Street, London W1X 3LA
Third impression June 1988

Flamingo is an imprint of
Fontana Paperbacks, a division of
the Collins Publishing Group

Printed and bound in Great Britain by
William Collins Sons & Co. Ltd, Glasgow

for Harry and Rosie

ONE

Crossing the road by the bombed-out public house on the corner and pondering the mystery which dominates vistas framed by a ruined door, I felt for some reason glad the place had not yet been rebuilt. A direct hit had excised even the ground floor, so that the basement was revealed as a sunken garden or site of archæological excavation long abandoned, where great sprays of willow herb and ragwort flowered through cracked paving stones; only a few broken milk bottles and a laceless boot recalling contemporary life. In the midst of this sombre grotto five or six fractured steps had withstood the explosion and formed a projecting island of masonry on the summit of which rose the door. Walls on both sides were shrunk away, but along its lintel, in niggling copybook handwriting, could still be distinguished the word *Ladies*. Beyond, on the far side of the twin pillars and crossbar, nothing whatever remained of that promised retreat, the threshold falling steeply to an abyss of rubble; a triumphal arch erected laboriously by dwarfs, or the gateway to some unknown, forbidden domain, the lair of sorcerers.

Then, all at once, as if such luxurious fantasy were not already enough, there came from this unexplored country the song, strong and marvellously sweet, of the blonde woman on crutches, that itinerant prima donna of the highways whose voice I had not heard since the day, years before, when Moreland and I had listened in Gerrard Street, the afternoon he had talked of getting married; when we had bought the bottle labelled *Tawny Wine* (*port flavour*) which even Moreland had been later unwilling to drink. Now once more above the rustle of traffic that same note swelled on the grimy air, contriving a transformation scene to recast those purlieus into the vision of an oriental

7

dreamland, artificial, if you like, but still quite alluring under the shifting clouds of a cheerless Soho sky.

'Pale hands I loved beside the Shalimar,
Where are you now? Who lies beneath your spell?'

In the end most things in life—perhaps all things—turn out to be appropriate. So it was now, for here before me lay the vestigial remains of the Mortimer where we had first met, the pub in which our friendship had begun. As an accompaniment to Moreland's memory music was natural, even imperative, but the repetition of a vocal performance so stupendously apt was scarcely to be foreseen. A floorless angle of the wall to which a few lumps of plaster and strips of embossed paper still adhered was all that remained of the alcove where we had sat, a recess which also enclosed the mechanical piano into which, periodically, Moreland would feed a penny to invoke one of those fortissimo tunes belonging to much the same period as the blonde singer's repertoire. She was closer now, herself hardly at all altered by the processes of time—perhaps a shade plumper—working her way down the middle of the empty street, until, framed within the rectangle of the doorway, she seemed to be gliding along under the instrumentality of some occult power and about to sail effortlessly through its enchanted portal:

'Pale hands, pink-tipped, like lotus buds that float
On those cool waters where we used to dwell . . .'

Moreland and I had afterwards discussed the whereabouts of the Shalimar, and why the locality should have been the haunt of pale hands and those addicted to them.
'A nightclub, do you think?' Moreland had said. 'A bordel, perhaps. Certainly an establishment catering for exotic tastes—and I expect not very healthy ones either. How I wish there were somewhere like that where we

could spend the afternoon. That woman's singing has unsettled me. What nostalgia. It was really splendid. "Whom do you lead on Rapture's roadway far?" What a pertinent question. But where can we go? I feel I must be amused. Do have a brilliant idea. I am in the depths of gloom to be precise. Let's live for the moment.'

'Tea at Casanova's Chinese Restaurant? That would be suitably oriental after the song.'

'What do you think? I haven't been there for ages. It wasn't very exciting on my last visit. Besides, I never felt quite the same about Casanova's after that business of Barnby and the waitress. It would be cheaper to drink tea at home—and no less Chinese as I have a packet of Lapsang.'

'As you like.'

'But why did they dwell *on* the cool waters? I can't understand the preposition. Were they in a boat?'

A habit of Moreland's was to persist eternally with any subject that caught his fancy, a characteristic to intensify in him resolute approach to a few things after jettisoning most outward forms of seriousness; a love of repetition sometimes fatiguing to friends, when Moreland would return unmercifully to some trivial matter less amusing to others than to himself.

'Do you think they *were* in a boat?' he went on. 'The poem is called a Kashmiri Love Song. My aunt used to sing it. Houseboats are a feature of Kashmir, aren't they?'

'Kipling characters go up there to spend their leave.'

'When we lived in Fulham my aunt used to sing that song to the accompaniment of the pianoforte.'

He paused in the street and offered there and then a version of the piece as loudly trilled by his aunt, interrupting himself once or twice to emphasise contrast with the rendering we had just heard. Moreland's parents had died when he was a child. This aunt, who played a large part in his personal mythology, had brought him up. Oppressed, no doubt, by her nephew's poor health and by thought of the tubercular complaint that had killed his

9

father (who had some name as a teacher of music), she was said to have 'spoiled' Moreland dreadfully. There were undeniable signs of something of the sort. She had probably been awed, too, by juvenile brilliance; for although Moreland had never been, like Carolo, an infant prodigy —that freakish, rather uncomfortable humour of only musical genius—he showed alarming promise as a boy. The aunt was also married to a musician, a man considerably older than herself whose generally impecunious circumstances had not prevented shadowy connexions with a more sublime world than that in which most of his daily life was spent. He had heard Wagner conduct at the Albert Hall; Liszt play at the Crystal Palace, seen the Abbé's black habit and shock of iron-grey hair pass through Sydenham; drunk a glass of wine with Tchaikovsky at Cambridge when the Russian composer had come to receive an honorary degree. These peaks are not to be exaggerated. Moreland had been brought up impecuniously too, but in a tradition of hearing famous men discussed on familiar terms; not merely prodigies read of in books, but also persons having to knock about the world like everyone else. The heredity was not unlike Barnby's, with music taking the place of the graphic arts.

'Perhaps this was a houseboat of ill fame.'

'What an enjoyable idea,' Moreland said. 'At the rapturous moments referred to in the lyric one would hear the water, if I may be so nautical, lapping beneath the keel. An overwhelming desire for something of the sort besets me this afternoon. Active emotional employment—like chasing an attractive person round some wet laurels.'

'Out of the question, I'm afraid.'

'What a pity London has not got a Luna Park. I should like to ride on merry-go-rounds and see freaks. Do you remember when we went on the Ghost Railway—when you dash towards closed doors and tear down hill towards a body across the line?'

In the end we decided against Casanova's Chinese Restaurant that day, instead experimenting, as I have said, with the adventitious vintages of Shaftesbury Avenue, a thoroughfare traversed on the way to Moreland's flat, which lay in an undistinguished alley on the far side of Oxford Street, within range of Mr Deacon's antique shop. Once there, after climbing an interminable staircase, you found an unexpectedly neat room. Unconformist, without discipline in many ways, Moreland had his precise, tidy side, instilled in him perhaps by his aunt; mirrored—so Maclintick used to say—in his musical technique. The walls were hung with framed caricatures of dancers in Diaghilev's early ballets, coloured pictures drawn by the Legat brothers, found by Moreland in a portfolio outside a second-hand book shop; Pavlova; Karsavina; Fokine; others, too, whom I have forgotten. The few books in a small bookcase by the bed included a tattered paper edition of Apollinaire's *Alcools*; one of the Sherlock Holmes volumes; Grinling's *History of the Great Northern Railway*. An upright piano stood against one wall, although Moreland, so he always insisted, was no great performer on that instrument. There were always flowers in the vase on the table when Moreland could afford them, which in those days was not often.

'Do you mind drinking wine from teacups, one of them short of a handle? Rather sordid, I'm afraid. I managed to break my three glasses the other night when I came home from a party and was trying to put them away so that the place might look more habitable when I woke up in the morning.'

Following a preliminary tasting, we poured the residue of the bottle down the lavatory.

'If you were legally allowed three wives,' asked Moreland, as we watched the cascade of amber foam gush noisily away, 'whom would you choose?'

Those were the days when I loved Jean Duport. Moreland knew nothing of her, nor did I propose to tell him. Instead, I offered three names from the group of female acquaintances we enjoyed in common, speaking without undue concern in making this triple decision. To tell the truth, in spite of what I felt for Jean, marriage, although looming up on all sides, still seemed a desperate venture to be postponed almost indefinitely.

'And you?'

Moreland possessed that quality, rather rare among men, of not divulging names. At the same time, the secretiveness he employed where his own love affairs were concerned was not without an element of exhibitionism. He was always willing to arouse a little unsatisfied curiosity.

'I am going to marry,' said Moreland, 'I have decided that. To make up my mind is always a rare thing with me, but the moment for decision has arrived. Otherwise I shall become just another of those depressed and depressing intellectual figures who wander from party to party, finding increasing difficulty in getting off with anyone—and in due course suspected of auto-erotic habits. Besides, Nietzsche advocates living dangerously.'

'If you have decided to base your life on the philosophy of writers of that period, Strindberg considered even the worst marriage better than no marriage at all.'

'And Strindberg earned the right to speak on that subject. As you probably know, his second wife kept a night-club, within living memory, not a thousand miles from this very spot. Maclintick, of all people, was once taken there.'

'But you haven't told me who your wife—your three wives —will be.'

'There is only one really. I don't know whether she will accept me.'

'Oh, come. You are talking like a Victorian novel.'

'I will tell you when we next meet.'

'This is intolerable after I offered my names.'

'But I am serious.'

I dismissed the notion that Moreland could be contemplating marriage with the heroine of a recent story of Barnby's about one of Mr Cochran's Young Ladies.

'Moreland pawned the gold cigarette case Sir Magnus

Donners gave him after writing the music for that film,' Barnby had said, 'just in order to stand her dinner at the Savoy. The girl had a headache that night—curse, too, I expect—and most of the money went on taking her back to Golders Green in a taxi.'

Even if that story were untrue, the toughness of Moreland's innate romanticism in matters of the heart certainly remained unimpaired by gravitating from one hopeless love affair to another. That fact had become clear after knowing him for even a few months. Wit, shrewdness about other aspects of life, grasp of the arts, fundamental good nature, none seemed any help in solving his emotional problems; to some extent these qualities, as displayed by him, were even a hindrance. Women found him amusing, were intrigued by his unusual appearance and untidy clothes, heard that he was brilliant, so naturally he had his 'successes'; but these, on the whole, were ladies with too desperate an enthusiasm for music. Moreland did not care for that. He liked wider horizons. His delicacy in coping with such eventualities need not be exaggerated. Undoubtedly, he allowed himself reasonable latitude with girls of that sort. Even so, the fact remained that, although fully aware of the existence, the greater effectiveness, of an attitude quite contrary to his own, he remained a hopeless addict of what he used to call, in the phrase of the day, a *princesse lointaine* complex'. This approach naturally involved him in falling in love with women connected in one way or another with the theatre.

'It doesn't matter whether it is the Leading Lady or Second Slave,' he said, 'I myself am always cast as a stage-door johnny of thirty or forty years back. As a matter of fact the hours I have to keep in my profession compel association with girls who have to stay up late—by which I do not necessarily mean tarts.'

All this was very alien to Barnby, himself enjoying to such a high degree the uncomplicated, direct powers of attack that often accompany a gift for painting or sculpture.

13

'Barnby never has to be in the mood to work,' Moreland used to say. 'The amount of material he can get through is proportionate to the hour he rises in the morning. In much the same way, if he sees a girl he likes, all he has to do is to ask her to sleep with him. Some do, some don't, it is one to him.'

Barnby would not in the least have endorsed this picture of himself. His own version was that of a man chronically overburdened, absolutely borne down by sensitive emotional stresses. All the same, in contrasting the two of them, there was something to be said for Moreland's over-simplification. Their different methods were, as it happened, displayed in high relief on the occasion of my first meeting with Moreland.

The Mortimer (now rebuilt in a displeasingly fashionable style and crowded with second-hand-car salesmen) was even in those days regarded by the enlightened as a haunt of 'bores'; but, although the beer was indifferent and the saloon bar draughty, a sprinkling of those connected with the arts, especially musicians, was usually to be found there. The chief charm of the Mortimer for Moreland, who at that time rather prided himself on living largely outside that professionally musical world which, towards the end of his life, so completely engulfed him, was provided by the mechanical piano. The clientèle was anathema; this Moreland always conceded, using that very phrase, a favourite one of his.

For my own part, I never cared for the place either. I had been introduced there by Barnby (met for the first time only a few weeks before) who was coming on to the Mortimer that evening after consultation with a frame-maker who lived in the neighbourhood. Barnby was preparing for a show in the near future. Those were the days when his studio was above Mr Deacon's antique shop; when he was pursuing Baby Wentworth and about to paint those murals for the Donners-Brebner Building, which were destroyed, like the Mortimer, by a bomb during the war. I had recently returned, I remember, from staying in the country with the Walpole-Wilsons. It must, indeed, have been only a week before Mr Deacon injured himself fatally by slipping on the stair at the Bronze Monkey (disqualified as licensed premises the same month as the result of a police raid), and died in hospital some days later, much regretted by the many elements—some of them less than tolerable—who made his antique shop their regular port of call.

It was pouring with rain that night and the weather had turned much colder. Barnby had not yet arrived when I came into the bar, which was emptier than usual. Two or three elderly women dressed in black, probably landladies off duty, were drinking Guinness and grumbling in one corner. In the other, where the mechanical piano was situated, sat Mr Deacon himself, hatless as usual, his whitening hair hanging lankly over a woollen muffler, the coarse mesh of which he might himself have knitted. His regular autumn exhalation of eucalyptus, or some other specific against the common cold (to which Mr Deacon was greatly subject), hung over that end of the room. He was always preoccupied with his health and the Mortimer's temperature was too low for comfort. His long, arthritic fingers curled round half a pint of bitter, making an irregular mould or beading about the glass, recalling a medieval receptacle for setting at rest a drinking horn. The sight of Mr Deacon always made me think of the Middle Ages because of his resemblance to a pilgrim, a mildly sinister pilgrim, with more than a streak of madness in him, but then in every epoch a proportion of pilgrims must have been sinister, some mad as well. I was rather snobbishly glad that the streets had been too wet for his sandals. Instead, his feet were encased in dark blue felt snowboots against the puddles. That evening Barnby and I had planned to see a von Stroheim revival —was it *Foolish Wives*? Possibly Barnby had suggested that Mr Deacon should accompany us to the cinema, although as a rule he could be induced to sit through only Soviet films, and those for purely ideological reasons. Mr Deacon was in the best of form that night. He was surrounded by a group of persons none of whom I knew.

'Good evening, Nicholas,' he said, in his deep, deep, consciously melodious voice, which for some reason always made me feel a trifle uneasy, 'what brings you to this humble hostelry? I thought you frequented marble halls.'

'I am meeting Ralph here. We are going to a film. Neither of us had an invitation to a marble hall tonight.'

'The cinema?' said Mr Deacon, with great contempt. 'I am astonished you young men can waste your time in the cinema. Have you nothing else to do with yourselves? I should have thought better of Barnby. Why, I'd as soon visit the Royal Academy. Sooner, in fact. There would be the chance of a good laugh there.'

Although it was by then many years since he had set brush to canvas, and in spite of his equal disdain for all manifestations of 'modern art', Mr Deacon never tired of expressing contempt for Academicians and their works.

'Are cinemas worse than haunting taverns on your part?'

'A just rebuke,' said Mr Deacon, delighted at this duplication of his own sententious tone, 'infinitely just. But, you see, I have come here to transact a little business. Not only to meet *les jeunes*. True, I would much rather be forwarding the cause of international disarmament tonight by selling *War Never Pays!* outside the Albert Hall, but we must all earn our bread and butter. My poor little broadsheet would bring in nothing to me personally. Just a penny for a noble cause. For my goods I have to make a charge. You seem to forget, Nicholas, that I am just a poor *antiquaire* these days.'

Mr Deacon spoke this last sentence rather unctuously. Inclined to mark his prices high, he was thought to make at least a respectable livelihood from his wares. The fact that a certain air of transgression still attached to his past added attraction in the eyes of some customers. It was a long time since the days when, as an artist of independent means living at Brighton, he had been acquainted with my

16

parents; days before that unfortunate incident in Battersea Park had led to Mr Deacon's prolonged residence abroad. A congenital taste for Greco-Roman themes, which had once found expression in his own paintings, now took the form of a pronounced weakness for buying up statuettes and medallions depicting gods and heroes of classical times. These objects, not always easily saleable, cluttered the shop, the fashion for such ornaments as an adjunct to Empire or Regency furniture having by then scarcely begun. Occasionally he would find on his hands some work of art too pagan in its acceptance of sexual licence to be openly displayed. Such dubious items were kept, according to Barnby, in a box under Mr Deacon's bed. In the underworld through which he now moved, business and pleasure, art and politics, life—as it turned out finally—death itself, all had become a shade disreputable where Mr Deacon was concerned. However, even in these morally reduced circumstances, he preferred to regard himself as not wholly cut off from a loftier society. He still, for example, enjoyed such triumphal contacts as the afternoon when Lady Huntercombe (wearing one of her Mrs Siddons hats) had arrived unexpectedly on his doorstep; after an hour bearing away with her an inlaid tea-caddy in Tunbridge-ware, for which, in spite of creditable haggling on her own part, she had been made to pay almost as much as if purchased in Bond Street. She had promised to return—in a phrase Mr Deacon loved to repeat—'When my ship comes in.'

'Ridiculous woman,' he used to say delightedly, 'as if we did not all know that the Huntercombes are as rich as Crœsus.'

One of the persons surrounding Mr Deacon at the table in the Mortimer, a young man muffled to the ears in a manner which gave him the appearance of a taxi-driver wearing several overcoats, now broke off the energetic conversation he had been carrying on with his neighbour, a fattish person in gold-rimmed spectacles, and tapped Mr Deacon lightly on the arm with a rolled-up newspaper.

'I should certainly not go near the Albert Hall if I were you, Edgar,' he said. 'It would be too great a risk. Someone might seize you and compel you to listen to Brahms. In fact, after the way you have been talking this evening, you would probably yield to temptation and enter of your own free will. I would not trust you an inch where Brahms is concerned, Edgar. Not an inch.'

Letting go his glass, Mr Deacon lifted a gnarled hand dramatically, at the same time crooking one of his heavily jointed fingers.

'Moreland,' he said, 'I wish to hear no more of your youthful prejudices—certainly no more of your sentiments regarding the orchestration of the Second Piano Concerto.'

The young man began to laugh derisively. Although giving this impression of wearing several overcoats, he was in fact dressed only in one, a threadbare, badly stained garment, from the pockets of which protruded several more newspapers in addition to that with which he had demanded Mr Deacon's attention.

'As I was remarking, Nicholas,' said Mr Deacon, turning once more in my own direction and giving at the same time a smile to express tolerance for youthful extremism of whatever colour, 'I have come to this gin palace primarily to inspect an object of virtu—a classical group in some unspecified material, to be precise. I shall buy it, if its beauty satisfies me. *Truth Unveiled by Time*—in the Villa Borghese, you remember. I must say in the original marble Bernini has made the wench look as unpalatable as the heartless quality she represents. A reproduction of this work was found at the Caledonian Market by a young person with whom I possess a slight acquaintance. He thought I might profitably dispose of same on his behalf.'

'I hope the young person is an object of virtue himself,' said Moreland. 'I presume the sex is masculine. We don't want anything in the nature of Youth, rather than Truth, being unveiled by Time. Can we trust you, Edgar?'

Mr Deacon gave one of his deep, rather stagy chuckles. He lightly twitched his shoulders.

'Nothing could be more proper than my relationship with this young gentleman,' he said. 'I met his mother in the summer when we were both reinvigorating ourselves at the same vegetarian communal holiday—she, I think, primarily as a measure of economy rather than on account of any deeply felt anti-carnivorous convictions on her own part. A most agreeable, sensible woman I found her, quite devoted to her boy. She reminded me in some ways of my own dear Mama, laid to rest in Kensal Green this many a long year. Her lad turned up to meet her at Paddington when we travelled back together. That was how he and I first came to know one another. Does that satisfy your rapacious taste for scandal, Moreland? I hope so.'

Mr Deacon spoke archly, rather than angrily. It was clear from his manner that he liked, even admired Moreland, from whom he seemed prepared to accept more teasing than he would ever have allowed to most of his circle.

'Anyway, the lad was not here when I arrived,' he went on, briskly turning once more towards myself, 'so I joined this little party of music-makers sitting by their desolate stream. I have been having some musical differences with Moreland here who becomes very dictatorial about his subject. I expect you know each other already. What? No? Then I must introduce you. This is Mr Jenkins—Mr Moreland, Mr Gossage, Mr Maclintick, Mr Carolo.'

The revolutionary bent of his political opinions had never modified the formality of Mr Deacon's manners. His companions, on the other hand, with the exception of Gossage who gave a smirk, displayed no outward mark of conventional politeness. In fact none of the rest of them showed the smallest wish to meet anyone outside their own apparently charmed circle. All the same, I immediately liked something about Hugh Moreland. Although I had never seen him in Mr Deacon's shop, nor in Barnby's studio, I knew of him already as a figure of some standing in the musical world: composer: conductor: pianist: I was uncertain of his precise activities. Barnby, talking about Moreland, had spoken of incidental music for a semi-private venture (a film version of *Lysistrata* made in France) which Sir Magnus Donners had backed. Since music holds for me none of that hard, cold-blooded, almost mathematical pleasure I take in writing and painting, I could only guess roughly where Moreland's work—enthusiastically received in some circles, heartily disliked in others—stood in relation to the other arts. In those days I had met no professional musicians. Later, when I ran across plenty of these through Moreland himself, I began to notice their special peculiarities, moral and physical. Several representative musical types were present, as it happened, that evening in addition to Moreland himself, Maclintick and Gossage being music critics, Carolo a violinist.

Only since knowing Barnby had I begun to frequent such society as was collected that night in the Mortimer, which, although it soon enough absorbed me, still at that time represented a world of high adventure. The hiatus between coming down from the university and finding a place for myself in London had comprised, with some bright spots, an eternity of boredom. I used to go out with unexciting former undergraduate acquaintances like Short (now a civil servant), less often with more dashing, if by then more remote, people like Peter Templer. Another friend, Charles Stringham, had recently risen from the earth to take me to Mrs Andriadis's party, only to disappear again; but that night had nevertheless opened the road that led ultimately to the Mortimer: as Mr Deacon used to say of Barnby's social activities, 'the pilgrimage from the sawdust floor to the Aubusson carpet and back again'. At the time, of course, none of this took shape in my mind; no pattern was apparent of the kind eventually to emerge.

Moreland, like myself, was then in his early twenties. He was formed physically in a 'musical' mould, classical in type, with a massive, Beethoven-shaped head, high fore-head, temples swelling outwards, eyes and nose somehow bunched together in a way to make him glare at times like a High Court judge about to pass sentence. On the other hand, his short, dark, curly hair recalled a dissipated cherub, a less aggressive, more intellectual version of Folly in Bronzino's picture, rubicund and mischievous, as he threatens with a fusillade of rose petals the embrace of Venus and Cupid; while Time in the background, whis-kered like the Emperor Franz-Josef, looms behind a blue curtain as if evasively vacating the bathroom. Moreland's face in repose, in spite of this cherubic, humorous char-acter, was not without melancholy too; his flush suggesting none of that riotously healthy physique enjoyed by Bron-zino's—and, I suppose, everyone else's—Folly. Moreland had at first taken little notice of Mr Deacon's introduction; now he suddenly caught my eye, and, laughing loudly, slapped the folded newspaper sharply on the table.

'Tell us more about your young friend, Edgar,' he said, still laughing and looking across at me. 'What does he do for a living? Are we to understand that he wholly supports himself by finding junk at the Caledonian Market and vending it to connoisseurs of beauty like yourself?'

'He has stage connexions, Moreland, since you are so inquisitive,' said Mr Deacon, still speaking with accen-tuated primness. 'He was trained to dance—as he quaintily puts it—"in panto". Drury Lane was the peg upon which he hung his dreams. Now he dares to nourish wider ambi-tions. I am told, by the way, that the good old-fashioned harlequinade which I used so much to enjoy as a small boy has become a thing of the past. This lad would have made a charming Harlequin. Another theatrical friend of mine—rather a naughty young man—knows this child and thinks highly of his talent.'

'Why is your other friend naughty?'

'You ask too many questions, Moreland.'

'But I am intrigued to know, Edgar. We all are.'

'I call him naughty for many reasons,' said Mr Deacon, giving a long-drawn sigh, 'not the least of them because some years ago at a party he introduced me to an Italian, a youth whose sole claim to distinction was his alleged profession of gondolier, who turned out merely to have worked for a short time as ticket-collector on the *vaporetto*. A delightfully witty pleasantry, no doubt.'

There was some laughter at this anecdote, in which Maclintick did not join. Indeed, Maclintick had been listening to the course of conversation with unconcealed distaste. It was clear that he approved neither of Mr Deacon himself, nor of the suggestions implicit in Moreland's badinage. Like Moreland, Maclintick belonged to the solidly built musical type, a physical heaviness already threatening obesity in early middle age. Broad-shouldered, yet somehow narrowing towards his lower extremities, his frontal elevation gave the impression of a large triangular kite about to float away into the sky upon the fumes of Irish whiskey, which, even above the endemic odours of the Mortimer and the superimposed insistence of Mr Deacon's eucalyptus, freely emanated from the quarter in which he sat. Maclintick's calculatedly humdrum appearance, although shabby, seemed aimed at concealing bohemian affiliations. The minute circular lenses of his gold-rimmed spectacles, set across the nose of a pug dog, made one think of caricatures of Thackeray or President Thiers, imposing upon him the air of a bad-tempered doctor. Maclintick, as I discovered in due course, was indeed bad-tempered, his manner habitually grumpy and disapproving, even with Moreland, to whom he was devoted; a congenital lack of amiability he appeared perpetually, though quite unsuccessfully, attempting to combat with copious draughts of Irish whiskey, a drink always lauded by him to the disadvantage of Scotch.

'I should be careful what you handle from the Caledonian Market, Deacon,' Maclintick said, 'I'm told stolen goods often drift up there. I don't expect you want a stiff sentence for receiving.'

He spoke for the first time since I had been sitting at the table, uttering the words in a high, caustic voice.

'Nonsense, Maclintick, nonsense,' said Mr Deacon shortly.

His tone made obvious that any dislike felt by Maclintick for himself—a sentiment not much concealed—was on his own side heartily reciprocated.

'Are you suggesting our friend Deacon is really a "fence"?' asked Gossage giggling, as if coy to admit knowledge of even this comparatively unexotic piece of thieves' jargon. 'I am sure he is nothing of the sort. Why, would you have us take him for a kind of modern Fagin?'

'I wouldn't go as far as that,' said Maclintick speaking more amicably this time, probably not wanting to exacerbate Mr Deacon beyond a certain point. 'Just warning him to take proper care of his reputation which I should not like to see tarnished.'

He smiled a little uneasily at Moreland to show this attack on Mr Deacon (which the victim seemed rather to enjoy) was not intended to include Moreland. I learnt later how much Moreland was the object of admiration, almost of reverence, on the part of Maclintick. This high regard was not only what Maclintick himself—on that rather dreadful subsequent occasion—called 'the proper respect of the poor interpretative hack for the true creative artist', but also because of an affection for Moreland as a friend that surpassed ordinary camaraderie, becoming something protective, almost maternal, if that word could be used of someone who looked like Maclintick. Indeed, under his splenetic exterior Maclintick harboured all kind of violent, imperfectly integrated sentiments. Moreland, for example, impressed him, perhaps rightly, as a young man of matchless talent, ill equipped to face a materialistic world. At the same time, Maclintick's own hag-ridden temperament also

23

punished him for indulging in what he regarded as sentimentality. His tremendous disapproval of sexual inversion, encountered intermittently in circles he chose to frequent, was compensation for his own sense of guilt at this hero-worshipping of Moreland; his severity with Gossage, another effort to right the balance.

'It's nice when you meet someone fresh like that once in a while,' said Gossage.

He was a lean, toothy little man, belonging to another common musical type, whose jerky movements gave him no rest. He toyed nervously with his bow tie, pince-nez and moustache, the last of which carried little conviction of masculinity. Gossage's voice was like that of a ventriloquist's doll. He giggled nervously, no doubt fearing Maclintick's castigation of such a remark.

'Personal charm,' said Mr Deacon trenchantly, 'has unfortunately no connexion with personal altruism. However, I fully expect to be made to wait at my age. Lateness is one of the punishments justly visited by youth upon those who have committed the atrocious crime of coming to riper years. Besides, quite apart from this moral and aesthetic justification, none of the younger generation seem to know the meaning of punctuality even when the practice of that cardinal virtue is in their own interests.'

All this time Carolo, the last member of the party to be introduced, had not opened his mouth. He sat in front of a mixed vermouth with an air of slighted genius. I thought, that evening, Carolo was about the same age as Moreland and myself, but found afterwards he was older than he appeared. His youthful aspect was perhaps in part legacy of his years as a child prodigy.

'Carolo's real name is Wilson or Wilkinson or Parker,' Moreland told me later, 'something rather practical and healthy like that. A surname felt to ring too much of plain common sense. Almost the first public performance of music I remember being taken to by my aunt was to hear Carolo play at the Wigmore Hall. I never thought then that one of these days Carolo and I would rub shoulders in the Mortimer.'

Carolo's face was pale and drawn, his black hair arranged in delicate waves, this consciously 'romantic' appearance and demeanour altogether misrepresenting his character, which was, according to Moreland, far from imaginative.

'Carolo is only interested in making money,' Moreland said, 'and who shall blame him? Unfortunately, he doesn't seem much good at getting it these days. He also likes the girls a bit.'

Daydreams of wealth or women must have given Carolo that faraway look which never left him; sad and silent, he contemplated huge bank balances and voluptuous revels.

'Why, there is my young friend,' said Mr Deacon, rising to his feet. 'If you will forgive me, Nicholas . . . Moreland . . . and the rest of you . . .'

On the whole Mr Deacon was inclined to conceal from his acquaintances such minor indiscretions in which he might still, in this his later life, indulge. He seemed to regret having allowed himself to give the impression that one of his '*petites folies*', as he liked to term them, was on foot that night. The temptation to present matters by implication in such a light had been too much for his vanity. Now, too late, he tried to be more guarded, striding forward hastily and blocking the immediate advance of the young man who had just entered the Mortimer, carrying in his arms, as if it were a baby, a large brown paper parcel.

'Why,' said Moreland, 'after all that, Edgar's mysterious friend turns out to be Norman. Did you ever hear such a thing?'

By suddenly sidestepping with an artificial elegance of movement, the young man bearing the parcel avoided Mr Deacon's attempt to exclude him from our company, and approached the table. He was lightly built, so thin that scarcely any torso seemed to exist under his coat. It was easy to see why Mr Deacon had assigned him the rôle of Harlequin. Sad-eyed and pert, he was an urchin with good looks of that curiously puppet-like formation which designate certain individuals as actors or dancers; anonymity of feature and flexibility of body fitting them from birth to play an assumed part.

'Hullo, my dear,' he said, addressing himself to Moreland. 'I hear you saw the new Stravinsky ballet when you were in Paris.'

His voice came out in a drawl, half cockney, half drawing-room comedy, as he changed the position of his feet, striking a pose that immediately proclaimed a dancer's professional training.

'Speaking choreographically——' Moreland began.

Mr Deacon, put out at finding his 'young friend' already known to most of the company, once more made an effort to intervene and keep the boy to himself, determined that any negotiations conducted between them should be transacted in at least comparative privacy.

'What?' he said, scarcely trying to hide his annoyance. 'You know each other, do you? How nice we should all be friends. However, Norman and I must discuss business of our own. The sacred rites of bargaining must not be overheard.'

He tittered angrily, and laid one of those gothic hands of his on the shoulder of the young man called Norman, who, as if to indicate that he must bow to the inevitable, waved dramatically to Moreland, as he allowed himself to be shepherded to the far end of the bar. There, he and Mr Deacon untied the parcel between them, at the same time folding the brown paper round it, so that they themselves should be, if possible, the sole persons to observe the contents. Mr Deacon must have felt immediately satisfied that he wanted to buy the cast (which reached his shop, although, as it turned out, only for a brief moment), because, after a muttered conversation, they wrapped up the parcel again and left the Mortimer together. As they went through the door Moreland shouted goodnight, a farewell

26

to which only the young man responded by giving another wave of his hand.

'Who is the juvenile lead?' asked Gossage.

He smiled vigorously, at the same time removing his pince-nez to polish them, as if he did not wish Maclintick to think him unduly interested in Mr Deacon and his friend.

'Don't you know Norman Chandler?' said Moreland. 'I should have thought you would have come across him. He is an actor. Also dances a bit. Rather a hand at the saxophone.'

'A talented young gentleman,' said Gossage.

Moreland took another newspaper from his pocket, flattened it out on the surface of the table, and began to read a re-hash of the Croydon murder. Maclintick's face had expressed the strongest distaste during the conversation with Chandler; now he dismissed his indignation and began to discuss the Albert Hall concert Gossage was attending that night. I caught the phrases 'rhythmic ensemble' and 'dynamic and tonal balance'. Carolo sat in complete silence, from time to time tasting his vermouth without relish. Maclintick and Gossage passed on to the Delius Festival at the Queen's Hall. All this musical 'shop', to which Moreland, without looking up from his paper, would intermittently contribute comment, began to make me feel rather out of it. I wished I had been less punctual. Moreland came to the end of the article and pushed the paper from him.

'Edgar was quite cross at my turning out to know Norman,' he said to me, speaking in a detached, friendly tone. 'Edgar loves to build up mystery about any young man he meets. There was a lot of excitement about an "ex-convict from Devil's Island" he met at a fancy dress party the other day dressed as a French *matelot*.'

He leaned forward and deftly thrust a penny into the slot of the mechanical piano, which took a second or two to digest the coin, then began to play raucously.

27

'Oh, good,' said Moreland. '*The Missouri Waltz.*'

'Deacon is probably right in assuming some of the persons he associates with are sinister enough,' said Maclintick sourly.

'It is the only pleasure he has left,' said Moreland. 'I can't imagine what Norman was selling. It looked like a bed-pan from the shape of the parcel.'

Gossage sniggered, incurring a frown from Maclintick. Probably fearing Maclintick might make him a new focus of disapproval, he remarked that he must be 'going soon'.

'Deacon will be getting himself into trouble one of these days,' Maclintick said, shaking his head and speaking as if he hoped the blow would fall speedily. 'Don't you agree, Gossage?'

'Oh, couldn't say, couldn't say at all,' said Gossage hurriedly. 'I hardly know the man, you see. Met him once or twice at the Proms last year. Join him sometimes over a mug of ale.'

Maclintick ignored these efforts to present a more bracing picture of Mr Deacon's activities.

'And it won't be the first time Deacon got into trouble,' he said in his grim, high-pitched voice.

'Well, I shall really have to go,' repeated Gossage, in answer to this further rebuke, speaking as if everyone present had been urging him to stay in the Mortimer for just a few minutes longer.

'You will read my views on Friday. I am keeping an open mind. One has to do that. Goodbye, Moreland, goodbye . . . Maclintick, goodbye . . .'

'I must be going too,' said Carolo unexpectedly.

He had a loud, harsh voice, and a North Country accent like Quiggin's. Tossing back the remains of his vermouth as if to the success of a desperate venture from which he was unlikely to return with his life, he finished the dregs at a gulp, and, inclining his head slightly in farewell to the company with an unconcerned movement in keeping with this devil-may-care mood, he followed Gossage from the saloon bar.

'Carolo wasn't exactly a chatterbox tonight,' said Moreland.

'Never has much to say for himself,' Maclintick agreed. 'Always brooding on the old days when he was playing Sarasate up and down the country clad as Little Lord Fauntleroy.'

'He must have been at least seventeen when he last appeared in his black velvet suit and white lace collar,' said Moreland. 'The coat was so tight he could hardly draw his bow across the fiddle.'

'They say Carolo is having trouble with his girl,' said Maclintick. 'Makes him even gloomier than usual.'

'Who is his girl?' asked Moreland indifferently.

'Quite young, I believe,' said Maclintick. 'Gossage was asking about her. Carolo doesn't find it as easy to get engagements as he used—and he won't teach.'

'Wasn't there talk of Mrs Andriadis helping him?' said Moreland. 'Arranging a performance at her house or something.'

I listened to what was being said without feeling—as I came to feel later—that I was, in one sense, part and parcel of the same community; that when people gossiped about matters like Carolo and his girl, one was listening to a morsel, if only an infinitesimal morsel, of one's own life. However, I heard no more about Carolo at that moment, because Barnby could now be seen standing in the doorway of the saloon bar, slowly apprising himself of the company present, the problem each individual might pose. By that hour the Mortimer had begun to fill. A man with a yellowish beard and black hat was buying drinks for two girls drawn from that indeterminate territory eternally disputed between tarts and art students; three pimply young men were arguing about economics; a couple of taxi-drivers conferred with the barmaid. For several seconds Barnby stared about him, viewing the people in the Mortimer with apparent disapproval. Then, thickset, his topcoat turned up to his ears, he moved slowly forward, at the same time casting an expert, all-embracing glance at the barmaid and the two art girls. Reaching the table at last by these easy stages, he nodded to the rest of us, but did not sit down. Instead, he regarded the party closely. Such evolutions were fairly typical of Barnby's behaviour in public; demeanour effective with most strangers, on whom he seemed ultimately to force friendliness by at first withholding himself. Later he would unfreeze. With women, that apparently negative method almost always achieved good results. It was impossible to say whether this manner of Barnby's was unconscious or deliberate. Moreland, for example, saw in Barnby a consummate actor.

'Ralph is the Garrick of our day,' Moreland used to say, 'or at least the Tree or Irving. Barnby never misses a gesture with women, not an inflection of the voice.'

The two of them, never close friends, used to see each other fairly often in those days. Moreland liked painting and held stronger views about pictures than most musicians.

'I can see Ralph has talent,' he said of Barnby, 'but why use combinations of colour that make you think he is a Frenchman or a Catalan?'

'I know nothing of music,' Barnby had, in turn, once remarked, 'but Hugh Moreland's accompaniment to that film sounded to me like a lot of owls quarrelling in a bicycle factory.'

All the same, in spite of mutual criticism, they were in general pretty well disposed to one another.

'Buy us a drink, Ralph,' said Moreland, as Barnby stood moodily contemplating us.

'I'm not sure I can afford that,' said Barnby. 'I'll have to think about it.'

'Take a generous view,' said Moreland, who liked being stood plenty of drinks.

After a minute or two's meditation Barnby drew some money from his pocket, glanced at the coins in the palm of his hand, and laid some of them on the bar. Then he brought the glasses across to the table.

'Had a look at the London Group this afternoon,' he said. Barnby sat down. He and Moreland began to talk of English painting. The subject evidently bored Maclintick, who seemed to like Barnby as little as he cared for Mr Deacon. Conversation moved on to painting in Paris. Finally, the idea of going to a film was abandoned. It was getting late in the evening. The programme would be too far advanced. Instead, we agreed to dine together. Maclintick went off upstairs to telephone to his wife and tell her he would not be home until later.

'There will be a row about that,' said Moreland, after Maclintick had disappeared.

'Do they quarrel?'

'Just a bit.'

'Where shall we dine?' said Barnby. 'Foppa's?'

'No, I lunched at Foppa's,' Moreland said. 'I can't stand Foppa's twice in a day. It would be like going back to one's old school. Do you know Casanova's Chinese Restaurant? It hasn't been open long. Let's eat there.'

'I am not sure my stomach is up to Chinese food,' said Barnby. 'I didn't get to bed until three this morning.'

'You can have eggs or something like that.'

'Won't the eggs be several hundred years old? Still, we will go there if you insist. Anything to save a restaurant argument. Where is the place?'

Maclintick returned from telephoning. He bought himself a final Irish whiskey and drank it off. Conversation with his wife had been, as Moreland predicted, acrimonious. When told our destination was Casanova's Chinese Restaurant Maclintick made a face; but he failed to establish any rival claim in favour of somewhere he would prefer to eat, so the decision was confirmed. I asked how such a recklessly hybrid name had ever been invented.

'There used to be the New Casanova,' said Moreland, 'where the cooking was Italian and the decoration French eighteenth century—some way, some considerable way, after Watteau. Further up the street was the Amoy, called by some Sam's Chinese Restaurant. The New Casanova went into liquidation. Sam's bought it up and moved over their pots and pans and chopsticks, so now you can eat eight treasure rice, or bamboo shoots fried with pork ribbons, under panels depicting scenes from the career of the Great Lover.'

'What are prices like?' asked Barnby.

'One might almost say cheap. On Sunday there is an orchestra of three and dainty afternoon tea is served. You can even dance. Maclintick has been there, haven't you, Maclintick?'

'Must it be Chinese food tonight?' said Maclintick peevishly. 'I've a touch of enteritis as it is.'

'Remember some of the waitresses are rather attractive,' said Moreland persuasively.

'Chinese?' I asked.

'No,' said Moreland, 'English.'

He laughed a little self-consciously.

'Bet you've got your eye on one,' said Barnby.

I think Barnby made this remark as a matter of routine, either without bothering to consider the matter at all carefully, or on the safe assumption that no one would take the trouble to mention the fact that any given group of girls was above the average in looks without having singled out at least one of them for himself. That would unquestionably have been Barnby's own procedure. Alternatively, Moreland may have spoken of Casanova's on an earlier occasion, thereby giving Barnby reason to suspect there must be something special that attracted Moreland personally to the place. In any case, the imputation was not surprising, although Barnby's own uninterrupted interest in the subject always made him perceptive where the question of a woman, or women, was concerned. However, Moreland went red at the enquiry. He was in one sense, easily embarrassed about any matter that touched him intimately;

although, at the same time, his own mind moved too quickly for him to be placed long at a disadvantage by those who hoped to tease. In such situations he was pretty adept at turning the tables.

'I had my eye on a girl there formerly,' he said, 'I admit that. It wasn't entirely the excellent pig's trotter soup that brought me back to Casanova's. However, I can visit that restaurant now without a tremor—not a concupiscent thought. My pleasure in the place has become purely that of *gourmet* of Cathay. A triumph of self-mastery. I will point the girl out to you, Ralph.'

'What happened?' asked Barnby. 'Did she leave you for the man who played the trombone?'

'One just wasn't a success,' said Moreland, reddening again. 'Anyway, I will show you the problem as it stood— no doubt as it stands. Nothing altered, so far as I know, except my own point of view. But let's be moving. I'm famished.'

The name Casanova's Chinese Restaurant offered one of those unequivocal blendings of disparate elements of the imagination which suggest a whole new state of mind or way of life. The idea of Casanova giving his name to a Chinese restaurant linked not only the East with the West, the present with the past, but also, more parochially, suggested by its own incongruity an immensely suitable place for all of us to have dinner that night. We arrived in two large rooms, in which most of the tables were filled. The clientèle, predominantly male and Asiatic, had a backbone of Chinese businessmen and Indian students. A few Negroes sat with very blonde white girls; a sprinkling of diners belonged to those ethnically indefinable races which colonise Soho and interbreed there. Along the walls frescoes tinted in pastel shades, executed with infinite feebleness of design, appealed to Heaven knows what nadir of aesthetic degradation. Almost as soon as we found a table, I marked down Moreland's waitress. She was tall, very thin, fair-haired and blue-eyed, at that moment carrying a lot of glasses on a tray. The girl was certainly noticeable in her white lace cap and small frilled white apron above a black dress and black cotton stockings, the severity of this uniform, her own pale colouring, lending a curious exoticism to her appearance in these pseudo-oriental surroundings. There was an air of childlike innocence about her that could easily be deceptive. Indeed, when more closely observed, she had some of the look of a very expensive, rather wicked little doll. Moreland's answer to Barnby's almost immediate request to have 'the girl we have come to see' pointed out to him, confirmed the correctness of this guess. Barnby took one of his lingering, professional stares.

'Rather an old man's piece, isn't she?' he said. 'Still, I see your point. Poorish legs, though.'

'You mustn't concentrate on legs if your interest is in waitresses,' said Moreland. 'The same is true of ballet dancers, I'm afraid.'

'She looks as if she might well be a nymphomaniac,' said Maclintick, 'those very fair, innocent-looking girls often are. I think I mentioned that to Moreland when he brought me here before.'

Maclintick had hardly spoken since we left the Mortimer. Now he uttered these words in a tone of deep pessimism, as if, so far, he had resented every moment of the evening. He greatly disapproved of Barnby, whose inclination for women was as irksome to him as Mr Deacon's so downright repudiation of the opposite sex. Maclintick possibly thought Barnby had a bad influence on Moreland.

'She showed no sign of being a nympho,' Moreland said. 'On the contrary. I could have done with a little nymphomania—anyway at the start.'

'What are we going to eat?' said Barnby. 'I can't make head or tail of this menu.'

Maclintick and Barnby ordered something unadventurous from the dishes available; under Moreland's guidance, I embarked upon one of the specialities of the house. Moreland's waitress came to take our order for drinks. Although a restaurant of some size, Casanova's had no licence, so that a member of the staff collected beer from the pub opposite, or wine from the shop round the corner. When she came up to the table the waitress gave Moreland a cold, formal smile of recognition, which freely acknowledged him as a regular customer, but suggested no more affectionate relationship. Close up, she looked, I thought, as hard as nails; I did not feel at all tempted to enter into competition. Barnby eyed her. She took no notice of him whatever, noting our orders in silence and disappearing.

'Too thin for my taste,' said Barnby. 'I like a good armful.'

'This lascivious conversation is very appropriate to the memory of the distinguished Venetian gentleman after whom the restaurant is named,' said Maclintick harshly. 'What a bore he must have been.'

He leant across the table, and, like an angry woodpecker, began to tap out his pipe against the side of a large Schweppes ashtray.

'Do you suppose one would have known Casanova?' I said.

'Oh, but of course,' said Moreland. 'In early life, Casanova played the violin—like Carolo. Casanova played in a band—I doubt if he would have been up to a solo performance. I can just imagine what he would have been like to deal with if one had been the conductor. Besides, he much fancied himself as a figure at the opera and musical parties. One would certainly have met him. At least I am sure I should.'

'Think of having to listen to interminable stories about his girls,' said Maclintick. 'I could never get through Casanova's Memoirs. Why should he be considered a great man just because he had a lot of women? Most men would have ended by being bored to death.'

'That is why he was a great man,' said Moreland. 'It wasn't the number of women he had, it was the fact that he

35

didn't get bored. But there are endless good things there apart from the women. Do you remember when in London he overhears someone remark: "Tommy has committed suicide and he did quite right"—to which another person replies: "on the contrary, he did a very foolish thing, for I am one of his creditors and know that he need not have made away with himself for six months".'

Barnby and I laughed at this anecdote. Maclintick did not smile. At the same time he seemed struck by the story. He was silent for some moments. When he spoke again it was in a manner at once more serious, more friendly, than any tone he had previously employed that evening.

'I see nothing particularly funny in their conversation,' he said. 'That is how I propose to behave myself when the time comes. But I agree that Tommy was a fool to misjudge his term of days. I shall not do that. I give myself at least five more years at the present rate. That should allow me time to finish my book.'

'Still,' said Moreland, 'however bent one may be on the idea of eventual suicide oneself, you must admit, Maclintick, that such sentiments must have sounded odd to a man of Casanova's *joie de vivre*. Anyway, professional seducers never commit suicide. They haven't time.'

'The notable thing about professional seducers,' said Maclintick, now returning to his former carping tone of voice, 'is the rot they talk when they are doing their seducing. There is not a single cliché they leave unsaid.'

'Although by definition the most egotistical of men,' said Moreland, 'they naturally have to develop a certain anonymity of style to make themselvs acceptable to all women. It is the case of the lowest common factor—or is it the highest common denominator? If you hope to rise to the top class in seducing, you must appeal to the majority. As the majority are not very intelligent, you must conceal your own intelligence—if you have the misfortune to possess such a thing—in order not to frighten the girls off. There is inevitably something critical, something alarming to personal vanity, in the very suggestion of intelligence in another. That is almost equally true of dealing with men, so don't think I hold it against women. All I say is, that someone like myself ought to restrict themselves to intelligent girls who see my own good points. Unfortunately, they are rarely the sort of girls I like.'

Barnby grunted, no doubt feeling some of these strictures in apart applicable to himself.

'What do you expect to do?' he asked. 'Give readings from *The Waste Land*?'

'Not a bad idea,' said Moreland.

'In my experience,' Barnby said, 'women like the obvious.'

'Just what we are complaining about,' said Maclintick, 'the very thing.'

'Seduction is to do and say/The banal thing in the banal way,' said Moreland. 'No one denies that. My own complaint is that people always talk about love affairs as if you spent the whole of your time in bed. I find most of my own emotional energy—not to say physical energy—is exhausted in making efforts to get there. Problems of Time and Space as usual.'

The relation of Time and Space, then rather fashionable, was, I found, a favourite subject of Moreland's.

'Surely we have long agreed the two elements are identical?' said Maclintick. 'This is going over old ground—perhaps I should say old hours.'

'You must differentiate for everyday purposes, don't you?' urged Barnby. 'I don't wonder seduction seems a problem, if you get Time and Space confused.'

'I suppose one might be said to be true to a woman in Time and unfaithful to her in Space,' said Moreland. 'That is what Dowson seems to have thought about Cynara—or is it just the reverse? The metaphysical position is not made wholly clear by the poet. Talking of pale lost lilies, how do you think Edgar and Norman are faring in their deal?'

37

'Remember Lot's wife,' said Maclintick sententiously. 'Besides, we have a cruet on the table. Here are the drinks at last, thank God. You know Pope says every woman is at heart a rake. I'd be equally prepared to postulate that every rake is at heart a woman. Don Juan—Casanova—Byron—the whole bloody lot of them.'

'But Don Juan was not at all the same as Casanova,' said Moreland. 'The opera makes that quite clear. Ralph here sometimes behaves like Casanova. He isn't in the least like Don Juan—are you, Ralph?'

I was myself not sure this assessment of Barnby's nature was wholly accurate; but, if distinction were to be drawn between those two legendary seducers, the matter was at least arguable. Barnby himself was now showing signs of becoming rather nettled by this conversation.

'Look here,' he said. 'My good name keeps on being bandied about in a most uncalled for manner. Perhaps you wouldn't mind defining the differences between these various personages with whom I am being so freely compared. I had better be told for certain, otherwise I shall be behaving in a way that is out of character, which would never do.'

'Don Juan merely liked power,' said Moreland. 'He obviously did not know what sensuality was. If he knew it at all, he hated it. Casanova, on the other hand, undoubtedly had his sensual moments, even though they may not have occurred very often. With Henriette, for example, or those threesomes with the nun, M.M. Of course, Casanova was interested in power too. No doubt he ended as a complete Narcissus, when love naturally became intolerable to him, since love involved him with another party emotionally. Every Narcissus dislikes that. None of us regards Ralph as only wanting power where a woman is concerned. We think too highly of you for that, Ralph.'

Barnby did not appear flattered by this analysis of his emotional life.

'Thanks awfully,' he said. 'But, to get down to more

38

immediate matters, how would you feel, Hugh, if I asked that waitress to sit for me? For reasons of trade, rather than power or sensuality. Of course she is bound to think I am trying to get off with her. Nothing could be further from the case—no, I assure you, Maclintick. Anyway, I don't expect she will agree. No harm in trying, though. I just wanted to make sure you had no objection. To show how little of a Casanova I am—or is it a Don Juan?'

'Take any step you think best,' said Moreland laughing, although perhaps not best pleased by what Barnby had asked. 'I have resigned all claims. I don't quite see her in your medium, but that is obviously the painter's own affair. If I have a passion for anyone, I prefer an academic, even pedestrian, naturalism of portraiture. It is a limitation I share with Edgar Deacon. Nothing I'd care for less than to have my girl painted by Lhote or Gleizes, however much I may admire those painters—literally—in the abstract.'

All the same, although he put a good face on it, Moreland looked a little cast down. No more was said on the subject until the time came to make our individual contributions to the bill. The waitress appeared again. She explained that she had omitted at an earlier stage of the meal to collect some of the money due for what we had drunk. She now presented her final account. At this point Barnby took the opportunity to allow himself certain pleasantries—these a trifle on the ponderous side, as he himself admitted later—to the effect that she was demanding money under false pretences. The waitress received these comments in good part, unbending so far as to hint that she had not levied the charge before, because, having taken one look at Barnby, she had been sure he would give a further order for drink; she had accordingly decided to wait until the account was complete. Barnby listened to this explanation gravely, making no attempt to answer in the breezy manner he had employed a few seconds earlier this imputation of possessing a bibulous appearance. Just as the girl was about to withdraw, he spoke.

'Look here,' he said, 'I'm an artist—I paint people's pictures.'

She did not look at him, or answer, but she stopped giggling, while at the same time making no attempt to move away from the table.

'I'd like to paint you.'

She still did not speak. Her expression changed in a very slight degree, registering what might have been embarrassment or cunning.

'Could you come and be painted by me some time?'

Barnby put the question in a quiet, almost exaggeratedly gentle voice; one I had never before heard him use.

'Don't know that I have time,' she said, very coolly.

'What about one week-end?'

'Can't come Sunday. Have to be here.'

'Saturday, then?'

'Saturday isn't any good either.'

'You can't have to work all the week.'

'Might manage a Thursday.'

'All right, let's make it a Thursday then.'

There was a pause. Maclintick, unable to bear the sight and sound of these negotiations, had taken a notebook from his pocket and begun a deep examination of his own affairs; making plans for the future; writing down great thoughts; perhaps even composing music. Moreland, unable to conceal his discomfort at what was taking place, started a conversation with me designed to carry further his Time-Space theories.

'What about next Thursday?' asked Barnby, in his most wheedling tone.

'I don't know.'

'Say you will.'

'I don't know.'

'Come on.'

'I suppose so, then.'

Barnby reached forward and took Maclintick's pencil from his hand—not without protest on Maclintick's part—

and wrote something on the back of an envelope. I suppose it was just the address of his studio, but painters form the individual letters of their handwriting so carefully, so separately, that he seemed to be drawing a picture specially for her.

'It's above a shop,' Barnby said.

Then, suddenly, he crumpled the envelope.

'On second thoughts,' he said, 'I will come and pick you up here, if that is all right.'

'As you like.'

She spoke indifferently, as if all had been decided long before and they had been going out together for years.

'What time?'

She told him; the two of them made some mutual arrangement. Then they smiled at each other, again without any sense of surprise or excitement, as if long on familiar terms, and the waitress retired from the table. Barnby handed the stump of pencil back to Maclintick. We vacated the restaurant.

'Like Glendower, Barnby,' said Maclintick, 'you can call spirits from the vasty deep. With Hotspur, I ask you, will they come?'

'That's to be seen,' said Barnby. 'By the way, what is her name? I forgot to ask.'

'Norma,' said Moreland, speaking without apology.

To complete the story, Barnby (whose personal arrangements were often vague) told me that when the day of assignation came, he arrived, owing to bad timing, three-quarters of an hour late for the appointment. The girl was still waiting for him. She came to his studio, where he began a picture of her, subsequently completing at least one oil painting and several drawings. The painting, which was in his more severe manner, he sold to Sir Magnus Donners; Sir Herbert Manasch bought one of the drawings, which were treated naturistically. Eventually, as might have been foretold, Barnby had some sort of a love affair with his model; although he always insisted she was 'not his type', that matters had come to a head one thundery afternoon when an overcast sky made painting impossible. Norma left Casanova's soon after this episode. She took a job which led to her marrying a man who kept a tobacconist's shop in Camden Town. There was no ill feeling after Barnby had done with her; keeping on good terms with his former mistresses was one of his gifts. In fact he used to visit Norma and her husband (who sometimes gave him racing tips) after they were married. Through them he found a studio in that part of London; he may even have been godfather to one of their children. All that is beside the point. The emphasis I lay upon the circumstances of this assignation at Casanova's Chinese Restaurant is to draw attention to the extreme ease with which Barnby conducted the preliminaries of his campaign. Anyone who heard things being fixed up might have supposed Norma to have spent much of her previous life as an artist's model; that she regarded making an engagement for a sitting as a matter of routine regulated only by aspects of her own immediate convenience. Perhaps she had; perhaps she did. In such case Barnby showed scarcely less mastery of the situation in at once assessing her potentialities in that rôle.

'Of course, Ralph is a painter,' said Moreland, afterwards. 'He has a studio. Time, place and a respectable motive for a visit are all at his command. None of these things are to be despised where girls are concerned.'

'Time and Space, as usual.'

'Time and Space,' said Moreland.

The incident was not only an illustration of Barnby's adroitness in that field, but also an example of Moreland's diffidence, a diffidence no doubt in part responsible for the admixture of secretiveness and exhibitionism with which he conducted his love affairs. By exhibitionism, I mean, in Moreland's case, no more than a taste for referring obliquely from time to time to some unrevealed love that possessed him. I supposed that this habit of his explained his talk of marriage the day—five or six years after our first meeting—

when we had listened together to the song of the blonde singer; especially when he refused to name the girl—or three girls—he might be considering as a wife. It was therefore a great surprise to me when his words turned out to be spoken seriously. However, I did not at first realise how serious they were; nor even when, some weeks later, more about the girl herself was revealed.

He suggested one day that we should go together to *The Duchess of Malfi*, which was being performed at a small theatre situated somewhat off the beaten track; one of those ventures that attempt, by introducing a few new names and effects, momentarily to dispel the tedium of dramatic routine.

'Webster is always a favourite of mine,' Moreland said. 'Norman Chandler has for the moment abandoned dancing and the saxophone, and is playing Bosola.'

'That should be enjoyable. Has he quite the weight?'

Chandler had moved a long way since the day when I had first seen him at the Mortimer, when Mr Deacon had spoken so archly of having acquired his friendship through a vegetarian holiday. Now Chandler had made some name for himself, not only as a dancer, but also as an actor; not in leading rôles, but specialising in smaller, unusual parts suitable to his accomplished, but always intensely personal, style. I used to run across him occasionally with Moreland, whose passion for mechanical pianos Chandler shared; music for which they would search London.

'I also happen to know the Cardinal's mistress,' said Moreland, speaking very casually.

This remark suddenly struck a chord of memory about something someone had said a few days before about the cast of this very play.

'But wasn't she Sir Magnus Donner's mistress too? I was hearing about that. It is Matilda Wilson, isn't it, who is playing that part—the *jolie laide* Donners used to be seen about with a year or two ago? I have always wanted to have a look at her.'

Moreland turned scarlet. I realised that I had shown colossal lack of tact. This must be his girl. I saw now why he had spoken almost apologetically about going to the play, as if some excuse were required for attending one of Webster's tragedies, even though Moreland himself was known by me to be greatly attached to the Elizabethan dramatists. When he made the suggestion that we should see the play together I had suspected no ulterior motive. Now, it looked as if something were on foot.

'She was mixed up with Donners for a time,' he said, 'that is quite true. But several years ago now. I thought we might go round and see her after the performance. Then we could have a drink—even eat if we felt like it—at the Café Royal or somewhere like that.'

To hold a friend in the background at a certain stage of a love affair is a technique some men like to employ; a method which spreads, as it were, the emotional load, ameliorating risks of dual conflict between the lovers themselves, although at the same time posing a certain hazard in the undue proximity of a third party unencumbered with emotional responsibility—and therefore almost always seen to better advantage than the lover himself. Close friends probably fall in love with the same woman less often in life than in books, though the female spirit of emulation will sometimes fix on a husband or lover's friend out of a mere desire to show that a woman can do even better than her partner in the same sphere. Moreland and I used to agree that, in principle, we liked the same kind of girl; but never, so long as I knew him, did we ever find ourselves in competition.

The news that he was involved with Matilda Wilson, might even be thinking of marrying her—for that was the shape things seemed to be taking—was surprising in a number of ways. I had never seen the girl herself, although often hearing about her during her interlude with Sir Magnus, a person round whom gossip accumulated easily, not only because he was very rich, but also on account of supposedly unconventional tastes in making love. Sir Magnus was said to be reasonably generous with his girls, and, provided he was from time to time indulged in certain respects, not unduly demanding. It was characteristic of the situations in which love lands people that someone as sensitive as Moreland to life's grotesque aspects should find himself handling so delicate an affair, where perhaps even marriage was the goal. When we arrived at the theatre we found Mark Members waiting in the foyer. Members was the kind of person who would know by instinct that Moreland was interested in Matilda Wilson, and might be expected to make some reference to her past with Sir Magnus with the object of teasing Moreland with whom he was on prickly terms. However, the subject did not arise. Members had just finished straightening his tie in a large looking-glass. He was now looking disdainfully round him.

'What a shabby lot of highbrows have turned out tonight,' he said, when he saw us. 'It makes me ashamed to be one.'

'Nobody guesses you are, Mark,' said Moreland. 'Not in that natty new suit. They think you are an actuary or an average adjuster.'

Members laughed his tinny laugh.

'How is sweet music?' he asked. 'How are your pale tunes irresolute, Moreland? When is that opera of yours we hear so much about going to appear?'

'I've knocked off work on the opera for the moment,' said Moreland. 'I'm concentrating on something slighter which I think should appeal to music-lovers of your temperament. It is to be called *Music for a Maison de Passe: A Suite*.'

We passed on to where Gossage was standing a short way off by the curtain that screened the foyer from the passage leading to the auditorium. Gossage was talking with a great display of respect to a lady dressed rather too exquisitely for the occasion; the audience that night, as Members had truly remarked, being decidedly unkempt. This lady, slight in

45

figure, I recognised at once as Mrs Foxe, mother of my old friend, Charles Stringham. I had not seen Stringham since Widmerpool and I had put him to bed after too much to drink at an Old Boy Dinner. Mrs Foxe herself I had not set eyes on for ten years; the day she and Commander Foxe had lunched with Stringham in his rooms in college to discuss whether or not he should 'go down' before taking a degree.

Mrs Foxe was quite unchanged. Beautiful in early middle age, she remained still untouched by time. She was accompanied by a girl of seventeen or eighteen, and two young men who looked like undergraduates. Evidently she was hostess to this party, whom I supposed to be relations; connexions possibly of her first husband, Lord Warrington, or her third husband, Buster Foxe. Stringham, child of the intermediate marriage of this South African millionaire's daughter, used to boast he had no relations; so they were presumably not cousins of his. Gossage, parting now from Mrs Foxe with many smiles and bows, nodded to Moreland with an air of considerable satisfaction as he hurried past. When we reached our seats I saw that Mrs Foxe and her party were sitting a long way away from us. Since I hardly supposed she would remember me, I decided not to approach her during the *entr'actes*. In any case, she and I had little in common except Stringham himself, of whom I then knew nothing except that his marriage had broken up and he was said to be still drinking too much. He had certainly drunk a lot the night Widmerpool and I had put him to bed. Another reason for taking no step in Mrs Foxe's direction was that a stage in my life had been reached when I felt that to spend even a short time with a party of that kind would be 'boring'. For the moment, I had put such things behind me. Perhaps at some future date I should return to them; for the time being I rather prided myself on preferring forms of social life where white ties were not worn. I was even glad there was no likelihood of chance recognition.

Julia, the Cardinal's mistress in *The Duchess of Malfi*,

does not come on to the stage until the fourth scene of the first act. Moreland was uneasy until that moment, fidgeting in his seat, giving deep breaths, a habit of his when inwardly disturbed. At the same time, he showed a great deal of enjoyment in Norman Chandler's earlier speeches as Bosola. Chandler had brought an unexpected solidity to this insidious part. The lightness of his build, and general air of being a dancer rather than an actor, had prepared neither Moreland nor myself for the rendering he presented of 'this fellow seven years in the galleys for a notorious murder'.

'Do you think Norman talked like Bosola the night he was bargaining with Edgar Deacon about that statuette?' said Moreland, in an undertone. 'If so, he must have got the best of it. Did I ever tell you that he hadn't been paid when Edgar died, so Norman nipped round to the shop and took the thing away again? That was in the Bosola tradition.'

When at last Matilda Wilson appeared as Julia, Moreland's face took on a look of intensity, almost of strain, more like worry than love. I had been looking forward to seeing her with the interest one feels in being shown for the first time the woman a close friend proposes to marry; for I now had no doubt from the manner in which the evening had been planned that Matilda must be the girl whom Moreland had in mind when he had spoken of taking a wife. When she first came towards the footlights I was disappointed. I have no talent for guessing what an actress will look like off the stage, but, even allowing for an appearance greatly changed by the removal of make-up and the stiffly angled dress in which she was playing the part, she seemed altogether lacking in conventional prettiness. A minute or two later I began to change my mind. She certainly possessed a forceful, enigmatic personality; none of the film-star looks of the waitress in Casanova's, but something, one of those resemblances impossible to put into words, made me recall that evening. Matilda Wilson moved gracefully. Apart from that, and the effectiveness of her slow, clear voice and sardonic enunciation, she was not a very 'finished' actress. Once or twice I was aware of Moreland glancing in my direction, as if he hoped to discover what I thought of her; but he asked no questions and made no comment when the curtain fell. He shuddered slightly when she replied to Bosola's lines: 'Know you me, I am a blunt soldier', with: 'The better; sure there wants fire where there are no lively sparks of roughness'.

When the play was over, we went round to the stage door, penetrating into regions where the habitually cramped accommodation of theatrical dressing-rooms was more than usually in evidence. For a time we wandered about narrow passages filled with lithe young men who had danced the Masque of Madmen, now dressing, undressing, chattering, washing, playing noisy games of their own, which gave the impression that the action of the play was continuing its course even though the curtain had come down. We found Matilda Wilson's room at last. She was wearing hardly any clothes, removing her make-up, while Norman Chandler, dressed in a mauve dressing-gown of simulated brocade, sat on a stool beside her, reading a book. I never feel greatly at ease 'backstage', and Moreland himself, although by then certainly used enough to such surroundings, was obviously disturbed by the responsibility of having to display his girl for the first time. He need not have worried; Matilda herself was completely at ease. I saw at once, now she was off the stage, how effortless her conquest of Moreland must have been. He possessed, it was true, a certain taste for rather conventional good looks which had to be overcome in favour of beauty of a less obvious kind; in other respects she seemed to have everything he demanded, yet never could find. Barnby always dismissed the idea of intelligence in a woman as no more than a characteristic to be endured. Moreland held different views.

'I don't want what Rembrandt or Cézanne or Barnby or any other painter may happen to want,' he used to say. 'I simply cling to my own preferences. I don't know what's good, but I know what I like—not a lot of intellectual snobbery about fat peasant women, or technical talk about masses and planes. After all, painters have to contend professionally with pictorial aspects of the eternal feminine which are quite beside the point where a musician like myself is concerned. With women, I can afford to cut out the chiaroscuro. Choosing the type of girl one likes is about the last thing left that one is allowed to approach subjectively. I shall continue to exercise the option.'

Matilda Wilson jumped up from her stool as soon as she saw Moreland. Throwing her arms round his neck, she kissed him on the nose. When a woman is described as a '*jolie laide*', the same particular combination of looks is, for some reason, implied; you expect a brunette, small rather than tall, with a face emphasised by eyebrows and mouth, features which would be too insistent if the eyes did not finally control the general effect—in fact what is also known as *beauté de singe*. Matilda Wilson was not at all like that. Off the stage, she was taller and thinner than I had supposed, her hair fairish, with large, rather sleepy green eyes. The upper half of her face was pretty enough; the lower, forcefully, even rather coarsely modelled. You felt the beauty of her figure was in some manner the consequence of her own self-control; that a less intelligent woman might have 'managed' her body without the same effectiveness.

'Oh, darling,' she said, in a voice that at once suggested her interlude in the world of Sir Magnus Donners, 'I am so glad you have turned up at last. Various awful men have been trying to make me go out with them. But I said you were calling for me. I hoped you would not forget as you did last week.'

'Oh, last week,' said Moreland, looking dreadfully put out, and making a characteristic gesture with his hand, as if about to begin conducting. 'That muddle was insane of me. Will you ever forgive me, Matty? It upset me so much. Do let me off further mention of it. I am so hopelessly forgetful.'

49

He looked rather wildly round him, as if he expected to find some explanation of the cause of bad memory in the furthest recesses of the dressing-room, finally turning to me for support.

'Nick, don't you find it absolutely impossible nowadays to remember anything?' he began. 'Do you know, I was in the Mortimer the other day——'

Up to that time he had made no attempt to tell Matilda Wilson my name, although no doubt she had been warned that I was probably going to join them at the end of the play. He would certainly have launched into a long train of reminiscence about something or other that had happened to him in the Mortimer, if she had not burst out laughing and kissed him again, this time on the ear. She held out her hand to me, still laughing, and Moreland, now red in the face, insisted that the time had passed for introductory formalities. Meanwhile, Norman Chandler had been finishing his chapter without taking any notice of what was going on round him. Now, he put a marker in his book (which I saw to be *Time and Western Man*), and, drawing the billowing robes of his rather too large dressing-gown more tightly round him, he rose to his feet.

' "A lot of awful men"?' he said, speaking in a voice of old-time melodrama. 'What do you mean, Matilda? I offered you a bite with Max and me, if your boy friend did not arrive. That was only because you said he was so forgetful, and might easily think he had made a date for the day after tomorrow. I never heard such ingratitude.'

Matilda put her arm round Chandler's waist and attempted to smoothe his hair with her brush.

'Oh, I didn't mean you, darling, of course I didn't,' she said. 'I don't call you a man. I love you much too much. I mean an awful man who telephoned—and then another awful man who left a note. How could anyone call you awful, Norman, darling?'

'Oh, I don't know so much about that,' said Chandler, now abandoning the consciously sinister, masculine tones of

Bosola, and returning to his more familiar chorus-boy drawl. 'I'm not always adored as much as you might think from looking at me. I don't quite know why that is.'

He put his head on one side, forefinger against cheek, transforming himself to some character of ballet, perhaps the Faun from *L'Après-midi*.

'You are adored by me,' said Matilda, kissing him twice before throwing down the hairbrush on the dressing-table. 'But I really must put a few clothes on.'

Chandler broke away from her, executing a series of little leaps in the air, although there was not much room for these *entrechats*. He whizzed round several times, collapsing at last upon his stool.

'Bravo, bravo,' said Matilda, clapping her hands. 'You will rival Nijinsky yet, Norman, my sweetie.'

'Be careful,' said Chandler. 'Your boy friend will be jealous. I can see him working himself up. He can be very violent when roused.'

Moreland had watched this display of high spirits with enjoyment, except when talk had been of other men taking out Matilda, when his face had clouded. Chandler had probably noticed that. So far from being jealous of Chandler, which would certainly have been absurd in the circumstances, Moreland seemed to welcome these antics as relaxing tension between himself and Matilda. He became more composed in manner. Paradoxically enough, something happened a moment later which paid an obvious tribute to Chandler's status as a ladies' man, however little regarded in that rôle by Moreland and the world at large.

'I will be very quick now,' said Matilda, 'and then we will go. I am dying for a bite.'

She retired behind a small screen calculated to heighten rather than diminish the dramatic effect of her toilet, since her long angular body was scarcely at all concealed, and, in any case, she continually reappeared on the floor of the room to rescue garments belonging to her which lay about there. The scene was a little like those depicted in French eighteenth-century engravings where propriety is archly threatened in the presence of an amorous *abbé* or two—powdered hair would have suited Matilda, I thought; Moreland, perhaps, too. However, the picture's static form was interrupted by the sound of some commotion in the passage which caused Chandler to stroll across the room and stand by the half-open door. Some people were passing who must have recognised him, because he suddenly said: 'Why, hullo, Mrs Foxe,' in a tone rather different from that used by him a moment before; a friendly tone, but one at the same time faintly deferential, possibly even a shade embarrassed. There was the sudden suggestion that Chandler was on his best behaviour.

'We were looking for you,' said a woman's voice, speaking almost appealingly, yet still with a note of command in it. 'We thought you would not mind if we came behind the scenes to see you. Such an adventure for us, you know. In fact we even wondered if there was any chance of persuading you to come to supper with us.'

The people in the passage could not be seen, but this was undoubtedly Stringham's mother. She introduced Chandler to the persons with her, but the names were inaudible.

'It would be so nice if you could come,' she said, quite humbly now. 'Your performance was wonderful. We adored it.'

Chandler had left the dressing-room now and was some way up the passage, but his voice could still be heard.

'It is terribly sweet of you, Mrs Foxe,' he said, with some hesitation. 'It would have been quite lovely. But as a matter of fact I was supposed to be meeting an old friend this evening.'

He seemed undecided whether or not to accept the invitation, to have lost suddenly all the animation he had been showing in the dressing-room a minute or two before. Moreland and Matilda had stopped talking and had also begun to listen, evidently with great enjoyment, to what was taking place outside.

'Oh, but if he is an old friend,' said Mrs Foxe, who seemed to make no doubt whatever of the sex of Chandler's companion for dinner, 'surely he might join us too. It would be so nice. What is his name?'

Although she was almost begging Chandler to accept her invitation, there was also in her voice the imperious note of the beauty of her younger days, the rich woman, well known in the world and used to being obeyed.

'Max Pilgrim.'

Chandler's voice, no less than Mrs Foxe's, suggested conflicting undertones of feeling: gratification at being so keenly desired as a guest; deference, in spite of himself, for the air of luxury and high living that Mrs Foxe bestowed about her; determination not to be jockeyed out of either his *gaminerie* or accustomed manner of ordering his own life by Mrs Foxe or anyone else.

'Not *the* Max Pilgrim?'

'He is at the Café de Madrid now. He sings there.'

'But, of course. "I want to dazzle Lady Sybil . . ." What a funny song that one is. Does he mean it to be about Sybil Huntercombe, do you think? It is so like her. We must certainly have Mr Pilgrim too. But will he come? He has probably planned something much more amusing. Oh, I do hope he will.'

'I think——'

'But how wonderful, if he would. Certainly you must ask him. Do telephone to him at once and beg him to join us.'

The exact words of Chandler's reply could not be heard, but there could be little doubt that he had been persuaded. Perhaps he was afraid of Max Pilgrim's annoyance if the supper party had been refused on behalf of both of them. In dealing with Mrs Foxe, Chandler seemed deprived, if only temporarily, of some of his effervescence of spirit. It looked as if he might be made her prisoner. This was an unguessed aspect of Mrs Foxe's life, a new departure in her career of domination. The party moved off, bearing Chandler with them; their voices died away as they reached the end of the passage. Moreland and Matilda continued to laugh. I asked what it was all about.

'Norman's grand lady,' said Matilda. 'She is someone called Mrs Foxe. Very smart. She sits on all sorts of committees and she met Norman a week or two ago at some charity performance. It was love at first sight.'

'You don't mean they are having an affair?'

'No, no, of course not,' said Moreland, speaking as if he were quite shocked at the notion, 'how absurd to suggest such a thing. You can have a passion for someone without having an affair with them. That is one of the things no one seems able to understand these days.'

'What is it then?'

'Just one of those fascinating mutual attractions between improbable people that take place from time to time. I should like to write a ballet round it.'

'Norman is interested too? He sounded a bit unwilling to go out to supper.'

'Perhaps not interested in the sense you mean,' said Moreland, 'but everyone likes being fallen in love with. People who pretend they don't are always the ones, beyond all others, to wring the last drop of pleasure—usually sadistic pleasure—out of it. Besides, Norman has begun to live rather a Ritzy life with her, he tells me. Some people like that too.'

'I think Norman is quite keen,' said Matilda, adding some final touches to her face that made completion of her toilet seem promising. 'Did you hear the way he was talking? Not at all like himself. I think the only thing that holds him back is fear of old friends like Max Pilgrim laughing.'

'Norman obviously represents the physical type of the future,' Moreland said, abandoning, as he so often did, the

54

particular aspect of the matter under discussion in favour of a more general aesthetic bearing. 'The great artists have always decided beforehand what form looks are to take in the world, and Norman is pure Picasso—one of those attenuated, androgynous mountebanks of the Blue Period, who haven't had a meal for weeks.'

'Come along, sweetie, and don't talk so much,' said Matilda, closing her bag and getting up from the dressing-table. 'If we don't have something to eat pretty soon we shall become attenuated, androgynous mountebanks ourselves.'

No phrase could have better described what she looked like. She had emerged at last in a purple satin dress and sequin mittens, the ultimate effect almost more exotic than if she had remained in the costume of the play. I found her decidedly impressive. It was evident from the manner in which she had spoken of Mrs Foxe that she was on easy terms with a world which Moreland, in principle, disliked, indeed entered only for professional purposes. A wife who could handle that side of his life would undoubtedly be an advantage to him. Conversationally, too, Matilda was equipped to meet him on his own ground. Moreland's talk when pursuing a girl varied little, if at all, from his conversation at any other time. Some women found this too severe an intellectual burden; others were flattered, even when incapable of keeping pace. With Matilda, this level of dialogue seemed just what was required. She was a clever girl, with a good all-round knowledge of the arts : one who liked to be treated as a serious person. This was apparent by the time we reached the restaurant, where Moreland at once began to discuss the play.

' "The lusty spring smells well; but drooping autumn tastes well," ' he said. 'How like:

> *Pauvre automne*
> *Meurs en blancheur et en richesse*
> *De neige et de fruits mûrs*

or : *Je suis soumis au Chef du Signe de l'Automne*
  Partant j'aime les fruits je déteste les fleurs

I was thinking the other day one might make an anthology
of the banker poets . . . Guillaume Apollinaire . . . T. S.
Eliot . . . Robert W. Service . . .'

He put down the menu which he had been studying.

'A wonderful idea,' said Matilda, who had been adding
magenta to her lips to emphasise the whiteness of her skin
or offset the colour of her dress, 'but first of all make up
your mind what you are going to eat. I have already decided
on Sole Bonne Femme, but I know we shall have to start all
over again when the waiter comes.'

Clearly she possessed a will of her own, and had already
learnt something of Moreland's habits; for example, that
persuading him to choose a dish at a restaurant was a pro-
tracted affair. When faced with a menu Moreland's first
thought was always to begin some lengthy discussion that
postponed indefinitely the need to make a decision about
food.

'What do you think I should like?' he said.

'Oeufs Meyerbeer,' she said. 'You always enjoy them.'

Moreland took up the menu again irresolutely.

'What do you think?' he said. 'I hate being hurried about
any of my appetites. What are you going to eat, Nick? I
am afraid you may order something that will make me
regret my own choice. You have done that in the past. It is
very disloyal of you. You know I think Gossage—in as much
as he possesses any sexual feelings at all—derives a certain
vicarious satisfaction from contemplating the loves of
Norman Chandler and Mrs Foxe. The situation manages to
embrace within one circumference Gossage's taste for rich
ladies and good-looking young men—together with a faint
spice of musical background.'

'Gossage says there is talk of putting on Marlowe's
Tamburlaine the Great,' said Matilda.

Moreland once again abandoned the menu.

' "Holla, ye pampered jades of Asia," ' he cried. ' "What, can ye draw but twenty miles a day?" That is rather what I feel about the newspaper criticism of Gossage and Maclintick. I should like them to drag me to concerts, as the kings drew Tamerlaine, in a triumphal coach. They would be far better employed doing that than pouring out all that stuff for their respective periodicals every week. Perhaps that is not fair to Maclintick. It is certainly true of Gossage.'

'I am sure Maclintick would draw you to the Queen's Hall in a rickshaw if you asked him,' said Matilda. 'He admires you so much.'

She turned to the waiter, ordered whatever she and I had agreed to eat, and Oeufs Meyerbeer for Moreland, who, still unable to come to a decision about food, accepted her ruling on this matter without dissent.

'I think there is just a chance I might be cast for Zenocrate,' she said, 'if they did ever do *Tamburlaine*. In any case, the show wouldn't be coming on for ages.'

'I wouldn't limit it to Maclintick and Gossage,' Moreland said. 'I should like to be dragged along by all the music critics, arranged in order of height, tallest in front, midgets at the back. That will give you some clue to what the procession would look like. I have always been interested in Tamerlaine. I found myself thinking of him the other day as part of that cruel, parched, Central Asian feeling one gets hearing *Prince Igor*. I am sure it was his bad leg that made him such a nuisance.'

'You may be interested in Tamerlaine, darling,' said Matilda, 'but you are not in the least interested in my career.'

'Oh, Matty, I am. I'm sorry. I am really. I want you to be the Duse of our time.'

He took her hand.

'I don't believe you, you old brute.'

In spite of saying that she smiled, and did not seem seriously annoyed. On the whole they appeared to understand one another pretty well. When the moment came to pay the bill, I flicked a note across to Moreland to cover my share. Matilda at once took charge of this, at the same time extracting another note from Moreland himself—always a great fumbler with money. These she handed over with a request for change. When the waiter returned with some money on a plate, she apportioned the silver equitably between Moreland and myself, leaving the correct tip; a series of operations that would have presented immense problems of manipulation to Moreland. All this enterprise made her appear to possess ideal, even miraculous, qualifications for becoming his wife. They were, indeed, married some months later. The ceremony took place in a registry office, almost secretly, because Moreland hated fuss. Not long after, perhaps a year, almost equally unexpectedly, I found myself married too; married to Isobel Tolland. Life—the sort of life Moreland and I used to live in those days—all became rather changed.

TWO

Sunday luncheon at Katherine, Lady Warminster's, never, as it were, specially dedicated to meetings of the family, had in the course of time grown into an occasion when, at fairly regular intervals, several—sometimes too many—of the Tollands were collected together. Now and then more distant relations were present, once in a way a friend; but on the whole immediate Tollands predominated. Everyone expected to meet their 'in-laws'; and, among other characteristics, these parties provided, at least superficially, a kind of parade of different approaches to marriage. There was in common a certain sense of couples being on their best behaviour in Lady Warminster's presence, but, in spite of that limited uniformity, routine at Hyde Park Gardens emphasised any individuality of matrimonial technique. Blanche, Robert, Hugo, and Priscilla Tolland still lived under the same roof as their step-mother, so that the two girls attended the meal more often than not; Robert, his social life always tempered with secrecy, was intermittently present; while Hugo, still tenuously keeping university terms accentuated by violent junctures when to be 'sent down' seemed unavoidable, could be seen there only during the vacation. This accommodation in the house of several younger members of the family had not resulted in much outward gaiety of atmosphere. On the contrary, the note struck as one entered the hall and ascended the staircase was quiet, almost despondent. The lack of exhilaration confirmed a favourite proposition of Moreland's as to the sadness of youth.

'I myself look forward ceaselessly to the irresponsibility of middle-age,' he was fond of stating.

It may, indeed, have been true that 'the children', rather than Lady Warminster herself, were to blame for this distinct air of melancholy. Certainly the environment was very different from the informality, the almost calculated disorder, surrounding the Jeavonses in South Kensington, a household I had scarcely visited since my marriage. Ted Jeavons's health had been even worse than usual; while Molly had given out that she was much occupied with reorganisation of the top floor (where her husband's old, bedridden—and recently deceased—cousin had lived), which was now to be done up as a flat for some friend or dependent. No doubt this reconditioning had reduced the Jeavons house to a depth of untidiness unthinkably greater than that which habitually prevailed there. The interior of Hyde Park Gardens was altogether in contrast with any such circumstance of invincible muddle. Hyde Park Gardens was unexceptional, indeed rather surprisingly ordinary, considering the personalities enclosed within, decorations and furniture expressing almost as profound an anonymity as Uncle Giles's private hotel, the Ufford; although, of course, more luxurious than the Ufford's, and kept just the right side of taste openly to be decried as 'bad', or even aggressively out of fashion.

Appreciably older than her sister Molly Jeavons—and, like her, childless—Lady Warminster had largely withdrawn from the world since her second husband's death in Kashmir eight or nine years before. Lord Warminster, who could claim some name as a sportsman, even as an amateur explorer, had formed the habit of visiting that country from time to time, not, so far as was known, on account of the sensual attractions extolled in the Kashmiri Love Song, but for pleasure in the more general beauty of its valleys, and the shooting of ibex there. On this last occasion, grazing his hand while opening a tin, he had contracted blood poisoning, an infection from which he subsequently died. Grieved in a remote way at her loss, although their comparatively brief married life together had been marked on his part by prolonged travel abroad, Lady Warminster had also been delighted to hand over Thrubworth to her eldest step-son,

Erridge; to settle herself permanently in London. She had always hated country life. Erridge had been less pleased to find himself head of the family at the age of eighteen or nineteen, saddled with the responsibilities of a large house and estate. Indeed, from that moment he had contended as little as possible with any but the most pressing duties contingent upon his 'position', devoting himself to his left-wing political interests, which merged into a not too exacting study of sociology.

Chips Lovell (with whom I had formerly been teamed up as a fellow script-writer in the film business), who was inclined to call almost everyone of an older generation than himself either 'Uncle' or 'Aunt', and was always prepared at a moment's notice to provide an *a priori* account of the personal history and problems of all his relations and acquaintances, had said: 'Like every other Ardglass, Aunt Katherine only really enjoys pottering about.' It was certainly true that Lady Warminster, as a widow, divided her time between her own ailments, real or imagined—opinion differed within the family on this point—and the writing of biographical studies devoted to the dominating, Amazonian women of history. Maria-Theresa, at the time of which I speak, had offered a theme sympathetic to the fashion of the moment for things Austrian. Lady Warminster enjoyed the reputation of having 'got on' pretty well with her step-children, even if no outstandingly warm sentiments existed between herself and any individual member of the family, except perhaps Blanche. In the past there had been, of course, occasional rows. Frederica and George found their step-mother's way of life too eccentric to wish to play much part in it themselves; Erridge and Norah, on the other hand, thought her hopelessly conventional. Such divergence of view was only to be expected in a large family, and most of her own contemporaries agreed on the whole that Katherine Warminster, so far as her step-children were concerned, was to be congratulated on having made a fairly good job of it. For my own part, I liked Lady

Warminster, although at the same time never wholly at ease in her presence. She was immaculately free from any of the traditional blemishes of a mother-in-law; agreeable always; entertaining; even, in her own way, affectionate; but always a little alarming: an elegant, deeply experienced bird—perhaps a bird of prey—ready to sweep down and attack from the frozen mountain peaks upon which she preferred herself to live apart.

Robert Tolland, seventh child and third son of his parents, was in the drawing-room at Hyde Park Gardens when, rather too early for the appointed time of the meal, I arrived there. He was a tall, cadaverous young man of about twenty-four, with his family's blue eyes and characteristic angularity of frame. Of my wife's brothers, Robert was the one with whom I felt myself generally most at home. He had some of the oddness, some of that complete disregard for public opinion, that distinguished Erridge (as I shall continue to call the eldest of the Tollands, since that was the name by which he was known within the family, rather than 'Alfred', or even 'Alf', preferred by his left-wing cronies like J. G. Quiggin), although at the same time Robert was without Erridge's political enthusiasm. He was not so conformist—'not so bloody boring', Chips Lovell had said—as his second brother, George Tolland (retired from the Brigade of Guards, now working in the City), although Robert to some extent haunted George's—to Chips Lovell—rather oppressive social world. In fact, outwardly, Robert was just as 'correct' as George, to use the term Molly Jeavons liked to apply to any of her relations whom she suspected of criticising her own manner of life. All the same, a faint suggestion of dissipation was also to be found in Robert; nothing like that thick sea mist of gossip which at an early age already encompassed his younger brother, Hugo, but something that affirmed to those with an instinct for recognising such things at long range, the existence in the neighbourhood of vaguely irregular behaviour. Chips Lovell, whose stories were always to be accepted with

62

caution, used to hint that Robert, a school contemporary of his, had a taste for night-club hostesses not always in their first youth. The case was non-proven. Robert would take girls out occasionally—girls other than the hypothetical 'peroxide blondes old enough to be his mother', so designated, probably imaginatively, by Lovell—but he never showed much interest in them for more than a week or two. By no means to be described as 'dotty' himself, there was perhaps something in Robert of his 'dotty' sister, Blanche: a side never fully realised, emotionally undeveloped. He sometimes reminded me of Archie Gilbert, that 'dancing man' of my early London days, whose life seemed exclusively lived at balls. Robert was, of course, more 'intelligent' than Archie Gilbert, intelligent at least in the crudest sense of being able to discourse comprehensibly about books he had read, or theatres, concerts and private views he had attended; conversational peaks to which Archie Gilbert had never in the least aspired. Robert, as it happened, was rather a keen concert-goer and frequenter of musical parties. He had a job in an export house trading with the Far East, employment he found perfectly congenial. No one seemed to know whether or not he was any good at the work, but Robert was thought by his sisters to possess a taste for making money. When I arrived in the drawing-room he was playing *Iberia* on the gramophone.

'How is Isobel?'

He threw the newspaper he had been reading to the ground and jumped to his feet, giving at the same time one of those brilliant smiles that suggested nothing could have come as a more delightful, a less expected, surprise than my own arrival in the room at just that moment. Although I was not exactly taken in by this reception, Robert's habitual exhibition of good manners never failed to charm me.

'Pretty well all right now. She is emerging tomorrow. I am going to see her this afternoon.'

'Do please give her my best love. I ought to have gone to see her in the nursing home myself. Somehow one never gets time for anything. What a bore it has been for you both. I was so sorry to hear about it.'

He spoke with solicitude, at the same time giving the impression that he was still, even at this late stage, unable wholly to conceal his wonder that someone should have chosen Isobel—or any other of his sisters—as a wife; nice girls, no doubt, beings for whom he felt the warmest affection, but creatures to be thought of always in terms of playing shops or putting their dolls to bed.

'Who will be at lunch?'

'I'll tell you. But shall we have the other side of this record first? I am playing them all in the wrong order. I love *Les Parfums de la Nuit*. I think that is really the bit I like best.'

'Do you adapt your music to the foreign news, Robert?'

'Rather suitable, isn't it? Now that the Alcazar has been relieved things seem to have become a bit static. I wonder who will win.'

He closed the lid of the gramophone, which began once more to diffuse the sombre, menacing notes adumbrating their Spanish background: tawny skies: dusty plains: bleak sierras: black marble sarcophagi of dead kings under arabesqued ceilings: *art nouveau* blocks of flats past which the squat trams rattled and clanged: patent-leather cocked hats of the Guardia Civil: leather cushions cast upon the sand under posters promulgating cures for impotence and the pox . . . these and a hundred other ever-changing cubist abstractions, merging their visual elements with the hurdy-gurdy music of the bull-ring . . . now—through this land-scape—baked by the sun, lorries, ramshackle as picadors' horses, crawled uphill in bottom gear and a stink of petrol . . . now, frozen by the wind and hooded like the muffled trio in Goya's *Winter*, Moorish levies convoyed pack-mules through the gorges veiled in snow . . .

'I expect you have heard about Erridge,' said Robert.

'That the Thrubworth woods will have to be sold?'

'Well, that, of course. But I mean his latest.'

'No?'

'He is going out there.'

'Where?'

Robert jerked his head in the direction of the shiny wooden cabinet from which Debussy quavered and tinkled and droned.

'Spain.'

'Indeed?'

'Can you imagine.'

'The International Brigade?'

'I don't know whether he will actually fight. As you know, he holds pacifist views. However, he will certainly be on the opposite side to General Franco. We can at least be sure of that. I can't think that Erry would be any great help to any army he joined, can you?'

The news that Erridge contemplated taking a comparatively active part in the Spanish civil war came as no great surprise to me. Politically, his sympathies would naturally be engaged with the extreme Left, whether Communist or Anarchist was not known. Possibly Erridge himself had not yet decided. He had been, of course, a supporter of Blum's 'Popular Front', but, within the periphery of 'Leftism', his shifting preferences were unpredictable; nor did he keep his relations informed on such matters. The only fact by then established was that Erridge had contributed relatively large sums of money to several of the organisations recently come into being, designed to assist the Spanish Republican forces. This news came from Quiggin, who like myself, visited from time to time the office of the weekly paper of which Mark Members was now assistant literary editor.

The fortunes of these two friends, Quiggin and Members, seemed to vary inversely. For a time Quiggin had been the more successful, supplanting Members as St John Clarke's secretary, finding congenial odd jobs in the world of letters, running away with the beautiful Mona, battening on Erridge; but ever since Mona had, in turn, deserted Quiggin for Erridge, Quiggin had begun to undergo a period of adversity. From taking a patronising line about Members, he now—like myself—found himself professionally dependent upon his old friend for books to review. The tide, on the other hand, seemed to be flowing in favour of Members. He had secured this presentable employment, not requiring so much work that he was unable to find time to write himself; his travel book, *Baroque Interlude*, had been a notable success; there was talk of his marrying a rich girl, who was also not bad-looking. So far as the affair of Mona was concerned, Quiggin had 'made it up' with Erridge; even declaring in his cups that Erridge had done him a good turn by taking her off his hands.

'After all,' said Quiggin, 'Mona has left him too. Poor Alf has nothing to congratulate himself about. He has just heaped up more guilt to carry round on his own back.'

After Erridge's return from the Far East, he and Quiggin had met at—of all places—a party given by Mrs Andriadis, whose sole interest now, so it appeared, was the Spanish war. Common sympathy in this cause made reconciliation possible without undue abasement on Quiggin's part, but the earlier project of founding a paper together was not revived for the moment, although Quiggin re-entered the sphere of Erridge's patronage.

'I correspond a certain amount with your brother-in-law,' he had remarked when we had last met, speaking, as he sometimes did, with that slight hint of warning in his voice.

'Which one?'

'Alf.'

'What do you correspond with him about?'

'Medical supplies for the Spanish Loyalists,' said Quiggin, pronouncing the words with quiet doggedness, 'Basque children—there is plenty to do for those with a political conscience.'

The whole business of Mona had made some strongly self-assertive action to be expected from Erridge; to be, in fact, all but certain to take place sooner or later. After leaving Quiggin, with whom she had been living during the period immediately prior to my own marriage, and setting sail with Erridge for China (where he planned to investigate the political situation), Mona had returned to England only a few months later by herself. No one had been told the cause of this severed relationship, although various stories—largely circulated by Quiggin himself—were current on the subject of Mona's adventures on the way home. She was the first woman in whom Erridge was known to have taken more than the most casual interest. It was not surprising that they should have found each other mutually incompatible. There was nothing easy-going about Mona's temperament; while Erridge, notwithstanding passionately humane and liberal principles, was used to having his own way in the smallest respect, his high-minded nonconformity of life in general absolving him, where other people were concerned, from even the irksome minor disciplines of everyday convention.

By leaving her husband, Peter Templer, in the first instance, Mona had undeniably shown aims directed to something less banal than mere marriage to a comparatively rich man. She would certainly never have put herself out for Erridge in order to retain him as husband or lover. What she did, in fact, desire from life was less explicable; perhaps, as Templer said after she left him, 'just to raise hell'. She had never, as once had been supposed, got herself married to Quiggin, so no question existed of further divorce proceedings. The Tolland family were less complacent about that fact than might have been expected.

'Personally, I think it was the greatest pity Erry failed to hold on to Minna, or whatever her name was,' Norah said. 'She sounds as if she might have done him a lot of good.'

Only George and Frederica dissented from this view among Erridge's brothers and sisters. More distant relations were probably divided about equally between those who resented, and those who thoroughly enjoyed, the idea of Erridge making a *mésalliance*. Lady Warminster's opinion was unknown. Possibly she too, in secret, considered—like Strindberg—any marriage better than none at all. Erridge himself, since his return from Asia, had remained alone, shut up in Thrubworth, occupying himself with those Spanish activities now to take a more decided form, refusing to attend to other more local matters, however pressing. The question of death duties had recently been reopened by the taxation authorities, the payment of which threatened a considerable sale of land to raise the money required. Only Norah, in face of opposition, had effected an entry into Thrubworth not long before this, reporting afterwards that her eldest brother had been 'pretty morose'. No one knew whether Erridge had achieved any degree of success in getting to the bottom of Far Eastern problems. Probably China and Japan, like his own estate, were now forgotten in contrast with a more fashionable preoccupation with Spain. To someone of Erridge's views and temperament, finding himself in the position he found himself, the Spanish war clearly offered a solution. Robert agreed in seeing nothing surprising in his brother's decision.

'Like big-game hunting in Edwardian days,' said Robert, 'or going to the Crusades a few years earlier. There will be one or two newspaper paragraphs about "the Red Earl", I suppose. Bound to be. Still, Erry gets remarkably little publicity as a rule, which is just as well. For some reason he has never become news. I hope he doesn't go and get killed. I shouldn't think he would, would you? Very well able to look after himself in his own way. All the same, a man I used to sit next to at school was shot in the street in Jerusalem the other day. In the back, just as he was getting into a taxi to go and have a spot of dinner. But he was a professional soldier and they have to expect that sort of thing. Rather different for someone like Erry who is a pacifist. I can't see the point of being a pacifist if you don't keep out of the way of fighting. Anyway, we can none of us be certain of surviving when the next war comes.'

'What will Erry do?'

'I suppose there will be a lot of the sort of people he likes out there already,' said Robert. 'His beard and those clothes will be all the go. He'll hang about Barcelona, lending a hand with the gardening, or the washing up, to show he isn't a snob. I think it is rather dashing of him to take this step considering his hypochondria. Of course, George would at least make some effort to keep up Thrubworth properly if he inherited. I say, I hope everyone is not going to be late. I am rather hungry this morning.'

'You haven't told me who is coming yet.'

'Nor I have. Well, the guest of honour is St John Clarke, the novelist. I expect you know him of old, as a brother of the pen.'

'As a matter of fact, Robert, I have never met St John Clarke. Who else?'

'Blanche, Priscilla—George and Veronica—Sue and Roddy.'

'But why St John Clarke?'

'I gather he more or less asked himself. His name is held on the books, you know. He used to turn up occasionally at Aunt Molly's. I remember Hugo being sick over him as a child. Probably St John Clarke sheered off the place after that. Of course he may be going to lend a hand with the Maria-Theresa book. I have only just thought of that possibility.'

Lady Warminster used sometimes to announce that she was receiving 'help' with one or another of her biographies from some fairly well-known figure—usually a distinguished politician or civil servant—although it was never explained what form this help took. Probably they adjusted the grammar.

'They tell me about punctuation,' she used to say.

This intermittent publication of an historical biography had in no way brought Lady Warminster into the literary world, nor could her house be said to present any of the features of a '*salon*'. A well-known author like St John Clarke was therefore an unexpected guest. At the Jeavonses' everything was possible. There was no one on earth who could occasion surprise there. Lady Warminster, on the contrary, living a very different sort of life, saw only relations and a few old friends. Even minor celebrities were rare, and, when they appeared, tended to be submerged by the family. Blanche and Priscilla entered the room at that moment, bearing between them on a tray a jigsaw puzzle, newly completed and brought downstairs to be admired.

When people called Blanche 'dotty', no question of incipient madness was implied, nor even mild imbecility. Indeed, after a first meeting it was possible to part company from her without suspicion that something might be slightly amiss. However, few who knew her well doubted that something, somewhere, had unquestionably gone a little wrong. Quieter than the rest of her sisters, good-looking, always friendly, always prepared to take on tedious tasks, Blanche would rarely initiate a conversation. She would answer with a perfectly appropriate phrase if herself addressed, but she never seemed to feel the need to comment on any but the most trivial topics. The world, the people amongst whom she moved, appeared to make no impression on her. Life was a dream that scarcely even purported to hold within its promise any semblance of reality. The cumulative effect of this chronic sleep-walking through her days—which far surpassed that vagueness of manner often to be found in persons well equipped to look after their own interest—together with her own acceptance of the fact that she was not quite like other people, did not care at all that she was different, had finally established Blanche's reputation for 'dottiness'. That was all. The impression of being undeveloped, unawakened, which perhaps in some degree Robert shared, may have caused both to prefer rather secret lives. Publicly, Blanche was almost always occupied with good works: girls' clubs in the East End; charities in which her uncle, Alfred Tolland, was concerned for which he sought her help. Blanche's practical activities were usually very successful so far as the end in view, although she herself never troubled to take much credit for them. Nor did she show any interest in getting married, though in her time not without admirers.

'We've finished it at last,' she said, indicating the puzzle. 'It took five months in all—with everyone who came to the house having a go. Then one afternoon the cats broke most of it up. The last few pieces were due to Priscilla's brilliance.'

She showed a huge representation of Venice, a blue-grey Santa Maria della Salute, reflected in blue-grey waters of the canal, against a blue-grey sky, Priscilla, six or seven years younger than her sister, longer-legged, with fairer, untidy hair, was then about twenty. In spite of his own good resolutions to marry an heiress, Chips Lovell had shown interest in her for a time; apparently without things coming to much. Priscilla had at present several beaux, successfully concealing her own feelings about them. She was not at all like her sister, Norah, in disparaging the whole male sex, but the young men she met at dances never seemed quite what she required. There was talk of her taking a job. A fund was being organised for the promotion of opera, and Robert, who knew some of the members of the board, thought he could find her a place in its office.

'How is Isobel?' Priscilla asked rather truculently, as if she had not yet forgiven her immediately elder sister, even after two years, for getting married before herself.

'Pretty well all right now. I am going to see her this afternoon.'

'I looked in the day before yesterday,' said Priscilla. 'It is a grimmish place, isn't it. I say, have you heard about Erry?'

'Robert told me this moment.'

'Erry is mad, of course. Do you know, I realised that for the first time when I was seven years old and he was grown up. Something about the way he was eating his pudding. I knew I must be growing up myself when I grasped that. Hullo, Veronica, hullo, George.'

The manner in which he wore his immensely discreet suit, rather than a slight, fair, fluffy moustache, caused George Tolland to retain the flavour of his service with the Brigade of Guards. Years before, when still a schoolboy, I had travelled to London with Sunny Farebrother, that business friend of Peter Templer's father, and he had remarked in the train : 'It helps to look like a soldier in the City. Fellows think they can get the better of you even before they start. That is always an advantage in doing a deal.' Perhaps George Tolland held the same theory. Certainly he had done nothing to modify this air of having just come off parade. Whether assumed consciously or not, the style rather suited him, and was quite unlike Ted Jeavons's down-at-heel look of being a wartime ex-officer. George was said to work like a slave in the City and seemed quite content with a social life offered chiefly by his own relations.

However, George had astonished everyone about eighteen months earlier by making an unexpected marriage. In some ways even Erridge's adventure with Mona had surprised his family less. Erridge was a recognised eccentric. He made a virtue of behaving oddly. In taking Mona abroad he had even, in a sense, improved his reputation for normality by showing himself capable of such an act. George, on the other hand, was fond of drawing attention—especially in contrasting himself with Erridge—to the exemplary, even, as he insisted, deliberately snobbish lines upon which his own life was run. 'I can never see the objection to being a snob,' George used to say. 'It seems far the most sensible thing to be.' Apparent simplicity of outlook is always suspicious. This remark should have put everyone on their guard. It was a sign that something was taking place under the surface of George's immaculate façade. However, since the vast majority accept at face value the personality any given individual puts forward as his own, no one in the least expected George to marry the woman he did. Veronica was the former wife of a businessman called Collins, whose job took him to Lagos for most of the year. She had two children by her first husband ('Native women,' said Chips Lovell, 'also some trouble about a cheque,') whom she had divorced a year or two before meeting George at some party given by City friends. A big brunette, not pretty, but with plenty of 'attack', Veronica was popular with her 'in-laws', especially Lady Warminster. She was older than George, now to all appearances completely under her thumb.

'How is Isobel, Nick?' Veronica asked. 'I went to see her last week. She was looking a bit washed out. I'd have gone again, but one of the kids was running a temperature and I got stuck in the house for a day or two. I hear St John Clarke is coming to lunch. Isn't that exciting? I used to love *Fields of Amaranth* when I was a girl. I never seem to get any time for reading now.'

George and Veronica were almost immediately followed into the room by Susan and her husband, Roddy Cutts, also in the City, now an M.P. Tall, sandy-haired, bland, Roddy smiled ceaselessly. The House of Commons had, if anything, increased a tendency, probably congenital, to behave with a shade more assiduity than ordinary politeness required; a trait that gave Roddy some of the bearing of a clergyman at a school-treat. Always smiling, his eyes roved for ever round the room, while he offered his hosts their own food, and made a point of talking chiefly to people he did not know, as if he felt these could not be altogether comfortable if still unacquainted with himself. In spite of accepting, indeed courting, this duty of putting young and old at their ease, he lacked the powerful memory—perhaps also the interest in individual differences of character—required to retain in the mind names and personal attributes; a weakness that sometimes impaired this eternal campaign of universal good-will. All the same, Roddy was able, ambitious, quite a formidable figure.

George and Roddy did not exactly dislike one another, but a certain faint sense of tension existed between them. Roddy, who came of a long line of bankers on his father's side, while his mother, Lady Augusta's, family could claim

73

an almost equal tradition of shrewd business grasp, undoubtedly regarded George as an amateur where money
matters were concerned. George, on the other hand, was
clearly made impatient when Roddy, speaking as a professional politician, explained in simple language the trend of
public affairs, particularly the military implications of world
strategy in relation to the growing strength of Germany.
Besides, Susan was George's favourite sister, so there may
have been a touch of jealousy about her too. Susan was a
pretty girl, not a beauty, but lively and, like her husband,
ambitious; possessing plenty of that taste for 'occcasion' so
necessary to the wife of a man committed to public life.

Lady Warminster now appeared in the room. She had
probably mastered her habitual unpunctuality at meals in
honour of St John Clarke. Slighter in build than her sister,
Molly Jeavons, she looked as usual like a very patrician sibyl
about to announce a calamitous disaster of which she had
personally given due and disregarded warning. This Cassan-
dra-like air of being closely in touch with sacred mysteries,
even with the Black Arts themselves, was not entirely misleading. Lady Warminster was prone to fortune-tellers and
those connected with divination. She was fond of retailing
their startling predictions. I found that, in her day, she
had even consulted Uncle Giles's fortune-telling friend, Mrs
Erdleigh, whom she rated high as an oracle, although the
two of them had long been out of touch, and had not 'put
the cards out' together for years.

'I asked Mr Clarke for half-past one,' said Lady Warminster. 'You know I had not seen him since one of those
rum parties Aunt Molly used to give, when I noticed him
at Bumpus's last week, browsing about among the books.
I think he only goes there to read the new ones, because
he showed no sign of wanting to buy anything. When he
caught sight of me, he immediately followed me out into
Oxford Street and began to talk about Shelley. He told me
a long story of how he wanted to see me again, how people
no longer liked him on account of his political opinions. He

is rather an old humbug, but I remember enjoying the first part of *Fields of Amaranth* when it came out. I always think one ought to be grateful to an author if one has liked even a small bit of a book.'

I had heard little of St John Clarke since the days when Mark Members and J. G. Quiggin had been, one after another in quick succession, his secretary; to be followed by the 'Trotskyist' German boy, Werner Guggenbühl; Guggenbühl, so Quiggin hinted, had been sacked as a result of political pressure, but did not mind leaving as he had found a better job. By this time, so many people of relative eminence were writing, speaking, or marching in one or another form of militant political expression that St John Clarke's adhesion to the Left was a matter of little general interest. He was said to have become at times resentful of a brand of politics he felt to lay a burden on his social life.

'The man has got it in him to be a traitor to any cause,' Quiggin said, when he reported this. 'We shall never see Clarke manning a machine-gun.'

This supposed backsliding on the part of St John Clarke was certainly not because any potential hostess objected to his being a 'Communist'. On the contrary, as an elderly, no longer very highly esteemed writer, such views may even have done something to re-establish his name. The younger people approved, while in rich, stuffy houses, where he was still sometimes to be seen on the strength of earlier reputation as a novelist, a left-wing standpoint was regarded as suitable to a man of letters, even creditable in a widely known, well-to-do author, who might at his age perfectly well have avoided the controversies of politics. However, St John Clarke himself apparently felt less and less capable, in practice, of taking part in the discussion of Marxist dialectic, with its ever-changing bearings. As a consequence of this laxity in 'keeping up', he had lost ground in the more exacting circles of the intellectual Left. His name was rarely seen except in alphabetical order among a score of nonentities signing at the foot of some letter to the press. St John

Clarke, according to Members (himself suspected by Quiggin of 'political cynicism') yearned for his former unregenerate life. If so, he must have felt himself too deeply committed, perhaps too old, to make a reversal of programme—which, at that period, would in any case have entailed swimming against a stream that brought to a writer certain advantages. Lady Warminster was probably better informed about St John Clarke than he supposed. Her phrase 'rather an old humbug' established within the family her own, as it were, official attitude. She now made some enquiry about the colds from which Veronica's two children, Angus and Iris, had been suffering.

'Oh, Angus is all right at last,' said George, speaking before his wife could reply. 'We have been looking about for a school for him. I am going down to see another next week.'

'They are both off to their Granny's on Friday,' said Veronica, 'where they will get fussed over a lot and probably catch colds all over again. But there it is. They have to go. The rest of the year will be spent getting them out of bad habits.'

'Talking of grandparents,' said George, who, although reputed to be very 'good' about Veronica's children, probably preferred relations on their father's side to be kept, in so far as possible, out of sight and out of mind, 'I was wondering whether I ought to try and reopen with Erry the question of getting the stained glass window put up to our own grandfather. I saw Uncle Alfred the other day—he has not been at all well, he tells me—who complained the matter had been allowed to drift for a number of years. I thought I would leave it for a time until Erry had settled down after his Chinese trip, then tackle him about it. There are always a mass of things to do after one has come home from abroad, especially after a long tour like that. I don't know what state of mind he is in at the moment. Do you happen to have seen anything of him lately?'

George's line about Erridge was pity rather than blame.

That was the tone in which these words had been spoken. Lady Warminster smiled to herself. She was known to regard the whole question of the stained glass window not only as at best a potential waste of money (out-of-date sentiment, threatening active production of ugliness) but also, no doubt correctly, as a matter to which Erridge would in no circumstances ever turn his attention; one, therefore, which was an even greater waste of time to discuss. She may have smiled for that reason alone. In addition, she was going to enjoy communicating to George news so highly charged with novelty as Erridge's latest project.

'You will have to be quick, George, if you want to get hold of Erry,' she said gently.

'Why?'

'He is going abroad again.'

'Where is he off to this time?'

'Spain.'

'What—to join in the war?'

'So he says.'

George took the information pretty well. He was by no means a fool, even if people like Chips Lovell did not find him a specially amusing companion. Like others who knew Erridge well, George had probably observed a cloud of that particular shape already forming on the horizon. Roddy Cutts, on the other hand, who, in the course of a couple of years of marriage to Susan, had only managed to meet her eldest brother once, was more surprised. Indeed, the whole Erridge legend, whenever it cropped up, always disturbed Roddy. He had clear-cut, practical ideas how people behaved. Erridge did not at all fit in with these.

'But surely Erridge isn't going to fight?' Roddy said. 'I suppose he has gone into the legal status of a British national taking part in a continental civil war. It is a most anomalous position—not to mention a great embarrassment to His Majesty's Government, whatever the party in power. I presume he will be anti-Franco, holding the views he does.'

'Of course he will be anti-Franco,' said George. 'But I

agree with you, Roddy, that I should not have thought actual fighting would have been in his line.'

All this talk was going on outside Lady Warminster's immediate orbit. Now she turned towards us to give one of her semi-official warnings.

'I believe Mr Clarke has something he wants to tell me about Erridge,' she said. 'It might entail a more or less private talk with him after luncheon. Don't any of you feel you have got to stay, if he decides to tell me some long rigmarole.'

She did not say, perhaps did not know, whether St John Clarke wanted to discuss Erridge's latest move or some more general matter that concerned Erridge's affairs. I had not heard that Erridge had been seeing more of St John Clarke recently. This indicated that their previous casual acquaintance must have grown in intimacy. The escapade with Mona, the decision to take part in the Spanish war, such things showed Erridge's more picturesque side, the aspect at which his beard and tattered clothes freely hinted. There were other, less dramatic matters to cause his family concern. The chief of these was the reopening of the question of death duties; but, in addition, the Thrubworth agent had died while Erridge was in China, revealing by vacation of office a situation often suspected by the rest of the family, that is to say gross, perhaps disastrous, mismanagement of the estate, which had been taking place over a long period. The account was seriously overdrawn at the bank. Thrubworth woods would probably have to be sold to meet the deficit. At least, selling the woods was Erridge's idea of the easiest way out; the trustees, too, were thought to be amenable to this solution. It was possible that Erridge, having no taste for meeting his step-mother to discuss business, had entrusted St John Clarke with some message on the subject, before he himself set off for Spain, where he could forget the trivialities of estate management in the turmoil of revolution. Perhaps Lady Warminster's last aside was intended to convey that, if business affairs

were to be discussed at all, they were not to be interrupte
If so, she made her announcement just in time, becau
a second later St John Clarke himself was announced. He
came hurriedly into the room, a hand held out in front of
him as if to grasp the handle of a railway carriage door
before the already moving train gathered speed and left the
platform.

'Lady Warminster, I am indeed ashamed of myself,' he
said in a high, rich, breathless, mincing voice, like that of
an experienced actor trying to get the best out of a minor
part in Restoration comedy. 'I must crave the forgiveness of
you and your guests.'

He gave a rapid glance round the room to discover whom
he had been asked to meet, at the same time diffusing about
him a considerable air of social discomfort. Lady Warminster accepted St John Clarke's hand carefully, almost
with surprise, immediately relinquishing it, as if the texture
or temperature of the flesh dissatisfied her.

'I hope you were not expecting a grand luncheon party,
Mr Clarke,' she said. 'There are only a few of the family
here, I am afraid.'

Plainly, that was only too true. There could be no doubt
from St John Clarke's face, flushed with running up the
stairs, that he had hoped for something better than what he
found; perhaps even a *tête-à-tête* with his hostess, rather
than this unwieldy domestic affair, offering neither intimacy
nor splendour. However, if disappointed at first sight, he
was an old campaigner in the ups and downs of luncheon
parties; he knew how to make the best of a bad job.

'Much, *much* pleasanter,' he murmured, still gazing sus-
piciously round the room. 'And I am sure you will agree
with me, Lady Warminster, in thinking, so far as company
is concerned, enough is as bad as a feast, and half a loaf in
many ways preferable to the alternative of a whole one or
the traditional no bread. How enjoyable, therefore, to be
just as we are.'

Although his strongly outlined features were familiar

from photographs in the papers, I had never before met this well-known author. Something about St John Clarke put him in the category—of which Widmerpool was another example—of persons at once absurd and threatening. St John Clarke's head recalled Blake's, a resemblance no doubt deliberately cultivated, because the folds and crannies of his face insistently suggested a self-applauding interior activity, a desire to let everyone know about his own 'mental strife'. I had seen him in person on a couple of occasions, though never before closely: once, five or six years earlier, walking up Bond Street with his then secretary Mark Members; a second time, on that misty afternoon in Hyde Park, propelled in a wheeled chair by Mona and Quiggin (who had replaced Members), while the three of them marched in procession as part of a political demonstration. Although he still carried himself with some degree of professional panache, St John Clarke did not look well. He might have been thought older than his years; his colour was not that of a man in good health. Once tall and gaunt in appearance, he had grown fat and flabby, a physical state which increased for some reason his air of being a dignitary of the Church temporarily passing, for some not very edifying reason, as a layman. Longish grey hair and sunken, haunted eyes recalled Mr Deacon's appearance, probably because both belonged to the same generation, rather than on account of much similarity about the way their lives had been lived. Certainly St John Clarke had never indulged himself in Mr Deacon's incurable leanings towards the openly disreputable. On the contrary, St John Clarke had been straitlaced, as much from inclination as from policy, during his decades of existence as a writer taken reasonably seriously. Even now, forgotten by the critics but remembered fairly faithfully by the circulating libraries, he had remained a minor public figure, occasionally asked to broadcast on some non-literary, non-political subject like the problem of litter or the abatement of smoke, talks into which he would always inject—so Members alleged—some small admixture of Marxist lore.

'And how is your sister, Lady Molly?' he asked, when we had moved into the dining-room and taken our places. 'It is many a year since I had the pleasure. Why, I scarcely seem to have seen her since she was châtelaine of Dogdene. How long ago seem those Edwardian summer afternoons.'

Lady Warminster, who was in one of her more playful moods, received the enquiry with kindly amusement, offering at once some formal statement which suggested no words of hers could do justice to conditions prevailing in the Jeavons house during redecoration. Lady Warminster had few illusions as to St John Clarke's preference for her sister as Marchioness of Sleaford, rich and presiding over a famous mansion, rather than married to Ted Jeavons and living in disorder and no great affluence in South Kensington. St John Clarke recalled that he had visited the Jeavons house, too, but also a long time ago. A minute or two later I heard her ask him whether he had read any of the two or three books I had written; a question calculated to produce more entertainment for Lady Warminster herself than gratification to St John Clarke or me. Aware, certainly, that I knew Members and Quiggin, he had given me a stiff, distrustful bow when introduced. Memories of his own dealings with that couple must have been unwelcome. Besides, Lady Warminster's buoyant manner was not of a kind to bring reassurance.

'Certainly, certainly,' said St John Clarke guardedly. 'I remember praising one of them. A laudable piece of work.'

He took a sip of the sickly white Bordeaux poured out for us. Lady Warminster possessed a horror of 'drink'. As a rule barely enough appeared at her table to satisfy the most modest requirements. This was perhaps her sole characteristic shared with Erridge. St John Clarke was abstemious too. Members, during his secretaryship, had tried to encourage in his master a taste for food and wine, but complained later that the only result had been a lot of talk about rare vintages and little known recipes, while the meals at St John Clarke's table grew worse than ever.

'Yes,' said St John Clarke, wiping his mouth and refolding the napkin on his knee, 'yes.'

It was true he had spoken favourably of my first book in a New York paper, when discoursing in general terms of younger English writers. That, so far as I was concerned, had been the first indication that St John Clarke—in the hands of Members—was undergoing some sort of aesthetic conversion. Kind words from him only a short time before would have been unthinkable. However, mention of a first novel at the safe remove of an American newspaper's bookpage is one thing : to be brought face to face with its author five or six years later, quite another. So, at least, St John Clarke must have keenly felt. Mutual relationship between writers, whatever their age, is always delicate, not so much—as commonly supposed—on account of jealousy, but because of the intensely personal nature of a writer's stock in trade. For example, St John Clarke seemed to me a 'bad' writer, that is to say a person to be treated (in those days) with reserve, if not thinly veiled hostility. Later, that question—the relationship of writers of different sorts—seemed, like so many others, less easily solved; in fact infinitely complicated. St John Clarke himself had made a living, indeed collected a small fortune, while giving pleasure to many by writing his books (pleasure even to myself when a boy, if it came to that), yet now was become an object of disapproval to me because his novels did not rise to a certain standard demanded by myself. Briefly, they seemed to me trivial, unreal, vulgar, badly put together, odiously phrased and 'insincere'. Yet, even allowing for these failings, was not St John Clarke still a person more like myself than anyone else sitting round the table? That was a sobering thought. He, too, for longer years, had existed in the imagination, even though this imagination led him (in my eyes) to a world ludicrously contrived, socially misleading, professionally nauseous. On top of that, had he not on this earlier occasion gone out of his way to speak a word of carefully hedged praise for my own work? Was that, therefore, an aspect of his critical faculty for which he should be given credit, or was it an even stronger reason for guarding against the possibility of corruption at the hands of one whose own writings could not be approved? Fortunately these speculations, heavily burdened with the idealistic sentiments of one's younger days, were put to no practical test; not only because St John Clarke was sitting at some distance from me, but also on account of the steps he himself immediately took to change a subject likely to be unfruitful to both of us. He quickly commented on the flowers in the vases, which were arranged with great skill, and turned out to be the work of Blanche.

'Flowers mean more to us in a city than in a garden,' said St John Clarke.

Lady Warminster nodded. She was determined not to abandon the subject of literature without a struggle.

'I expect you are writing a new book yourself, Mr Clarke,' she said. 'We have not had one from you for a long time.'

'Nor from you, Lady Warminster.'

'But I am not a famous writer,' she said. 'I just amuse myself with people like Maria-Theresa who take my fancy. For you, it is quite another matter.'

St John Clarke shook his head energetically, like a dog emerging from a pond. It was ten or fifteen years since he had published anything but occasional pieces.

'Sometimes I add a paragraph to my memoirs, Lady Warminster,' he said. 'There is little about the critics of the present day to encourage an author of my age and experience to expose his goods in the market place. To tell the truth, Lady Warminster, I get more pleasure from watching the confabulation of sparrows in their parliament on the roof-tops opposite my study window, or from seeing the clouds scudding over the Serpentine in windy weather, than

I do from covering sheets of foolscap with spidery script that only a few sympathetic souls, some now passed on to the Great Unknown, would even care to read.

> No sparrow on any roof was ever lonely
> As I am, nor any animal untamed.

Doesn't Petrarch say that somewhere? He is a great stay to me. Childish pleasures, you may tell me, Lady Warminster, but I answer you that growing old consists abundantly in growing young.'

Lady Warminster was about to reply, whether in agreement or not with this paradox was never revealed, because St John Clarke suddenly realised that his words belonged to an outdated, even decadent state of mind, wholly inconsistent with political regeneration. He could hardly have been carried away by the white wine. Probably it was some time since he had attended a luncheon party of this sort, the comparative unfamiliarity of which must have made him feel for a minute or two back in some much earlier sequence of his social career.

'Of course I was speaking of when the errant mind strays,' he added in a different, firmer tone, 'as I fear the mind of that unreliable fellow, the intellectual, does from time to time. I meant to imply that, when there are so many causes to claim one's attention, it seems a waste of time to write about the trivial encounters of an individual like myself, who has spent so much of his time pursuing selfish, and, I fear, often frivolous aims. We shall have to learn to live more collectively, Lady Warminster. There is no doubt about it.'

'That was just what a fellow in the City was saying to me the other day,' said George. 'We were talking about those trials for treason in Russia. I can't make head or tail of them. He seemed full of information about Zinoviev and Kamenev and the rest of them. He was quite well disposed to Russia. A bill-broker named Widmerpool. You probably

84

remember him at school, Nick. Some story about an overcoat, wasn't there?'

'I've met him,' said Roddy. 'Used to be with Donners-Brebner. Heavy-looking chap with thick spectacles. As a matter of fact, he was always regarded as rather a joke in our family at the time when my sister, Mercy, was going to dances. He was the absolute last resort when a man had dropped out for a dinner party. Didn't some girl pour sugar over his head once at a ball?'

'What's happened to Widmerpool?' I asked. 'I haven't seen him for a year or two. Not since Isobel and I were married, as a matter of fact. I've known him for ages.'

'Fettiplace-Jones was giving him dinner at the House,' said Roddy, 'the night of the India debate.'

'Is he thinking of standing?' George asked. 'He is rather the type.'

'Not as a Tory,' Roddy said. 'Widmerpool is far from being a Tory.'

Roddy looked a shade resentful at George's probably quite artless judgment that Widmerpool was the sort of man likely to make an M.P.

'I ran across him somewhere,' said George. 'Then he was sitting at the next table one day at Sweeting's. He struck me as a knowledgeable chap. We had him to dinner as a matter of fact. Now I come to think of it, he said he knew you, Nick. My firm does a certain amount of business with Donners-Brebner, where Widmerpool used to be. He may be going back there in an advisory capacity, anyway temporarily, he told me.'

'I didn't at all take to Mr Widmerpool,' said Veronica, breaking off conversation with Susan on the subject of the best place to buy curtain material. 'He could talk of nothing but Mrs Simpson the night he came to us. You couldn't get him off the subject.'

St John Clarke, who had begun to look a little petulant at all this chatter about persons in general unknown to him, brightened at that name. He seemed about to speak; then some inner prompting must have caused him to think better of expressing any reflections stirring within his mind, because finally he remained silent, crumbling his bread thoughtfully.

'I met Mr Widmerpool once at Aunt Molly's,' said Susan. 'There was that business of his engagement being broken off, wasn't there—with that rather dreadful lady, one of the Vowchurches?'

'I hear poor Uncle Ted is a little better,' said Lady Warminster.

She referred to the war wound from which Jeavons intermittently suffered, at the same time managing to convey also a sense of moral or social improvement in Jeavons's condition which appeared for some reason to forbid further discussion of Widmerpool's unsuccessful attempt of a year or two before to marry Mrs Haycock.

'Roddy and I were at the Jeavonses' last week,' said Susan. 'The worst of the redecorating is over now, although one still falls over ladders and pails of whitewash. Aunt Molly's friend Miss Weedon—whom I can't stand—has moved in permanently now. She has a kind of flat on the top floor. And do you know who is living there too? Charles Stringham of all people. Do you remember him? Miss Weedon is said to be "looking after him".'

'Was that the Stringham we were at school with?' George asked me, but with no idea of what amazement I felt at this news, 'He was another contemporary of Widmerpool's.'

'I used to think Charles Stringham so attractive when he occasionally turned up at dances,' said Susan reminiscently, speaking as if at least half a century had passed since she herself had been seen on a dance floor. 'Then he absolutely disappeared from the scene. What happened to him? Why does he need "looking after"?'

'Charles Stringham isn't exactly a teetotaller, darling,' said Roddy, showing slight resentment at the expression by his own wife of such unqualified praise of another man's charms.

Lady Warminster shuddered visibly at the thought of what that understatement about Stringham's habits must comprehend. I asked Susan how this indeed extraordinary situation had come about: that Miss Weedon and String-ham should be living under the same roof at the Jeavonses.'

'Charles Stringham went to see Miss Weedon there one evening—she was his mother's secretary once, and has always been friends with Charles. He was in an awful state apparently, with 'flu coming on, practically delirious. So Miss Weedon kept him there until he recovered. In fact he has been there ever since. That is Aunt Molly's story.'

'Molly mentioned something about it to me,' said Lady Warminster.

She spoke very calmly, as if in reassuring confirmation that there was really nothing whatever for anyone to worry about. Having once registered her own illimitable horror of alcohol, Lady Warminster was fully prepared to discuss Stringham's predicament, about which, as usual, she prob-ably knew a great deal more than her own family supposed. The information about Stringham was not only entirely new to me, but full of all kind of implications of other things deep rooted in the past; far more surprising, far more dramatic, for example, than Erridge's setting off for Spain.

'Charles is Amy Foxe's son by her second husband,' said Lady Warminster. 'There was a daughter, too—divorced from that not very nice man with one arm—who is married to an American called Wisebite. Amy has had trouble with both her children.'

Stringham's mother was an old friend of Lady War-minster's, although the two of them now saw each other rarely. That was chiefly because Mrs Foxe's unrelenting social activities allowed little time for visits to the drowsy, unruffled backwater in which the barque of Lady War-minster's widowhood had come to rest; unruffled, that is

87

to say, in the eyes of someone like Mrs Foxe. In fact, life at Hyde Park Gardens could not always be so described, although its tenor was very different from the constant rotation of parties, committee meetings, visits, through which Mrs Foxe untiringly moved. Perhaps this description of Mrs Foxe's existence was less exact since she had become so taken up with Norman Chandler; but, although she might now frequent a less formal social world (her charity organising remained unabated), she had been, on the other hand, correspondingly drawn into Chandler's own milieu of the theatre and music.

'It is really very good of Miss Weedon to look after Charles Stringham,' Lady Warminster continued. 'His mother, what with her hospitals and those terrible wars over them with Lady Bridgnorth, is always so dreadfully busy. Miss Weedon—Tuffy, everyone used to call her— was Flavia Stringham's governess before she became her mother's secretary. Such a nice, capable woman. I don't know why you should not like her, Sue.'

This speech did not make absolutely clear whether Lady Warminster cared as little as Susan for Mrs Foxe's former secretary, or whether, as the words outwardly indicated, she indeed approved of Miss Weedon and liked meeting her. Lady Warminster's pronouncements in such fields were often enigmatic. Possibly we were all intended to infer from her tone a shade of doubt as to whether Miss Weedon should have been allowed to take such absolute control over Stringham as now seemed to prevail. I felt uncertainty on that subject myself. This new situation might be good; it might be bad. I remembered Miss Weedon's unconcealed adoration for him when still a boy; the signs she had shown later at Jeavonses' of hoping to play some authoritarian rôle in Stringham's life.

'I am doing what I can to help,' Miss Weedon had said, when we had met at the Jeavons house not long before my marriage.

Then, I had wondered what she meant. Now I saw that

restraint, even actual physical restraint, might have been in her mind. Perhaps nothing short of physical restraint would meet Stringham's case. It was at least arguable. Miss Weedon was providing something of the sort.

'Molly will be glad of the additional rent,' said Lady Warminster, who seemed to be warming to the subject, now that its alcoholic aspects had faded into the background. 'She has been complaining a lot lately about being hard up. I tremble to think what Ted's doctor's bill must be like at any time. What difficulties he has with his inside. However, he is off slops again, I hear.'

'Have the Stringhams any money?' George asked.

'Oh, I don't think so,' said Lady Warminster, speaking as if the mere suggestion of anyone, let alone the Stringhams, having any money was in itself a whimsical enough notion. 'But I believe Amy was considered quite an heiress when she first appeared in London and old Lady Amesbury took her about a lot. She was South African, you know. Most of it spent now, I should think. Amy has always been quite thoughtless about money. She is very wilful. People said she was brought up in a very silly way. I suppose she probably lives now on what her first husband, Lord Warrington, left in trust. I don't think Charles's father—"Boffles", as he used to be called—had a halfpenny to bless himself with. He used to be very handsome, and so amusing. He looked wonderful on a horse. He is married now to a Frenchwoman he met at a tennis tournament in Cannes, and he farms in Kenya. Poor Amy, she has some rather odd friends.'

In making this last comment, Lady Warminster was no doubt thinking of Norman Chandler; although no one could say how much, or how little, she knew of this association, nor what she thought about it. Robert caught my eye across the table. Within the family, he was regarded as the chief authority on their step-mother's obliquity of speech. Robert, strangely enough, had turned out to be one of the young men I had seen with Mrs Foxe at that performance

of *The Duchess of Malfi* three or four years before. Mrs
Foxe's other two guests had been John Mountfichet, the
Bridgnorth's eldest son, and Venetia Penistone, one of the
Huntercombes' daughters. After we had become brothers-
in-law, and later talked of this occasion, Robert had described to me the excitement shown by Mrs Foxe that
night at the prospect of seeing Chandler after the play was
over. It was only a week or two since they had met for
the first time.

'You know Mrs Foxe is rather daunting in her way,'
Robert had said. 'At least she always rather daunts me.
Well, she was trembling that night like a leaf. I think she
was absolutely mad about that young actor we eventually
took out to supper. She didn't get much opportunity to
talk to him, because Max Pilgrim came too and spent the
whole evening giving imitations of elderly ladies.'

This companionship between Mrs Foxe and Chandler
still flourished. She was said to give him 'wonderful' pre-
sents, expecting nothing in return but the pleasure of seeing
him when he had the time to spare. That one of the most
exigent of women should find satisfaction in playing this
humble rôle was certainly remarkable. Chandler, lively and
easy-going, was quite willing to fall in with her whim. They
were continually seen about together, linked in a relationship somewhere between lover with mistress and mother to
son.

'I could understand it if Norman were a sadist,' Moreland
used to say. 'A mental one, I mean, who cut her dates and
suchlike. On the contrary, he is always charming to her. Yet
it still goes on. Women are inexplicable.'

During all this talk about Stringham and his parents, St
John Clarke had once more dropped out of the conversation.
His face was beginning to show that, although aware a self-
invited guest must submit to certain periods of inattention
on the part of his hostess, these had been allowed to become
too frequent to be tolerated by a man of his position. He
began to shift about in his chair as if he had something on

his mind, perhaps wondering if he would finally be given a chance of being alone with Lady Warminster, or whether he had better say whatever he had to say in public. He must have decided that a *tête-à-tête* was unlikely, because he now spoke to her in a low confidential tone.

'There was a matter I wanted to put to you, Lady Warminster, which, in the hurried circumstances of our meeting at Bumpus's, I hardly liked to bring up. That was why I invited myself so incontinently to your house, to which you so graciously replied with an invitation to this charming lunch party. Lord Warminster—your eldest stepson—Alfred, I have begun to call him.'

St John Clarke paused, laughed a little coyly, and put his head on one side.

'*We* call him Erridge,' said Lady Warminster kindly, 'I never quite know why. It was not the custom in my own family, but then we were different from the Tollands in many ways. The Tollands have always called their eldest son by the second title. I suppose he could perfectly well be called Alfred. And yet, somehow, Erridge is not quite an Alfred.'

She considered a moment, her face clouding, as if the problem of why Erridge was not quite an Alfred worried her more than a little, even made her momentarily sad.

'Lady Priscilla mentioned her brother's political sympathies just now,' said St John Clarke, smiling gently in return, as if to express the ease with which he could cope with social fences of the kind Lady Warminster set in his way. 'I expect you may know he is leaving for Spain almost immediately.'

'He told me so himself,' said Lady Warminster.

'The fact is,' said St John Clarke, getting rather red in the face and losing some of his courtliness of manner, 'the fact is, Lady Warminster, your stepson has asked me to look after his business affairs while he is away. Of course I do not mean his estate, nothing like that. His interests of a politico-literary kind——'

He took up his glass, but it was empty.

'Lord Warminster and I have been seeing a good deal of each other since his return from the East,' he said, stifling a sigh probably caused by thoughts of Mona.

'At Thrubworth?' asked Lady Warminster.

She showed sudden interest. In fact everyone at the table pricked up their ears at the supposition that St John Clarke had been received at Thrubworth. Guests at Thrubworth were rare. A new name in the visitors' book would be a significant matter.

'At Thrubworth,' said St John Clarke reverently. 'We talked there until the wee, small hours. During the past few years both of us have undergone strains and stresses, Lady Warminster. Alfred has been very good to me.'

He stared glassily down the table, as if he thought I myself might well be largely to blame for Members and Quiggin; for the disturbances the two of them must have evoked in his personal life.

'No one can tell what may happen to Lord Warminster in Spain,' St John Clarke said, speaking now more dramatically. 'He knows me to be a strong supporter of the democratically elected Spanish Government. He knows I feel an equally strong admiration for himself.'

'Yes, of course,' said Lady Warminster encouragingly.

'At the same time, Lady Warminster, I am an author, a man of letters, not a man of affairs. I thought it only right you should know the position. I want to do nothing behind your back. Besides that, Alfred has occasional dealings with persons known to me in the past with whom I should be unwilling . . . I do not mean of course . . .'

These phrases, which seemed to appeal to Lady Warminster's better feelings, certainly referred in the main to Quiggin.

'Oh, I am sure he does,' said Lady Warminster fervently. 'I do so much sympathise with you in feeling that.'

She plainly accepted St John Clarke's halting sentences as reprobating every friend Erridge possessed.

'In short I wondered if I could from time to time ask your advice, Lady Warminster—might get in touch with you if necessary, perhaps even rely on you to speak with acquaintances of your stepson's with whom—for purely personal reasons, nothing worse I assure you—I should find it distasteful to deal.'

St John Clarke made a gesture to show that he was throwing himself on Lady Warminster's mercy. She, on her part, did not appear at all unwilling to learn something of Erridge's affairs in this manner, although she can have had no very clear picture of St John Clarke's aims, which were certainly not easy to clarify. No doubt he himself liked the idea of interfering in Erridge's business, but at the same time did not wish to be brought once more in contact with Quiggin. Lady Warminster must have found it flattering to be offered the position of St John Clarke's confidante, which would at once satisfy curiosity and be in the best interests of the family. If Erridge never came back from Spain—an eventuality which had to be considered—there was no knowing what messes might have to be cleared up. Besides, Erridge's plans often changed. His doings had to be coped with empirically. Like less idealistic persons, he was primarily interested in pleasing himself, even though his pleasures took unusual form. Little could be guessed from an outward examination of these enthusiasms at any given moment.

'Write to me, Mr Clarke, or telephone,' said Lady Warminster, 'whenever you think I can be of help. Should my health not allow me to see you at that moment, we will arrange something later.'

I had by then seen too much of Lady Warminster and her stepchildren to be surprised by the calm with which news of this sort was accepted. My own temper was in sympathy with such an attitude of mind. I looked forward to hearing Quiggin's account of the current Erridge situation. Possibly Quiggin himself might decide to go to Spain. Such a move was not to be ruled out. No doubt he too intended to keep an eye on Erridge's affairs; the best way to do that might be to attach himself to Erridge's person. The development of St John Clarke as a close friend of Erridge must be very unsympathetic to Quiggin. St John Clarke's appeal to Lady Warminster was unexpected. He had managed to get most of it said without attracting much attention from the rest of the party, who were discussing their own affairs, but the general drift of his muttered words probably caused the turn conversation took when it became general once more.

'Do you hold any view on what the outcome in Spain will be, Mr Clarke?' asked George.

St John Clarke made a gesture with his fingers to be interpreted as a much watered-down version of the Popular Front's clenched fist. Now that he had had his word with Lady Warminster about Erridge, he seemed more cheerful, although I was again struck by the worn, unhealthy texture of his skin. He still possessed plenty of nervous energy, but had lost his earlier flush. His cheeks were grey and pasty in tone. He looked a sick man.

'Franco cannot win,' he said.

'What about the Germans and Italians?' said George. 'It doesn't look as if non-intervention will work. It has been a failure from the start.'

'In that case,' said St John Clarke, evidently glad to find an opportunity to pronounce this sentence, 'can you blame Caballero for looking elsewhere for assistance.'

'Russia?'

'In support of Spain's elected government.'

'Personally, I am inclined to think Franco will win,' said George.

'Is that to your taste?' asked St John Clarke mildly.

'Not particularly,' George said. 'Especially if that has got to include Hitler and Mussolini. But then Russia isn't to my taste either. It is hard to feel much enthusiasm for the way the Government side go on, or, for that matter, the way they were going before the war broke out.'

'People like myself look forward to a social revolution in

a country that has remained feudal far too long,' said St John Clarke, speaking now almost benignly, as if the war in Spain was being carried on just to please him personally, and he himself could not help being flattered by the fact. 'We cannot always be living in the past.'

This expressed preference for upheaval for its own sake roused Roddy Cutts. He began to move forward his knives and forks so that they made a pattern on the table, evidently a preliminary to some sort of a speech. St John Clarke was about to expand his view on revolution, when Roddy cut him short in measured, moderate, parliamentary tones.

'The question is,' Roddy said, 'whether the breakdown of the internal administration of Spain—and nobody seriously denies the existence of a breakdown—justified a military *coup d'état*. Some people think it did, others disagree entirely. My own view is that we should not put ourselves in the position of seeming to encourage a political adventurer of admittedly Fascist stamp, while at the same time expressing in no uncertain terms our complete lack of sympathy for any party or parties which allow the country's rapid disintegration into a state of lawlessness, which can only lead, through Soviet intrigue, to the establishment of a Communist régime.'

'I think both sides are odious,' said Priscilla. 'Norah backs the Reds, like Erry. She and Eleanor Walpole-Wilson have got a picture of La Pasionaria stuck up on the mantelpiece of their sitting-room. I asked them if they approved of shooting nuns.'

St John Clarke's expression suggested absolute neutrality on that point.

'The tradition of anti-clericalism in Spain goes back a long way, Lady Priscilla,' he said, 'especially in Catalonia.'

Roddy Cutts had no doubt been studying Spanish history too, because he said: 'You will find an almost equally unbroken record of Royalism in Navarre, Mr Clarke.'

'I haven't been in Spain for years,' said Lady Warminster, in her low, musical voice, speaking scarcely above a whisper. 'I liked the women better than the men. Of course they all have English nannies.'

Luncheon at an end, St John Clarke established himself with Blanche in a corner of the drawing-room, where he discoursed of the humour of Dickens in a rich, sonorous voice, quite unlike the almost falsetto social diction he had employed on arrival. Blanche smiled gently, while with many gestures and grimaces St John Clarke spoke of Mr Micawber and Mrs Nickleby. They were still there, just beginning on *Great Expectations*, when I set out for the nursing home, carrying messages of good-will to Isobel from the rest of the family.

A future marriage, or a past one, may be investigated and explained in terms of writing by one of its parties, but it is doubtful whether an existing marriage can ever be described directly in the first person and convey a sense of reality. Even those writers who suggest some of the substance of married life best, stylise heavily, losing the subtlety of the relationship at the price of a few accurately recorded, but isolated, aspects. To think at all objectively about one's own marriage is impossible, while a balanced view of other people's marriage is almost equally hard to achieve with so much information available, so little to be believed. Objectivity is not, of course, everything in writing; but if one has cast objectivity aside, the difficulties of presenting marriage are inordinate. Its forms are at once so varied, yet so constant, providing a kaleidoscope, the colours of which are always changing, always the same. The moods of a love affair, the contradictions of friendship, the jealousy of business partners, the fellow feeling of opposed commanders in total war, these are all in their way to be charted. Marriage, partaking of such—and a thousand more —dual antagonisms and participations, finally defies definition. I thought of some of these things on the way to the nursing home.

'How were they all?' asked Isobel.

We went over the luncheon party in detail; discussed

the news about Erridge. Isobel was returning the following day, so that there were domestic arrangements to be rehearsed, mysteries of the labyrinth of married life, fallen into abeyance with her imprisonment, now to be renewed with her release.

'I shan't be sorry to come home.'

'I shan't be sorry for you to be home again.'

Late in the afternoon I left the place. Its passages somewhat like those of Uncle Giles's *pied-à-terre*, the Ufford, were additionally laden with the odour of disinfectant, more haunted with human kind. As in the Ufford, it was easy to lose your way. Turning a corner that led to the stairs, I suddenly saw in front of me, of all people, Moreland, talking to a tall, grey-haired man, evidently a doctor, because he carried in his hand, like a stage property in a farce, a small black bag. Moreland looked hopelessly out of place in these surroundings, so that the two of them had some of the appearance of taking part in a play. The doctor was talking earnestly, Moreland fidgeting about on his feet, evidently trying to get away without too great a display of bad manners. We had not met for over a year—although occasionally exchanging picture postcards—because Moreland had taken a job at a seaside resort known for pride in its musical activities. Sooner or later to be a conductor in the provinces was a destiny Moreland had often predicted for himself in moods of despondency. I knew little or nothing about his life there, nor how his marriage was going. The postcards dealt usually with some esoteric matter that had caught his attention—a peculiar bathing dress on the beach, peepshows on the pier, the performance of pierrots —rather than the material of daily life. In the earlier stages of marriage, Matilda was keeping pace pretty well with circumstances not always easy from shortage of money. When he caught sight of me, Moreland looked quite cross, as if I had surprised him in some situation of which he was almost ashamed.

'What on earth are you doing here?' he asked brusquely.

'Visiting my wife.'

'Like me.'

'Is Matilda in this awful place too?'

'But of course.'

He, too, had seemed in the depths of gloom when I first saw him; now, delighted at encountering a friend in these unpromising surroundings, he began to laugh and slap a rolled-up newspaper against his leg. Matilda had made him buy a new suit, in general cleaned up his appearance.

'So you have come back to London.'

'Inevitably.'

'For good?'

'I had to. I couldn't stand the seaside any longer. Matilda is about to have a baby, as a matter of fact. That is why I am haunting these portals.'

'Isobel has just had a miscarriage.'

'Oh, Lord,' said Moreland, 'I am always hearing about miscarriages. I used to think such things were quite out of date, and took place only in Victorian times when ladies—as Sir Magnus Donners would say—laced themselves up "a teeny, teeny little bit too tight". Rather one of Sir Magnus's subjects. I may add I shall be quite bankrupt unless Matilda makes up her mind fairly soon. She keeps on having false alarms. It is costing a fortune.'

He began to look desperately worried. The man with the black bag took a step forward.

'Both you gentlemen might be surprised if I told you the incidence of abortion recently quoted in medical journals,' he said in a thin, rasping voice.

'Oh, sorry,' said Moreland. 'This is Dr Brandreth.'

I saw the man to be the Brandreth who had been at school with me. Four or five years older, he had probably been unaware of my existence at that time, but I had seen him again at least once in later life, notably at that Old Boy Dinner at which our former housemaster, Le Bas, had fainted, an occasion when Brandreth, as a doctor, had taken charge of the situation. Tall and bony, with hair like the locks of a young actor who has dusted over his skull to play a more aged part in the last act, Brandreth possessed those desiccated good looks which also suggest the theatre. I began to explain that I knew him already, that we had been schoolboys together, but he brushed the words aside with a severe 'Yes, yes, yes . . .' at the same time taking my hand in a firm, smooth, interrogatory, medical grip, no doubt intended to give confidence to a patient, but in fact striking at once a disturbing interior dread at the possibilities of swift and devastating diagnosis.

'Another of my woman patients,' he went on, 'happens to be in here. Rather a difficult case for the gynaecologist. I've been giving him a hand with the after-treatment—from the temperamental point of view.'

Brandreth continued to hold Moreland with his eye, as if to make sure his attention did not wander too far afield. At the same time he took up a position closer to myself that seemed to imply appeal to me, as one probably familiar with Moreland's straying mind, to help if necessary in preventing his escape before the time was ripe. Penning us both in, Brandreth was evidently determined to obstruct with all the forces at his command further conversation between us which, by its personal nature, might exclude himself. However, at the critical moment, just as Brandreth was beginning to speak, he was interrupted by the competition of a new, impelling force. A stoutly built man, wearing a Jaeger dressing-gown, pushed past us without ceremony, making towards a door of frosted glass in front of which we were grouped. In his manner of moving, this person gave the impression that he thought we were taking up too much room in the passage—which may have been true—and that he himself was determined to convey, if necessary by calculated discourtesy, demonstrated by his own aggressive, jerky progress, a sense of strong moral disapproval towards those who had time to waste gossiping. Brandreth had already opened his mouth, probably to make some further pronouncement about obstetrics, but now he closed it quickly, catching the man in the dressing-gown by the sleeve.

'Widmerpool, my dear fellow,' he said, 'I want you to meet another patient of mine—one of England's most promising young musicians.'

Widmerpool, whose well-worn dressing-gown covered a suit of grubby pyjamas in grey and blue stripe, stopped unwillingly. Without friendliness, he rotated his body towards us. Brandreth he disregarded, staring first at Moreland, then myself, frowning hard through his thick spectacles, relaxing this severe regard a little when he recognised in me a person he knew.

'Why, Nicholas,' he said, 'what are you doing here?'

Like Moreland, Widmerpool too seemed aggrieved at finding me within the precincts of the nursing home.

'Ha!' said Brandreth. 'Of course you know one another. Fellow pupils of Le Bas. Strange coincidence. I could tell you some stranger ones. We were speaking of the high incidence of abortion, my dear Widmerpool.'

Widmerpool started violently.

'Not abortion, Dr Brandreth,' said Moreland, laughing. 'Miscarriage—nothing against the law.'

'I'm using the word,' said Brandreth, treating our ignorance with genial amusement, 'in the strictly medical sense that doesn't necessarily connote anything illegal. I had been talking to Mr Moreland,' he added, 'about Wagner, a chronic sufferer, I understand, from some form of dermatitis, though he finally succumbed, I believe, to a cardiac lesion—unlike Schubert and his abdominal trouble. They were both, I imagine, temperamental men.'

The fact that Widmerpool and I knew each other at least as well as Brandreth knew Widmerpool, prevented Brandreth from dominating the situation so completely as he had intended before Widmerpool's arrival. His tone in addressing Widmerpool was at once hearty and obsequious, almost servile in its unconcealed desire to make a good impression by play with Moreland's musical celebrity. Brandreth obviously considered Widmerpool a person of greater importance than Moreland, but also one who might be interested to come in contact with sides of life different from his own. In supposing this, Brandreth showed his acquaintance with Widmerpool to be superficial. Widmerpool remained totally unimpressed by the arts. He was even accustomed to show an open contempt for them in *tête-à-tête* conversation. In public, for social reasons, he had acquired the merest working knowledge to carry him through a dinner party, content with St John Clarke as a writer, Isbister as a painter.

'I don't know about those things,' he had once said to me. 'If I don't know about things, they do not interest me. Even if artistic matters attracted me—which they do not—I should not allow myself to dissipate my energies on them.'

Now, he stood staring at me as if my presence in the nursing home was an insoluble, an irritating, mystery. I explained once more that I had been visiting Isobel.

'Oh, yes,' said Widmerpool. 'You married one of the Tollands, did you not, Nicholas? I was sorry not to have come to your wedding. That was some time ago . . . nearly . . . as a matter of fact, I was far too busy. I should like to give you a wedding present. You must tell me something you want, even though I was not able to turn up at the ceremony. After all, we have known each other a long time now. A little piece of silver perhaps. I will consult my mother who arranges such things. Your wife is not suffering from anything serious, I hope. I believe I once met her at her aunt's, Lady Molly Jeavons. Perhaps it was one of her sisters.'

The meeting had, indeed, taken place. Isobel had mentioned it. She had not cared for Widmerpool. That was one of the reasons why I had made no effort to keep in touch with him. In any case I should never have gone out of my way to seek him, knowing, as one does with certain people, that the rhythm of life would sooner or later be bound to bring us together again. However, I remembered

that I owed him a meal. Guilt as to this unfulfilled obliga-
tion was strengthened by awareness that he was capable of
complaining publicly that I had never invited him in
return. Preferring to avoid this possibility, I decided on the
spot to ask Widmerpool, before we parted company, to
lunch at my club; in fact while Isobel's convalescence gave
an excuse for not bringing him to our flat.

'I have been enjoying a brief rest here,' he said. 'An
opportunity to put right a slight mischief with boils. Some
tests have been made. I leave tomorrow, agog for work
again.'

'Isobel goes tomorrow, too. She will keep rather quiet for
a week or two.'

'Quite so, quite so,' said Widmerpool, dismissing the
subject.

He turned abruptly on his heel, muttering something
about 'arranging a meeting in the near future', at the same
time making a rapid movement towards the door of frosted
glass at which he had been aiming when first accosted by
Brandreth.

'Can you lunch with me next Tuesday—at my club?'

Widmerpool paused for a second to give thought to this
question, once more began to frown.

'Tuesday? Tuesday? Let me think. I have something on
Tuesday. I must have. No, perhaps I haven't. Wait a
minute. Let me look at my book. Yes . . . Yes. As it happens, I can lunch with you on Tuesday. But not before
half-past one. Certainly not before one-thirty. More likely
one-thirty-five.'

Quickening his step, drawing his dressing-gown round
him as if to keep himself more separate from us, he passed
through the door almost at a run. His displacement immediately readjusted in Moreland's favour Brandreth's social
posture.

'To return to Wagner,' Brandreth said, 'you remember
Wanderlust, Mr Moreland, of course you do, when Siegfried
sings: "From the wood forth I wander, never to return!"

—how does it go?—"*Aus dem Wald fort in die Welt zieh'n: nimmer kehr'ich zurück!*" Now, it always seems to me the greatest pity that in none of the productions of *The Ring* I have ever heard, has the deeper pessimism of these words been given full weight . . .'

Brandreth began to make movements with his hands as if he were climbing an invisible rope. Moreland disengaged us brutally from him. We descended the stairs.

'Who was the man in the dressing-gown with spectacles?' Moreland asked, when we had reached the street.

'He is called Kenneth Widmerpool. In the City. I have known him a long time.'

'I can't say I took to him,' Moreland said. 'But, look here, what a business married life is. I hope to goodness Matilda will be all right. There are various worrying aspects. I sometimes think I shall go off my head. Perhaps I am off it already. That would explain a lot. What are you doing tonight? I am on my way to the Maclinticks. Why not come too?'

Without waiting for an answer, he began to recount all that had been happening to Matilda and himself since we had last met; various absurd experiences they had shared; how they sometimes got on each other's nerves; why they had returned to London; where they were going to live. There had been some sort of a row with the municipal authorities at the seaside resort. Moreland held decided professional opinions; he could be obstinate. Some people, usually not the most intelligent, found working with him difficult. I heard some of his story, telling him in return how the film company for which I had been script-writing had decided against renewing my contract; that I was now appearing on the book page of a daily paper; also reviewing from time to time for the weekly of which Mark Members was assistant literary editor.

'Mark recommended Dr Brandreth to us,' Moreland said. 'A typical piece of malice on his part. Brandreth is St John Clarke's doctor—or was when Mark was St John Clarke's secretary. Gossip is the passion of his life, his only true emotion—but he can also put you on the rack about music.'

'Is he looking after Matilda?'

'A gynaecologist does that. He is not a music-lover, thank God. Of course, a lot of women have babies. One must admit that. No doubt it will be all right. It just makes one a bit jumpy. Look here, Nick, you must come to the Maclinticks'. It would be more cheerful if there were two of us.'

'Should I be welcome?'

'Why not? Have you developed undesirable habits since we last met?'

'I never think Maclintick much likes me.'

'Likes you?' said Moreland. 'What egotism on your part. Of course he doesn't like you. Maclintick doesn't like anybody.'

'He likes you.'

'We have professional ties. As a matter of fact, Maclintick doesn't really hate everyone as much as he pretends. I was being heavily humorous.'

'All the same, he shows small visible pleasure in meeting most people.'

'One must rise above that. It is a kindness to do so. Maclintick does not get on too well with his wife. The occasional company of friends eases the situation.'

'You do make this social call sound tempting.'

'If nobody ever goes there, I am afraid Maclintick will jump into the river one of these days, or hang himself with his braces after a more than usually gruelling domestic difference. You must come.'

'All right. Since you present it as a matter of life and death.'

We took a bus to Victoria, then passed on foot into a vast, desolate region of stucco streets and squares upon which a doom seemed to have fallen. The gloom was cosmic. We traversed these pavements for some distance, proceeding from haunts of seedy, grudging gentility into an area of indeterminate, but on the whole increasingly unsavoury, complexion.

'Maclintick is devoted to this part of London,' Moreland said. 'I am not sure that I agree with him. He says his mood is for ever Pimlico. I grant that a sympathetic atmosphere is an important point in choosing a residence. It helps one's work. All the same, tastes differ. Maclintick is always to be found in this neighbourhood, though never for long in the same place.'

'He never seems very cheerful when I meet him.'

I had run across Maclintick only a few times with Moreland since our first meeting in the Mortimer.

'He is a very melancholy man,' Moreland agreed. 'Maclintick is very melancholy. He is disappointed, of course.'

'About himself as a musician?'

'That—and other things. He is always hard up. Then he has an aptitude for quarrelling with anyone who might be of use to him professionally. He is writing a great tome on musical theory which never seems to get finished.'

'What is his wife like?'

'Like a wife.'

'Is that how you feel about marriage?'

'Well, not exactly,' said Moreland laughing. 'But you know one does begin to understand all the music-hall jokes and comic-strips about matrimony after you have tried a spell of it yourself. Don't you agree?'

'And Mrs Maclintick is a good example?'

'You will see what I mean.'

'What is Maclintick's form about women? I can never quite make out.'

'I think he hates them really—only likes whores.'

'Ah.'

'At least that is what Gossage used to say.'

'That's a known type.'

'All the same, Maclintick is also full of deeply romantic, hidden away sentiments about *Wein, Weib and Gesang*. That is his passionate, carefully concealed side. The gruffness is intended to cover all that. Maclintick is terrified of being thought sentimental. I suppose all his bottled-up feelings came to the surface when he met Audrey.'

'And the prostitutes?'

'He told Gossage he found them easier to converse with than respectable ladies. Of course, Gossage—you can imagine how he jumped about telling me this—was speaking of a period before Maclintick's marriage. No reason to suppose that sort of thing takes place now.'

'But if he hates women, why do you say he is so passionate?'

'It just seems to have worked out that way. Audrey is one of the answers, I suppose.'

The house, when we reached it, turned out to be a small, infinitely decayed two-storey dwelling that had seen better days; now threatened by a row of mean shops advancing from one end of the street and a fearful slum crowding up from the other. Moreland's loyalty to his friends—in a quiet way considerable—prevented me from being fully prepared for Mrs Maclintick. That she should have come as a surprise was largely my own fault. Knowing Moreland, I ought to have gathered more from his disjointed, though on the whole decidedly cautionary, account of the Maclintick household. Besides, from the first time of meeting Maclintick—when he had gone to the telephone in the Mortimer— the matrimonial rows of the Maclinticks had been an accepted legend. However much one hears about individuals, the picture formed in the mind rarely approximates to the reality. So it was with Mrs Maclintick. I was not prepared for her in the flesh. When she opened the door to us, her formidable discontent with life swept across the threshold in scorching, blasting waves. She was a small dark woman with a touch of gipsy about her, this last possibility suggested by sallow skin and bright black eyes. Her black hair was worn in a fringe. Some men might have found her attractive. I was not among them, although at the same time not blind to the fact that she might be capable of causing trouble where men were concerned. Mrs Maclintick said nothing at the sight of us, only shrugging her shoulders. Then, standing starkly aside, as if resigned to our entry in spite of an overpowering distaste she felt for the two of us, she held the door open wide. We passed within the Maclintick threshold.

'It's Moreland—and another man.'

Mrs Maclintick shouted, almost shrieked these words, while at the same time she twisted her head sideways and upwards towards a flight of stairs leading to a floor above, where Maclintick might be presumed to sit at work. We followed her into a sitting-room in which a purposeful banality of style had been observed; only a glass-fronted bookcase full of composers' biographies and works of musical reference giving some indication of Maclintick's profession.

'Find somewhere to sit,' said Mrs Maclintick, speaking as if the day, bad enough before, had been finally ruined by our arrival. '*He* will be down soon.'

Moreland seemed no more at ease in face of this reception than myself. At the same time he was evidently used to such welcomes in that house. Apart from reddening slightly, he showed no sign of expecting anything different in the way of reception. After telling Mrs Maclintick my name, he spoke a few desultory words about the weather, then made for the bookcase. I had the impression this was his accustomed gambit on arrival in that room. Opening its glass doors, he began to examine the contents of the shelves, as if—a most unlikely proposition—he had never before had time to consider Maclintick's library. After a minute or two, during which we all sat in silence, he extracted a volume and began to turn over its pages. At this firm treatment, which plainly showed he was not going to allow his hostess's ill humour to perturb him, Mrs Maclintick unbent a little.

'How is your wife, Moreland?' she asked, after picking up and rearranging some sewing upon which she must have been engaged on our arrival. 'She is having a baby, isn't she?'

'Any day now,' said Moreland.

Either he scarcely took in what she said, or did not consider her a person before whom he was prepared to display the anxiety he had earlier expressed to me on that subject, because he did not raise his eyes from the book, and, a second after she had spoken, gave one of his sudden loud bursts of laughter. The amusement was obviously caused by something he had just read. For a minute or two he continued to turn the pages, laughing to himself.

'This life of Chabrier is enjoyable,' he said, still without looking up. 'How wonderful he must have been dressed as a bull-fighter at the fancy dress ball at Granada. What fun it all was in those days. Much gayer than we are now. Why wasn't one a nineteenth-century composer living in Paris and hobnobbing with the Impressionist painters?'

Mrs Maclintick made no reply to this rhetorical question, which appeared in no way to fire within her nostalgic daydreams. She was about to turn her attention, as if unwillingly, towards myself, with the air of a woman who had given Moreland a fair chance and found him wanting, when Maclintick came into the room. He was moving unhurriedly, as if he had arrived downstairs to search for something he had forgotten, and was surprised to find his wife entertaining guests. Despondency, as usual, seemed to have laid an icy grip on him. He wore bedroom slippers and was pulling at a pipe. However, he brightened a little when he saw Moreland, screwing up his eyes behind the small spectacles and beginning to nod his head as if humming gently to himself. I offered some explanation of my presence in the house, to which Maclintick muttered a brief, comparatively affirmative acknowledgement. Without saying more, he made straight for a cupboard from which he took bottles and glasses.

'What have you been up to all day?' asked Mrs Maclintick. 'I thought you were going to get the man to see about the gas fire. You haven't moved from the house as far as I know. I wish you'd stick to what you say. I could have got hold of him myself, if I'd known you weren't going to do it.'

Maclintick did not answer. He removed the cork from a bottle, the slight 'pop' of its emergence appearing to embody the material of a reply to his wife, at least all the reply he intended to give.

'I've been looking at this book on Chabrier,' said Moreland. 'What an enjoyable time he had in Spain.'

Maclintick grunted. He hummed a little. Chabrier did not appear to interest him. He poured out liberal drinks for everyone and handed them round. Then he sat down.

'Have you become a father yet, Moreland?' he asked.

He spoke as if he grudged having to make so formal an enquiry of so close a friend.

'Not yet, 'said Moreland. 'I find it rather a trial waiting. Like the minute or two before the lights go out when you are going to conduct.'

Maclintick continued to hum.

'Can't imagine why people want a row of kids,' he said. 'Life is bad enough without adding that worry to the rest of one's other troubles.'

Being given a drink must have improved Mrs Maclintick's temper for the moment, because she asked me if I too were married. I told her about Isobel being about to leave a nursing home.

'Everyone seems to want babies nowadays,' said Mrs Maclintick. 'It's extraordinary. Maclintick and I never cared for the idea.'

She was about to enlarge on this subject when the bell rang, at the sound of which she went off to open the front door.

'How are you finding things now that you are back in London?' Maclintick asked.

'So-so,' said Moreland. 'Having to do a lot of hack work to keep alive.'

From the passage came sounds of disconnected talk. It was a man's voice. Whomever Mrs Maclintick had admitted to the house, instead of joining us in the sitting-room continued downstairs to the basement, making a lot of noise with his boots on the uncarpeted stairs. Mrs Maclintick returned to her chair and the knickers she was mending. Maclintick raised his eyebrows.

'Carolo?' he asked.

'Yes.'

'What's happened to his key?'

'He lost it.'

'Again?'

'Yes.'

'Carolo is always losing keys,' said Maclintick. 'He'll have to pay for a new one himself this time. It costs a fortune keeping him in keys. I can't remember whether I told you Carolo has come to us as a lodger, Moreland.'

'No,' said Moreland, 'you didn't. How did that happen?'

Moreland seemed surprised, for some reason not best pleased at this piece of information.

'He was in low water,' Maclintick said, speaking as if he were himself not specially anxious to go into detailed explanations. 'So were we. It seemed a good idea at the time. I'm not so sure now. In fact I've been thinking of getting rid of him.'

'How is he doing?' asked Moreland. 'Carolo is always very particular about what jobs he will take on. All that business about teaching being beneath his dignity.'

'He says he likes time for that work of his he is always tinkering about with,' said Maclintick. 'I shall be very surprised if anything ever comes of it.'

'I like Carolo here,' said Mrs Maclintick. 'He gives very little trouble. I don't want to die of melancholia, never seeing a soul.'

'What do you mean?' said Maclintick. 'Look at the company we have got tonight. What I can't stick is having Carolo scratching away at the other end of the room when

I am eating. Why can't he keep the same hours as other people?'

'You are always saying artists ought to be judged by different standards from other people,' said Mrs Maclintick fiercely. 'Why shouldn't Carolo keep the hours he likes? He is an artist, isn't he?'

'Carolo may be an artist,' said Maclintick, puffing out a long jet of smoke from his mouth, 'but he is a bloody unsuccessful one nowadays. One of those talents that have dried up, in my opinion. I certainly don't see him blossoming out as a composer. Look here, you two had better stay to supper. As Audrey says, we don't often have company. You can see Carolo then. Judge for yourselves. It is going to be one of his nights in. I can tell from the way he went down the stairs.'

'He has got to work somewhere, hasn't he?' said Mrs Maclintick, whose anger appeared to be rising again after a period of relative calm. 'His bedroom is much too cold in this weather. You use the room with a gas fire in it yourself, the only room where you can keep warm. Even then you can't be bothered to get it repaired. Do you want Carolo to freeze to death?'

'It's my house, isn't it?'

'You say you don't want him in the sitting-room. Why did you tell him he could work in the room off the kitchen if you don't want him there?'

'I am not grumbling,' said Maclintick. 'I am just warning these two gentlemen what to expect—that is to say Carolo scribbling away at a sheet of music at one end of the room, and some cold beef and pickles at the other.'

'Mutton,' said Mrs Maclintick.

'Mutton, then. We can get some beer in a jug from the local.'

'Doesn't Carolo ever eat himself?' Moreland asked.

'He often meals with us as a matter of fact,' said Mrs Maclintick. 'I don't know why Maclintick should make all this fuss suddenly. It is just when Carolo has other plans that he works while we are having supper. Then he eats out later. He likes living on snacks. I tell him it's bad for him, but he doesn't care. What is so very extraordinary about all that?'

Her husband disregarded her.

'Then you are both going to stay,' he said, almost anxiously. 'That is fixed. Where is the big jug, Audrey? I'll get some beer. What does everyone like? Bitter? Mild-and-bitter?'

Moreland had probably been expecting this invitation from the start, but the Maclinticks' bickering about Carolo seemed to have put him out, so that, giving a hasty glance in my direction as if to learn whether or not I was prepared to fall in with this suggestion, he made some rambling, inconclusive answer which left the whole question in the air. Moreland was subject to fits of jumpiness of that sort; certainly the Maclinticks, between them, were enough to make anyone ill at ease. However, Maclintick now obviously regarded the matter as settled. The prospect of enjoying Moreland's company for the rest of the evening evidently cheered him. His tone in suggesting different brews of beer sounded like a gesture of conciliation towards his wife and the world in general. I did not much look forward to supper at the Maclinticks, but there seemed no easy way out. Moreland's earlier remarks about Maclintick's need for occasional companionship were certainly borne out by this visit. The Maclinticks, indeed, as a married couple, gave the impression of being near the end of their tether. When, for example, Mona and Peter Templer had quarrelled—or, later, when Mona's interlude with Quiggin had been punctuated with bad temper and sulkiness—the horror had been less acute, more amenable to adjustment, than the bleak despair of the Maclinticks' union. Mrs Maclintick's hatred of everything and everybody—except, apparently, Carolo, praise of whom was in any case apparently little more than a stick with which to beat Maclintick—caused mere existence in the same room with her to be disturbing. She now made for the basement, telling us she would shout in due course an invitation to descend. Simultaneously, Maclintick set off for the pub at the end of the street, taking with him a large, badly chipped china jug to hold the beer.

'I am afraid I've rather let you in for this,' said Moreland, when we were alone.

His face displayed that helpless, worried look which it would sometimes take on; occasions when Matilda, now-adays, probably took charge of the situation. No doubt he found life both worrying and irksome, waiting for her to give birth, himself by this time out of the habit of living on his own.

'Is it usually like this here?'

'Rather tougher than usual.'

We waited for some minutes in the sitting-room, More-land returning to the life of Chabrier, while I turned over the pages of an illustrated book about opera, chiefly looking at the pictures, but thinking, too, of the curious, special humour of musicians, and also of the manner in which they write; ideas, words and phrases gushing out like water from a fountain, so utterly unlike the stiff formality of painters' prose. After a time, Mrs Maclintick yelled from the depths that we were to join her. Almost at the same moment, Maclintick returned with the beer. We followed him downstairs to the basement. There, in a room next to the kitchen, a table was laid. We settled ourselves round it. Maclintick filled some tumblers; Mrs Maclintick began to carve the mutton. Carolo was immediately manifest. Al-though, architecturally speaking, divided into separate parts, the Maclinticks' dining-room was not a large one, the table taking up most of one end. Maclintick's objection to their lodger working while he and his wife were making a meal seemed valid enough when the circumstances re-vealed themselves. Carolo sat, his face to the wall, engrossed with a pile of music. He looked round when Moreland and I entered the room, at the same time giving some sort of a hurried greeting, but he did not rise, or pause from his work, for more than a second. Mrs Maclintick's temper had improved again; now she appeared almost glad that Moreland and I had stayed.

'Have some beetroot,' she said. 'It is fresh today.'

Moreland and Maclintick did not take long to penetrate into a region of musical technicality from which I was excluded by ignorance; so that while they talked, and Carolo scratched away in the corner, just as Maclintick had described, I found Mrs Maclintick thrown on my hands. In her latest mood, she turned out to have a side to her no less tense than her temper displayed on arrival, but more loquacious. In fact a flow of words began to stem from her which seemed to have been dammed up for months. No doubt Maclintick was as silent in the home as out of it, and his wife was glad of an outlet for her reflections. Indeed, her desire to talk was now so great that it was hard to understand why we had been received in the first instance with so little warmth. Mrs Maclintick's dissatisfaction with life had probably reached so advanced a stage that she was unable to approach any new event amiably, even when proffered temporary alleviation of her own chronic spleen. Possibly Moreland's friendship with her husband irked her, suggesting a mental intimacy from which she was excluded, more galling in its disinterested companionship than any pursuit of other women on Maclintick's part. She began to review her married life aloud.

'I can't think why Maclintick goes about looking as he does. He just won't buy a new suit. He could easily afford one. Of course, Maclintick doesn't care what he looks like. He takes no notice of anything I say. I suppose he is right in one way. It doesn't matter what he looks like the way we live. I don't know what he does care about except Irish whiskey and the Russian composers and writing that book of his. Do you think it will ever get finished? You know he has been at it for seven years. That's as long as we've been married. No, I'm wrong. He told me he started it before he met me. Eight or nine years, then. I tell him no one will read it when it is finished. Who wants to read a book about the theory of music, I should like to know? He says himself there is too much of that sort of thing published as it is. It is not that the man hasn't got ability. He is bright enough in his way. It is just that he doesn't know how to go about things. Then all these friends of his, like Moreland and you, encourage him, tell him he's a genius, and the book will sell in thousands. What do you do? Are you a musician? A critic, I expect. I suppose you are writing a book yourself.'

'I am not a music critic. I am writing a book.'

'Musical?'

'No—a novel.'

'A novel?' said Mrs Maclintick.

The idea of writing a novel seemed to displease her only a little less than the production of a work on musical theory.

'What is it to be called?'

'I don't know yet.'

'Have you written any other novels?'

I told her. She shook her head, no more in the mood for literature than music. All the time she treated Maclintick as if he were not present in the flesh; and, since he and Moreland were deeply engaged with questions of pitch and rhythm, both were probably unaware of these reflections on her domestic situation.

'And then this house. You can see for yourself it is like a pig-sty. I slave sixteen hours a day to keep it clean. No good. Might as well not attempt it. Maclintick isn't interested in whether his house is clean or not. What I say is, why can't we go and live in Putney? Where *I* want to live is never considered, of course. Maclintick likes Pimlico, so Pimlico it has to be. The place gives me the pip. Well, don't you agree yourself? Even if we move, it has to be somewhere else in Pimlico, and the packing up is more trouble than it is worth. I should like a bit of garden. Can't have that here. Not even a window-box. Of course Maclintick hates the sight of a flower.'

I quoted St John Clarke's opinion that the beauty of

flowers is enhanced by metropolitan surroundings. Mrs Maclintick did not reply. Her attention had been distracted by Carolo, who had begun to pile his sheets of music together and stow them away in a portfolio.

'Come and have a drink with us, Carolo, before you go,' she said, with greater warmth than she had shown until that moment. 'Maclintick will get some more beer. We could all do with another drop. Here is the jug, Maclintick. Don't take all the cheese, Moreland. Leave a little for the rest of us.'

Maclintick did not look specially pleased at this suggestion of Carolo joining us at the table, but he too welcomed the idea of more beer, immediately picking up the chipped jug and once more setting off with it to the pub. A chair was drawn up for Carolo, who accepted the invitation with no more than mumbled, ungracious agreement; to which he added the statement that he would not be able to stay long. I had not set eyes on him since that night in the Mortimer. Carolo looked just the same : pale; unromantic; black wavy hair a shade longer and greasier than before. Mrs Maclintick gave him a glance that was almost affectionate.

'Have you got to go out tonight, Carolo?' she said. 'There is a little mutton left.'

Carolo shook his head, looking wearily at the residue of the joint, the remains of which were not specially tempting. He seemed in a thoughtful mood, but, when Maclintick reappeared with the jug and poured him out a glass, he drank a deep draught of the beer with apparent gratification. After wiping his mouth with a handkerchief, he spoke in his harsh, North Country voice.

'How have you been, Moreland?' he asked.

'Much as usual,' said Moreland. 'And you?'

'Pretty middling. How's Matilda?'

'Having a baby,' said Moreland flushing; and, as if he preferred to speak no more for the moment about that particular subject, went on : 'You know, in that book I was

116

reading upstairs, Chabrier says that the Spanish fleas have their own national song—a three-four tune in F major that Berlioz introduces into the *Damnation of Faust*.'

'The Spanish fleas must be having a splendid time nowadays,' said Maclintick, 'biting both sides indiscriminately.'

'The International Brigade could certainly make a tasty dish,' said Moreland, 'not to mention the German and Italian "volunteers". As a matter of fact the fleas probably prefer the Germans. More blonds.'

'I hope to God Franco doesn't win,' said Mrs Maclintick, as if that possibility had at this moment just struck her.

'Who do you want to win?' said Maclintick gruffly. 'The Communists?'

Up till then Maclintick had been on the whole in a better temper than usual. The arrival at the table of Carolo had unsettled him. He now showed signs of wanting to pick a quarrel with someone. His wife was clearly the easiest person present with whom to come into conflict. Biting and sucking noisily at his pipe he glared at her. It looked as if the Spanish war might be a matter of controversy of some standing between them; a source of contention as a married couple, rather than a political difference. Maclintick's views on politics could never be foretold. Violent, changeable, unorthodox, he tended to dislike the Left as much as the Right. He had spoken very bitterly.

'I would rather have the Communists than the Fascists,' said Mrs Maclintick, compressing her lips.

'Only because you think it is the done thing to be on the Left,' said Maclintick, with an enraging smile. 'There isn't a middle-brow in the country who isn't expressing the same sentiment. They should try a little practical Communism and see how they like it. You are no exception, I assure you.'

He removed his pipe from his mouth and swallowed hard. Moreland was obviously becoming uneasy at the turn things were taking. He began kicking his foot against the side of his chair.

'I am Pinkish myself,' he said laughing.

'And you want the Communists?' asked Maclintick.

'Not necessarily.'

'And Marxist music?'

'I long to hear some.'

'Shostakovitch, Russia's only reputable post-Revolution composer, not allowed to have his opera performed because the dictatorship of the proletariat finds that work musically decadent, bourgeois, formalist?'

'I'm not defending the Soviet régime,' said Moreland, still laughing. 'I'm all for *Lady Macbeth of the Mtsensk District*—my favourite title. Wasn't there a period in the Middle Ages when the Pope forbade certain chords under pain of excommunication? All I said—apropos of the war in Spain—I am Pinkish. No more, no less.'

This attempt to lighten the tension was not very successful. Maclintick leaned down and tapped his pipe against his heel. Mrs Maclintick, though silent, was white with anger.

'What about Toscanini?' she demanded suddenly.

'What about him?' said Maclintick.

'The Fascists slapped his face.'

'Well?'

'I suppose you approve of that.'

'I don't like the Fascists any more than you do,' said Maclintick. 'You know that perfectly well. It was me that Blackshirt insisted on taking to the police station in Florence, not you. You tried to truckle to him.'

'Anyway,' said Mrs Maclintick, 'I want the Government in Spain to win—not the Communists.'

'How are you going to arrange that, if they do defeat Franco? As it is, the extremists have taken over on the side of "the Government", as you call it. How are you going to arrange that the nice, liberal ones come out on top?'

'What do you know about it?' said his wife, speaking now with real hatred. 'What do you know about politics?'

'More than you.'

'I doubt it.'

'Doubt it, then.'

There was a moment during the pause that followed this exchange of opinion when I thought she might pick up one of the battered table knives and stick it into him. All this time, Carolo had remained absolutely silent, as if unaware that anything unusual was going on round him, unaware of Spain, unaware of civil war there, unaware of Communists, unaware of Fascists, his expression registering no more than its accustomed air of endurance of the triviality of those who inhabited the world in which he unhappily found himself. Now he finished the beer, wiped his mouth again with the pocket handkerchief, and rose from the table.

'Got to remove myself,' he said in his North Country burr.

'What time will you be back?' asked Maclintick.

'Don't know.'

'I suppose someone will have to let you in.'

'Suppose they will.'

'Oh, shut up,' burst out Mrs Maclintick. 'I'll let him in, you fool. What does it matter to you? You never open a door for anyone, not even your precious friends. It's me that does all the drudgery in this house. You never do a hand's turn, except sitting upstairs messing about with a lot of stuff that is really out of your reach—that you are not quite up to.'

By this time everyone was standing up.

'I think probably Nick and I ought to be going too,' said Moreland, the extent of his own discomposure making him sound more formal than usual. 'I've got to get up early tomorrow . . . go and see Matilda . . . one thing and another . . .'

He succeeded in suggesting no more than the fact that the Maclintick's house had become unbearable to him. Maclintick showed no sign of surprise at this sudden truncation of our visit, although he smiled to himself rather grimly.

'Do you want to take the book about Chabrier?' he asked. 'Borrow it by all means if you would like to read the rest of it.'

'Not at the moment, thanks,' said Moreland. 'I have got too much on hand.'

Carolo had already left the house by the time we reached the front door. Without bidding us farewell, Mrs Maclintick had retired in silence to the kitchen, where she could be heard clattering pots and pans and crockery. Maclintick stood on the doorstep biting his pipe.

'Come again,' he said, 'if you can stand it. I'm not sure how long I shall be able to.'

'It won't be till after Matilda has given birth,' Moreland said.

'Oh, I forgot about that,' said Maclintick. 'You're going to become a father. Well, good night to you both. Pleasant dreams.'

He shut the door. We set off up the street.

'Let's walk by the river for a bit to recover,' Moreland said. 'I'm sorry to have let you in for all that.'

'Was it a representative Maclintick evening?'

'Not one of their best. But they understand each other in an odd way. Of course, that is the sort of thing people say just before murder takes place. Still, you grasp what I mean when I insist it is good for Maclintick to see friends occasionally. But what on earth can Carolo be doing there? Everyone must be pretty short of cash for Carolo to live with the Maclinticks as a lodger. I should not have thought either party would have chosen that. All the pubs are shut by now in this area, aren't they?'

Cutting down to the Embankment, we walked for a time beside the moonlit, sparkling river, towards Vauxhall Bridge and along Millbank, past the Donners-Brebner Building dominating the far shore like a vast penitentiary, where I had called for Stringham one night years before, when he had been working there.

'Married life is unquestionably difficult,' Moreland said.

'One may make a slightly better shot at it than the Maclinticks, but that doesn't mean one has no problems. I shall be
glad when this baby is born. Matilda has not been at all easy
to deal with since it started. Of course, I know that is
in the best possible tradition. All the same, it makes one
wonder, with Maclintick, how long one will be able to
remain married. No, I don't mean that exactly. It is not
that I am any less fond of Matilda, so much as that marriage
—this quite separate entity—somehow comes between us.
However, I expect things will be all right as soon as the
baby arrives. Forgive these morbid reflections. I should
really write them for the Sunday papers, get paid a huge
fortune for it and receive an enormous fan-mail. The fact
is, I am going through one of those awful periods when I
cannot work. You know what hell that is.'

Moreland and I parted company, making arrangements to
meet soon. The subject of marriage cropped up again,
although in a different manner, when Widmerpool lunched
with me the following week.

'We will not take too long over our meal, if you do not
mind,' he said, speaking only after he had hung his hat,
topcoat and umbrella on a peg in the hall. 'I am, as usual,
very busy. That is why I am a minute or two after time.
There is a lot of work on hand as a matter of fact. You probably know that I have accepted the commitment of advising
Donners-Brebner regarding the investment of funds for
their pension scheme. Sir Magnus, in general an excellent
man of business for immediate negotiation, is sometimes
surprisingly hesitant in matters of policy. Unexpectedly
changeable, too. In short Sir Magnus doesn't always know
his own mind. Above all, he is difficult to get hold of. He
will think nothing of altering the hour of appointment
three or four times. I have had to point out to his secretary
more than once that I must make a schedule of my day just
as much as Sir Magnus must plan his.'

All the same, in spite of petty annoyances like Sir
Magnus's lack of decision, Widmerpool was in far better

form than at our last luncheon together, two or three years before, a time when he had himself been thinking of marriage. He ate more than on that occasion, although for drink he still restricted himself to a glass of water, swallowing pills both before and after the meal.

'Brandreth recommended these tablets,' he said. 'He says they are soothing. I find him on the whole a satisfactory medical adviser. He is rather too fond of the sound of his own voice, but he has a sensible attitude towards things. Brandreth is by no means a fool. Nothing narrow about him like so many doctors.'

'Did you go to him because you knew him at school?'

'No, no,' said Widmerpool. 'What an idea. For a man to have shared one's education is, in my eyes, no special recommendation to my good graces. I suppose I could have formed some early impression of his character and efficiency. I regret to say that few, if any, of my school contemporaries struck me sufficiently favourably for me to go out of my way to employ their services. In any case, Brandreth was that amount older than myself to make it difficult to judge his capabilities—certainly his capabilities as a medical man. At the same time, it is true to say that our connexion has something to do with the fact that we were at school together. Do you remember that Old Boy Dinner at which Le Bas fainted? I was impressed by the manner in which Brandreth handled that situation—told the rest of the party to go about their business and leave Le Bas to him. I liked that. It is one of my principles in life to surround myself with persons whose conduct has satisfied me. Usually the people themselves are quite unaware that they have benefited by the fact that, at one time or another, they made a good impression on me. Brandreth is a case in point.'

'The opposite process to entertaining angels unawares?'

'I don't quite know what you mean,' said Widmerpool. 'But tell me about yourself, your married life, Nicholas.

Where are you living? I dined with your brother-in-law, George Tolland, not long ago. I am never sure that it is a wise thing for soldiers to go into business. If fellows enter the army, let them stay in the army. That is true of most professions. However, he gave me some acceptable advice regarding raising money for my Territorials. The mess fund balance always seems low.'

Widmerpool rarely showed great interest in other people's affairs, but his good humour that day was such that he listened with more attention than usual when subjects unconnected with himself were ventilated. I wondered if some business deal had put him in such a genial mood. Conversation drifted to such matters.

'Things are looking up a little in the City,' he said, when luncheon was over. 'I foresee that the rhythm of the trade circle is moving towards improvement. I have been doing some small calculations on my own account to verify how matters stand. It will interest you to hear my findings. As you know, the general level of dividends is the major determinant of general stock values and market prices over a long period of time. Over shorter periods stock prices fluctuate more widely than dividends. That is obvious, of course. I worked out, for example, that since the Slump, stock prices have risen between 217⅜ per cent and 218½ per cent. So far as I could ascertain, dividends have not exceeded 62¾ per cent to 64⅝ per cent. Those are my own figures. I do not put them forward as conclusive. You follow me?'

'Perfectly.'

'Setting aside a European war,' said Widmerpool, 'which I do not consider a strong probability in spite of certain disturbing features, I favour a reasoned optimism. I hold views, as it happens, on the interplay of motions and emotions of the Stock Exchange, which, in my opinion, are far more amenable to appraisement than may be supposed by the tyro. My method could not be simpler. I periodically divide the market price of stocks—as expressed by some reliable index—by the dividend paid on the index. What could be easier than that. You agree?'

'Of course.'

'But lest I should seem to pontificate upon my own subject, to be over-occupied with the sordid details of commerce, let me tell you, Nicholas, that I have been allowing myself certain relaxations.'

'You have?'

'As you know, my mother has always urged me to spend more time seeking amusement. She thinks I work too hard.'

'I remember your telling me.'

I did not know what he was aiming at. There was no doubt he was pleased about something. He seemed uncertain whether or not to reveal the reason for that. Then, suddenly, his gratification was explained.

'I have been moving in rather exalted circles lately,' he said, giving a very satisfied smile.

'Indeed?'

'Not exactly royal—that is hardly the word yet . . . You understand me . . . ?'

'I think so.'

'It was an interesting experience.'

'Have you actually met . . .'

Widmerpool bowed his head, suggesting by this movement the knowledge of enviable secrets. At the same time he would allow no admission that might be thought compromising either to himself or those in high places whose reputation must rightly be shielded. I tried to extort more from him without any success.

'When did this happen?'

'Please do not press me for details.'

He was now on his dignity. There was a moment of silence. Widmerpool took a deep breath, as if drawing into his lungs all the health-giving breezes of the open sea of an elevated social life.

'I think we are going to see some great changes, Nicholas,' he said, 'and welcome ones. There is much—as I have often said before—to be swept away. I feel sure the things I speak of will be swept away. A new broom will soon get to work. I venture to hope that I may even myself participate in this healthier society to which we may look forward.'

'And you think we shall avoid war?'

'Certainly, I do. But I was speaking for once of society in its narrower sense—the fashionable world. There is much in the prospect before us that attracts me.'

I wondered if he were again planning to marry. Widmerpool, as I had noticed in the past, possessed certain telepathic powers, sometimes to be found in persons insensitive to the processes of thought of other people except in so far as they concern themselves; that is to say he seemed to know immediately that some idea about him was germinating in a given person's mind—in this case that I was recalling his fiasco with Mrs Haycock.

'I expect you remember that the last time you were lunching with me I was planning matrimony myself,' he said. 'How fortunate that nothing came of it. That would have been a great mistake. Mildred would not have made at all a suitable wife for me. Her subsequent conduct has caused that to become very plain. It was in the end a relief to my mother that things fell out as they did.'

'How is your mother?'

'As usual, she is positively growing younger,' said Widmerpool, pleased by this enquiry. 'And together with her always keen appreciation of youth, she tries, as I have said, to persuade me to venture more often into a social world. She is right. I know she is right. I made an effort to follow her advice—with the satisfactory consequence that I have more than half imparted to you.'

It was no good hoping to hear any more. Like Moreland dropping hints about his love affairs, Widmerpool hoped only to whet my curiosity. He seemed anxious to convince me that, although his own engagement had been broken off in embarrassing circumstances, he had been left without any feeling of bitterness.

'I hear Mildred Haycock has returned to the South of France,' he said. 'Really the best place for her. I won't repeat to you a story I was told about her the other day. For my own part, I see no reason to hurry into marriage. Perhaps, after all, forty is the age at which to find a mate. I believe Léon Blum says so in his book. He is a shrewd man, Monsieur Blum.'

THREE

People talked as if it were a kind of phenomenon that Matilda should ever have given birth to a child at all: the unwillingness of the world to believe that anyone—especially a girl who has lived fairly adventurously—might exist for a time in one manner, then at a later date choose quite another way of life. The baby, a daughter, survived only a few hours. Matilda herself was very ill. Even when she recovered, Moreland remained in the deepest dejection. He had worried so much about his wife's condition before the child was born that he seemed almost to have foreseen what would happen. That made things no better. About that time, too, there was a return of trouble with his lung: money difficulties obtruded: everything went wrong: depression reigned. Then, after some disagreeable weeks, two unexpected jobs turned up. Almost from one day to the next Moreland recovered his spirits. There was, after all, no reason why they should not in due course have another child. The financial crisis was over: the rent paid: things began to look better. All the same, it had to be admitted the Morelands did not live very domestically. The routine into which married life is designed inexorably to fall was still largely avoided by them. They kept rigorously late hours. They were always about together. A child would not have fitted easily into the circumstances of their small, rather bleak flat (no longer what Moreland had begun to call 'my former apolaustic bachelor quarters') where they were, in fact, rarely to be found.

We used to see a good deal of the Morelands in those days, dining together sometimes at Foppa's, sometimes at the Strasbourg, afterwards going to a film, or, as Moreland really preferred, sitting in a pub and talking. He would develop a passion for one particular drinking place—never the Mortimer after marriage—then tire of it, inclination turning to active aversion. Isobel and Matilda got on well together. They were about the same age; they had the nursing home in common. Matilda had recovered quickly, after an unpromising start. She found apparent relief in describing the discomfort she had suffered, although speaking always in a manner to cast a veil of unreality over the experience. Lively, violent, generous, she was subject, like Moreland himself, to bouts of deep depression. On the whole the life they lived together—so wholly together—seemed to suit her.. Perhaps, after all, people were right to think of her as intended by nature for a man's mistress and companion, rather than cast for the rôle of mother.

'Matilda's father was a chemist,' Moreland once remarked, when we were alone together, 'but he is dead now —so one cannot get special terms for purges and sleeping pills.'

'And her mother?'

'Married again. They were never on very good terms. Matty left home very young. I think everyone was rather glad when she struck out on her own.'

Two of my sisters-in-law, as it happened, had come across Matilda in pre-Moreland days. These were Veronica, George Tolland's wife, and Norah, who shared a flat with Eleanor Walpole-Wilson. Veronica, whose father was an auctioneer in a country town not far from Stourwater Castle, was one of the few people to know something of Matilda's early life. They had, indeed, been at school together.

'I was much older, of course,' Veronica said. 'I just remember her right down at the bottom of the junior school, a little girl you couldn't help noticing. She was called Betty Updike then.'

'How did you ever discover Matilda was the same girl?'

'When I was living at home and divorcing Fred, I met a local girl in the High Street who'd got a job on the *Daily Mail*. She began to talk about Sir Magnus Donners and said: "Do you know the piece called Matilda Wilson he is always seen around with is really Betty Updike".'

There was nothing particularly surprising about Matilda having taken a new name for the stage. Many people did that. It was something to be expected. The manner in which Matilda had first met Sir Magnus was more interesting.

'This girl told me Matilda Wilson came down one term to help the school dramatic society do *A Midsummer Night's Dream*,' said Veronica. 'They had got permission to act the play at Stourwater. Sir Magnus, wandering round, came across Matilda Wilson dressing up a lot of little girls as elves. That went pretty well.'

It seemed as credible a story as any other. Once involved with Sir Magnus, Matilda had, of course, been 'seen everywhere'; within the limitations of the fact that Sir Magnus preferred to keep his girl of the moment as much as possible to himself, allowing her to meet no more of his own friends than strictly necessary for his own entertainment when the two of them could not be alone together. Certainly that had been true of the time when Sir Magnus was associated with Baby Wentworth, alleged by Barnby to have 'given notice' on this very account. There had been a lot of gossip about Matilda when she was 'with' Sir Magnus. When, not long before my own marriage, I had stayed with Quiggin and Mona in the cottage lent them by Erridge, Quiggin had even talked too much about Matilda for Mona's taste.

'Oh, yes,' Mona had said, in her irritated drawl, 'Matilda Wilson—one of those plain girls men for some extraordinary reason like running after. Because they are not much trouble, I suppose.'

Norah Tolland had encountered Matilda in quite different circumstances; in fact having drinks with Heather Hopkins, the pianist, who had formerly inhabited one of the lower floors of the house in Chelsea where Norah and Eleanor Walpole-Wilson occupied the attics. At the period of which I am speaking—about two years after my own marriage—Norah and Eleanor had both found themselves jobs and become very 'serious', talking a lot about politics and economics and how best to put the world right. They were now rather ashamed of their Heather Hopkins days.

'Poor old Hopkins,' Norah said, when I mentioned her once: 'Such a pity she goes round looking and talking like the most boring kind of man. Her flat might be the bar in a golf club. She is a good-hearted creature in her own way.'

'You get tired of all that clumping about,' said Eleanor, kicking some bedroom slippers out of sight under the sofa. 'And besides, Heather isn't in the least interested in world affairs. One does ask a little sense of responsibility in people.'

However, things had been very different some years before. Then, Hopkins had thrilled Norah and Eleanor with her eyeglass and her dinner-jacket and her barrack-room phrases. Matilda had been brought to the Hopkins flat by a young actress at that time much admired by the hostess. The gathering was, of course, predominantly female, and Matilda, often found attractive by her own sex, but herself preferring men even in an unaggressively masculine form, had spent most of the evening talking to Norman Chandler. She met him for the first time at this Hopkins party. Through Chandler, Matilda had subsequently obtained a foothold in that branch of the theatre which had led in due course to her part in *The Duchess of Malfi*. Norah, usually sparing of praise, had been impressed by Matilda, to whom, as it happened, she only managed to speak a couple of words in the course of the evening.

'I thought she was rather wonderful,' said Norah.

Moreland himself had first met his future wife at a time when Matilda's connexion with Sir Magnus, if not completely severed, had been at least considerably relaxed. Moreland's behaviour on this occasion had been characteristic. He had fallen deeply in love, immediately overwhelming

Matilda with that combination of attention and forgetfulness which most women found so disconcerting in his addresses. For once, however, that approach worked very well. Matilda was won. There had already been some ups and downs in their relationship by the time I was allowed to meet her, but, in principle, they were satisfied enough with each other before marriage; they still seemed satisfied when we used to meet them and dine together at Foppa's or the Strasbourg. I discounted Moreland's casual outbursts against marriage as an institution; indeed, took his word for it that, as he used to explain, these complaints were a sign of living in a world of reality, not a palace of dreams.

'People always treat me as if I was a kind of 1880 bohemian,' he used to say. 'On the contrary, I am the sane Englishman with his pipe.'

It was one of those evenings at the Strasbourg that he announced his symphony was finished and about to be performed. Although Moreland never talked much about his own compositions, I knew he had been working on the symphony for a long time.

'Norman's friend, Mrs Foxe, is going to give a party for it,' he said.

'But how lovely,' said Isobel. 'Will Mrs Foxe and Norman stand at the top of the stairs, side by side, receiving the guests?'

'I hope so,' said Moreland. 'An example to all of us. A fidelity extremely rare among one's friends.'

'Does Mrs Foxe still live in a house somewhere off Berkeley Square?' I asked.

'That's it,' said Moreland. 'With objects like mammoth ice-cream cornets on either side of the front door for putting out the torches after you have paid off your sedan chair.'

'I am not sure that I like parties at that house,' said Matilda. 'We have been there once or twice. I can stand grand parties less and less anyway.'

She was having one of her moods that night, but it was

on the whole true to say that since marriage Moreland had increasingly enjoyed going to parties, especially parties like that offered by Mrs Foxe; Matilda, less and less.

'You talk as if we spent our life in a whirl of champagne and diamonds,' Moreland said. 'Anyway, it won't be as grand as all that. Mrs Foxe has promised just to ask our own sordid friends.'

'Who,' asked Isobel, 'apart from us?'

'I'd far rather go off quietly by ourselves somewhere after the thing is over and have supper with Isobel and Nick,' Matilda said. 'That would be much more fun.'

'It is rather an occasion, darling,' said Moreland, vexed at these objections. 'After all, I am noted among composers for the smallness of my output. I don't turn out a symphony every week like some people. A new work by me ought to be celebrated with a certain flourish—if only to encourage the composer himself.'

'I just hate parties nowadays.'

'There are only going to be about twenty or thirty people,' Moreland said. 'I know Edgar Deacon used to assure us that "the saloon, rather than the *salon*, is the true artist's milieu", but his own pictures were no great advertisement for that principle. Personally, I feel neither subservience nor resentment at the prospect of being entertained by Mrs Foxe in luxurious style.'

'Have you ever talked to her naval husband?' I asked.

'There is a smooth, hearty fellow about the house sometimes,' Moreland said. 'A well-fed air, and likes a good mahogany-coloured whisky. I once heard him give an anguished cry when the footman began to splash in too much soda. I never knew he was her husband. He doesn't look in the least like a husband.'

'Of course he is her husband,' said Matilda. 'What an ass you are. He pinched my leg the night we were having supper with them after *Turandot*. That is one of the reasons I turned against the house.'

'Darling, I'm sure he didn't. Just your swank.'

'I told you when we got home. I even showed you the bruise. You must have been too tight to see it.'

'He always seems scrupulously well behaved to me,' Moreland said. 'Rather afraid of Mrs Foxe, as a matter of fact. I understand why, now she turns out to be his wife.'

Soon after this meeting with the Morelands came the period of crisis leading up to the Abdication, one of those public events which occupied the minds not only of those dedicated by temperament to eternal discussion of what they read about in the newspapers, but of everyone else in the country of whatever age, sex, or social class. The constitutional and emotional issues were left threadbare by debate. Barnby would give his views on the controversy in his most down-to-earth manner; Roddy Cutts treated it with antiseptic discretion; Frederica's connexion with the Court caused her to show herself in public as little as possible, but she did not wholly avoid persecution at the hands of friends and relations vainly hoping for some unreleased titbit.

'I shall have a nervous breakdown if they don't settle things soon,' said Robert Tolland. 'I don't expect you hear any news, Frederica?'

'I can assure you, Robert, my own position is equally nerve-racking,' said Frederica. 'And I hear no news.'

She certainly looked dreadfully worried. I found Members and Quiggin discussing the ineluctable topic when I went to collect a book for review.

'I am of course opposed in principle to monarchy, like all other feudal survivals,' Quiggin was saying. 'But if the country must have a king, I consider it desirable, indeed essential that he should marry a divorcée. Two divorces—double as good. I am no friend of the civilisation of Big Business, but at least an American marriage is better than affiliation with our own so-called aristocracy.'

Members laughed dryly.

'Have you taken part in a procession of protest yet, J.G.?' he asked, now in a sufficiently strong economic position vis-à-vis his old friend to treat Quiggin's indignation with amused irony. 'I believe all kinds of distinguished people from the intellectual world have been parading the streets with sandwich boards expressing outraged royalist sentiments.'

'I regard the whole matter as utterly trivial in any case,' said Quiggin, irritably shoving a handful of recently published novels back into the shelf behind Members's desk, tearing the paper wrappers of two of them by the violence of his action. 'You asked me my views, Mark, and I've told you what they are. Like Gibbon, I dismiss the subject with impatience. Perhaps you will produce a book of some interest this week, a change from these interminable autobiographies of minor criminals which flow so freely from the press and to which I am for ever condemned by you.'

I met Moreland in the street just after the story had broken in the newspapers.

'Isn't this just my luck?' he said. 'Now nobody is going to listen to music, look at a picture, or read a book, for months on end. We can all settle down happily to discussions every evening about Love and Duty.'

'Fascinating subjects.'

'They are in one's own life. Less so, where others are concerned.'

'You speak with feeling.'

'Do I? Just my naturally vehement way of expressing myself.'

As it turned out, once the step had been taken, the Abdication become a matter of history, everything resumed an accustomed routine with much greater ease than popularly foreseen. There appeared no reason to suppose the box office for Moreland's symphony would suffer. Priscilla (who had eventually taken the job in the organisation raising money for the promotion of opera) reported, for example, that the cross-section of the public seen through this particular miscroscope seemed to have settled down, after some weeks of upheaval, to its normal condition. Priscilla was not particularly interested in music—less so than Robert—but naturally this employment had brought her in touch to some degree with the musical world. At the same time, I was surprised when, the day before Moreland's work was to be performed, Priscilla rang up and asked if she could come with us the following evening. Isobel answered the telephone.

'I didn't know you often went to concerts,' she said.

'I don't unless I have a free ticket,' said Priscilla.

'Did you get a free ticket for this one?'

'Yes.'

'Who gave it you?'

'One of the persons whose music is going to be played.'

'I thought they were all dead, or living abroad, except Hugh Moreland.'

'Hugh Moreland gave me the ticket.'

'I didn't know you knew him.'

'Of course I do.'

'Oh, yes. You met him with us, didn't you?'

'And other times too. I meet him in my office.'

'You never mentioned it.'

'Look here, can I come with you and Nick, or can't I?' said Priscilla. 'I am just asking. If you think being seen in my company will get you a bad name, I'll go alone and pretend I don't know either of you if we meet in the bar. Nothing easier.'

This conversation was reported later by Isobel, with the information that Priscilla was dining with us the following night.

'Typical of Hugh to present a ticket to Priscilla, who is not in the least interested in music,' I said, 'when all sorts of people who might be useful to him would have been delighted to be remembered in that way.'

The statement was true, at the same time disingenuous. I was a little aware of that at the time. It was a priggish remark; not even genuinely priggish. There seemed no point in adding that it was obviously more fun to give a ticket to a pretty girl like Priscilla, rather than to some uncouth musical hanger-on whose gratification might ultimately pay a doubtful dividend. I felt it one of those occasions when a show of worldliness might be used as a smoke-screen. But why should a smoke-screen be required?

'I suppose Hugh had a few drinks at some party,' I said, 'and distributed tickets broadcast.'

In the end I convinced myself of the probability of this surmise. Isobel did not express any views on the subject. However, when she arrived at the flat, Priscilla explained that Moreland, the day before, had visited, in some professional capacity, the place where the Opera fund was administered. There, 'rummaging about in his pocket for his cigarettes', he found this spare ticket 'crumpled up among a lot of newspaper cuttings, bits of string, and paper-clips'. He had given the ticket to Priscilla, suggesting at the same time that she should come on to Mrs Foxe's party after the concert. That was a convincing story. It had all the mark of Moreland's behaviour. We talked of other things; of Erridge, who had cabled for thicker underclothes to be sent him in Barcelona, indicating in this manner that he was not, as some prophesied, likely to return immediately. We discussed Erridge's prospects in Spain. By the time we reached the concert hall, Priscilla seemed to have come with us that evening by long previous arrangement.

Moreland was fond of insisting that whatever the critics say, good or bad, all works of art must go through a maturing process before taking their allotted place in the scheme of things. There is nothing particularly original in that opinion, but those who hold firmly to it are on the whole less likely to be spoiled by praise or cast down by blame than others—not necessarily worse artists—who find heaven or hell in each individual press notice. The symphony was, in fact, greeted as a success, but not as an overwhelming success; a solid piece of work that would add to Moreland's reputation, rather than a detonation of unexampled brilliance. Gossage, fiddling about with the mustard pot at some restaurant, had once remarked (when Moreland was out of the room) that he would be wise to build up his name with a work of just that sort. In the concert hall, there had been a lot of applause; at the same time a faint sense of anti-climax. Even for the most self-disciplined of artists, a public taken by surprise is more stimulating than a public relieved to find that what is offered can be swallowed without the least sharpness on the palate. This was especially true of Moreland, who possessed his healthy share of liking to startle, in spite of his own innate antagonism to professional startlers. However, if the symphony turned out to be a little disappointing to those who may have hoped for something more barbed, the reception was warm enough to cast no suggestion of shadow over a party of celebration.

'That went all right, didn't it?' said Isobel.

'It seemed to.'

'I thought it absolutely wonderful,' said Priscilla.

I felt great curiosity at the prospect of seeing Mrs Foxe's house again, not entered since the day when, still a school-boy, I had lunched there with Stringham and his mother. Nothing had changed in the pillared entrance hall. There was, of course, absolutely no reason why anything should have changed, but I had an odd feeling of incongruity about reappearing there as a married man. The transition against this same backcloth was too abrupt. Some interim state, like steps in the gradations of freemasonry, seemed to have been omitted. We were shown up to a crimson damask drawing-room on the first floor, at one end of which sliding doors were open, revealing the room at right angles to be the 'library'—with its huge malachite urn, Romney portrait, Regency bookcases—into which Stringham had brought me on that earlier visit. There I had first encountered the chilly elegance of Commander

Foxe; also witnessed Stringham's method of dealing with his mother's 'current husband'.

Commander Foxe, as it happened, was the first person I saw when we came through the door. He was talking to Lady Huntercombe. From a certain bravado in his manner of addressing her, I suspected he had probably let himself off attending the concert. Mrs Foxe came forward to meet us as we were announced, looking just as she looked at *The Duchess of Malfi*, changeless, dazzling, dominating. As an old friend of Lady Warminster's, she had, of course, known Isobel and Priscilla as children. She spoke to them for a moment about their stepmother's health, then turned to me. I was about to recall to her the circumstances in which we had formerly met in what was now so dim a past, wondering at the same time what on earth I was going to say about Stringham, mention of whose name was clearly unavoidable, when Mrs Foxe herself forestalled me.

'How well I remember when Charles brought you to luncheon here. Do you remember that too? It was just before he sailed for Kenya. We all went to the Russian Ballet that night. Such a pity you could not have come with us. What fun it was in those days ... Poor Charles ... He has had such a lot of trouble . . . You know, of course . . . But he is happier now. Tuffy looks after him—Miss Weedon; you met her too when you came here, didn't you?—and Charles has taken to painting. It has done wonders.'

'I remember his caricatures.'

Stringham could not draw at all in the technical sense, but he was a master of his own particular form of graphic representation, executed in a convention of blobs and spidery lines, very effective for producing likenesses of Le Bas or the other masters at school. I could not imagine what Stringham's 'painting' could be. This terminology put the activity into quite another setting.

'Charles uses gouache now,' said Mrs Foxe, speaking with that bright firmness of manner people apply especially to close relations attempting to recover from more or less disastrous mismanagement of their own lives, 'designing theatrical costumes and that sort of thing. Norman says they are really quite good. Of course, Charles has had no training, so it is probably too late for him to do anything professionally. But the designs have originality, Norman thinks. You know Norman talks a lot about you and Isobel. He adores you both. Norman made me read one of your books. I liked it very much.'

She looked a bit pathetic when she said that, making me feel in this respect perhaps Chandler had gone too far in his exercise of power. However, other guests coming up the stairs at our heels compelled a forward movement. Moreland, red in the face, appeared in Mrs Foxe's immediate background. We offered our congratulations. He muttered a word or two about the horror of having a new work performed; seemed very happy about everything. We left him talking to Priscilla, herself rather pink, too, with the excitement of arrival. The party began to take more coherent shape. Mrs Foxe had, on the whole, most dutifully followed Moreland's wishes in collecting together his old friends, rather than arranging a smart affair of her own picking and choosing. Indeed, the far end of the crimson drawing-room could almost have been a corner of the Mortimer on one of its better nights; the group collected there making one feel that at any moment the strains of the mechanical piano would suddenly burst forth. The Maclinticks, Carolo, Gossage, with several other musicians and critics known to me only by sight, were present, including a famous conductor of a generation older than Moreland's, invited probably through acquaintance with Mrs Foxe in a social way rather than because of occasional professional contacts between Moreland and himself. This distinguished person was conversing a little loudly and self-consciously, with a great deal of gesticulation, to show there was no question of condescension from himself towards his less successful colleagues. Near this knot of musicians stood Chandler's old friend, Max Pilgrim, trying to get a word or two out of Rupert Wise, another of Chandler's friends—indeed, a great admiration of Chandler's—a male dancer known for his strict morals and lack of small talk. Wise's engagement to an equally respectable female member of the *corps de ballet* had recently been announced. Mrs Foxe had promised to give them a refrigerator as a wedding present.

'Not colder than Rupe's heart,' Chandler had commented. 'It was my suggestion. He may have a profile like Apollo, but he's got a mind like Hampstead Garden Suburb.'

The Huntercombes, as well as the celebrated conductor, were certainly contributed to the party by Mrs Foxe rather than by Moreland. Once—as I knew from remarks let fall by Stringham in the past—Mrs Foxe would have regarded Lady Huntercombe as dreadfully 'slow', and laughed at her clothes, which were usually more dramatic than fashionable. However, now that Mrs Foxe's energies were so largely directed towards seeking ways of benefiting Chandler and his friends, Lord Huntercombe's many activities in the art world had to be taken into account. In his capacity as trustee of more than one public gallery, Lord Huntercombe was, it was true, concerned with pictures rather than with music or the theatre. At the same time, his well recognised abilities in his own field had brought him a seat on several committees connected with other branches of the arts or activities of a generally 'cultural' sort. Lord Huntercombe, small and immensely neat, was indeed a man to be reckoned with. He had caught napping one of the best known Bond Street dealers in the matter of a Virgin and Child by Benozzo Gozzoli (acquired from the gallery as the work of a lesser master, later resoundingly identified), also so nicely chosen the moment to dispose of his father's collection of English pastels that he obtained nearly twice their market value.

Lady Huntercombe, as usual majestically dressed in a black velvet gown, wore a black ribbon round her neck clipped with an elaborate ornament in diamonds. She took a keen interest in music, more so than her husband, who liked to be able himself to excel in his own spheres of patronage, and was not musically inclined. I remembered Lady Huntercombe expressing her disappointment after Stringham's wedding at the manner in which the choir had sung the anthem. 'Dreadfully sharp,' I heard her say at the reception. 'It set my teeth on edge.' Now she was talking to Matilda, to the accompaniment of animated and delighted shakings of her forefinger, no doubt indicative of some special pleasure she had taken in Moreland's symphony; apparently at the same time trying to persuade Matilda—who seemed disposed to resist these advances—to accept some invitation or other similar commitment.

Moving towards the inner room, I observed that Chandler's small bronze of *Truth Unveiled by Time*, long ago bought from the Caledonian Market and rescued from Mr Deacon's shop after his death, had now come finally to rest on the console table under the Romney. Chandler himself was standing beside the table, stirring a glass of champagne with a gold swizzle-stick borrowed from Commander Foxe. Although Chandler might hold Mrs Foxe under his sway, she, on her part, had in some degree tamed him too. His demeanour had been modified by prolonged association with her. He was no longer quite the *gamin* of the Mortimer.

'Hullo, my dear,' he said. 'Fizz always gives me terrible hiccups, unless I take the bubbles away. You know Buster, of course.'

Commander Foxe, greyer now, a shade bulkier than when I had last seen him, was at the same time, if possible, more dignified as a result of these outward marks of maturity. He retained in his dress that utter perfection of turn-out that stopped so brilliantly short of seeming no more than the trappings of a tailor's dummy. His manner, on the other hand, had greatly changed. He had become chastened, almost humble. I could not imagine how I had ever found him alarming; although, even with this later development of geniality, there still existed a suggestion that below the surface he knew how to make himself disagreeable if need be. I mentioned where we had last met. He at once recollected, or pretended to recollect, the occasion; the essence of good manners and friendliness, almost obsequious in his desire to please.

'Poor old Charles,' he said. 'Of course I remember you were a friend of his. Do you ever see him these days? Well, of course, nobody does much, do they? All the same, it hasn't worked out too badly. Do you remember Miss Weedon, Amy's secretary? Rather a formidable lady. Oh, you know all about that, do you? Yes, Molly Jeavons is an aunt of your wife's, of course. Quite a solution for Charles in a way. It gives him the opportunity to live a quiet life for a time. Norman goes round and sees Charles sometimes, don't you, Norman?'

'I simply adore Charles,' said Chandler, 'but I'm rather afraid of that gorgon who looks after him—I believe you are too, Buster.'

Buster laughed, almost achieving his savage sneer of former times. He did not like Miss Weedon. I remembered that. He was no doubt glad to have ridded the house of Stringham too. They had never got on well together.

'At least Tuffy keeps Charles in order,' Buster said. 'If one hasn't any self-discipline, something of the sort unfortunately has to be applied from the outside. It is a hard thing to say, but there it is. Are you in this musical racket yourself? I hear Hugh Moreland's symphony was very fine. I couldn't manage to get there myself, much to my regret.'

I felt a pang of horror at the way his family now talked of Stringham: as if he had been put away from view like a person suffering from a horrible, unmentionable disease, or become some terrifying legendary figure, fearful as the Glamis monster, about whom it was appropriate to joke as dreadful to behold, but at the same time a being past serious credence. All the same, it was hard to know what else they could do about him, how better behave towards him. Stringham, after all, was their problem, not mine. I myself could offer no better solution than Miss Weedon; was in no position to disparage his own relations so far as their conduct towards Stringham was concerned.

'They were a bit hurried in seeing our former King off the premises, weren't they?' said Buster, changing the subject to public events, possibly because he feared his last words might provoke musical conversation. 'Some of one's friends have been caught on the wrong foot about it all. Still, I expect he will have a much better time on his own in the long run. His latter job was not one I should care to take on.'

'My dear, you'd do it superbly,' said Chandler. 'I always think that when I look at that photograph of you in tropical uniform.'

'No, no, nonsense, Norman,' said Buster, not displeased at this attribution to himself of potentially royal aptitudes. 'I should be bored to death. I can't in the least imagine myself opening Parliament and all that sort of thing.'

Chandler signified his absolute disagreement.

'I must go off and have a word with Auntie Gossage now,' he said, 'or the old witch will fly off on a broomstick and complain about being cut. See you both later.'

'What a wonderful chap Norman is,' said Buster, speaking with unaccustomed warmth. 'You know I sometimes wonder what Amy would do without him. Or me, either, for that matter. He runs the whole of our lives. He can do anything from arranging the flowers to mixing the best Tom Collins I have ever drunk. So talented in other ways too. Ever seen him act? Then, as for dancing and playing the saxophone . . . Well, I've never met a man like him.'

There seemed no end to Buster's admiration for Chandler. I did not disagree, although surprised, rather impressed, by Buster's complete freedom from jealousy. It was not that anyone supposed that Chandler was 'having an affair' with Mrs Foxe—although no one can speak with certainty, as Barnby used to insist, about any two people in that connexion—but, apart from any question of physical relationship, she obviously loved Chandler, even if this might not be love of quite the usual sort A husband, even a husband as unprejudiced as Buster, might have felt objection on personal, or merely general, grounds. Many men who outwardly resembled Buster would, on principle, have disliked a young man of Chandler's appearance and demeanour; certainly disliked for ever seeing someone like this about the house. Either natural tolerance had developed in Buster as he had grown older, or there were other reasons why his wife's infatuation with Chandler satisfied him; after all Matilda had alleged the pinching of her leg. Possibly Chandler kept Mrs Foxe from disturbing Buster in his own amusements. If that was the reason, Buster showed a good grace in the manner in which he followed his convenience; in itself a virtue not universally practised. Perhaps he was a little aware that he had displayed himself to me in an unexpected light.

'Amy needs a good deal of looking after,' he said. 'I am sometimes rather busy. Get caught up in things. Business engagements and so on. Most husbands are like that, I suppose. Can't give a wife all the attention she requires. Know what I mean?'

This self-revelation was so unlike the Buster I remembered, that I was not sure whether to attribute the marked alteration in his bearing in some degree to changes in myself. Perhaps development in both of us had made a mutually new attitude possible. However, before Buster could particularise further on the subject of married life, a subject about which I should have liked to hear more from him, Maclintick, moving with the accustomed lurching walk he employed drunk or sober, at that moment approached us.

'Any hope of getting Irish in a house like this?' he asked me in an undertone. 'Champagne always gives me diarrhoea. It would be just like the rich only to keep Scotch. Do you think it would be all right if I accosted one of the flunkeys? I don't want to let Moreland down in front of his grand friends.'

I referred to Buster this demand for Irish whiskey on Maclintick's part.

'Irish?' said Buster briskly. 'I believe you've got us there. I can't think why we shouldn't have any in the cellar, because I rather like the stuff myself. Plenty of Scotch, of course. I expect they told you that. Wait here. I'll go and make some investigations.'

'Who is that kind and beautiful gentleman?' asked Maclintick acidly, not showing the least gratitude at Buster's prompt effort to satisfy his need for Irish whiskey. 'Is he part of the management?'

'Commander Foxe.'

'I am no wiser.'

'Our hostess's husband.'

'I thought she was married to Chandler. He is the man I always see her with at the ballet—if you call him a man. I suppose I have shown my usual bad manners again. I ought never to have come to a place like this. Quite against my principles. All the same, I hope Baron Scarpia will unearth a drop of Irish. Must be an unenviable position to be married to a woman like his wife.'

His own matrimonial state seemed to me so greatly worse than Commander Foxe's that I was surprised to find Maclintick deploring any other marriage whatever. Gossage —'that old witch', as Chandler had called him—joined us before I could answer. He seemed to be enjoying the party, clasping together his fingers and agitating his hands up and down in the air.

'What did you think of Moreland's work, Maclintick?' he asked. 'A splendid affair, splendidly received. Simply wonderful. I rarely saw such enthusiasm. Didn't you think so, Maclintick?'

'No, I didn't,' said Maclintick, speaking with finality. 'So far as reception was concerned, I thought it just missed being a disaster. The work itself was all right. I liked it.'

Gossage was not in the least put out by the acerbity of Maclintick's disagreement. He stood on his toes, placing the tips of his fingers together in front of him like a wedge.

'You judged that, did you, Maclintick?' he said thoughtfully, as if a whole new panorama had been set in front of him. 'You judged that. Well, perhaps there is something in what you say. All the same, I considered it a great personal triumph for Moreland, a great triumph.'

'You know as well as I do, Gossage, that it was not a triumph,' said Maclintick, whose temper had risen suddenly. 'We are all friends of Moreland's—we shouldn't have come to this bloody awful party tonight, dressed up in these clothes, if we weren't—but it is no help to Moreland to go round saying his symphony was received as a triumph, that it is the greatest piece of music ever written, when we all know it wasn't and it isn't. It is a very respectable piece of work. I enjoyed it. But it wasn't a triumph.'

Gossage looked as if he did not at all agree with Maclintick's strictures on Mrs Foxe's party and the burden of wearing evening clothes, but was prepared at the same time to allow these complaints to pass, as well as any views on Moreland as a composer, in the light of his colleague's notorious reputation for being cantankerous.

'There may be opposition from some quarters,' Gossage said. 'I recognise that. Some of the Old Gang may get on their hind legs. A piece of music is none the worse for causing that to happen.'

'I don't see why there should be opposition,' said Maclintick, as if he found actual physical relief in contradicting Gossage on all counts. 'A certain amount of brick-throwing might even be a good thing. There comes a moment in the career of most artists, if they are any good, when attacks on their work take a form almost more acceptable than praise. That happens at different moments in different careers. This may turn out to be the moment with Moreland. I don't know. I doubt it. All I know is that going round pretending the symphony is a lot of things it isn't, does Moreland more harm than good.'

'Ah, well,' said Gossage, speaking now with conscious resignation, 'we shall see what everyone says by the week-end. I liked the thing myself. It seemed to have a lot of life in it. Obvious failings, of course. All the same, I fully appreciate the points you make, Maclintick. But here is Mrs Maclintick. And how is Mrs Maclintick this evening?'

Mrs Maclintick had the air of being about to make trouble. She was wearing a fluffy, pale pink dress covered with rosettes and small bows, from which her arms and neck emerged surrounded by concentric circles of frills. On her head was set a cap, medieval or pre-Raphaelite in conception, which, above dark elfin locks, swarthy skin and angry black eyes, gave her the appearance of having come to the party in fancy dress.

'Do take your hands out of your pockets, Maclintick,' she said at once. 'You always stand about everywhere as if you were in a public bar. I don't know what the people here must think of you. We are not in the Nag's Head now, you know. Try to remember not to knock your pipe out on the carpet.'

Maclintick took no notice of his wife whatsoever. Instead, he addressed to Gossage some casual remarks about Smetana which seemed to have occurred to him at that moment. Mrs Maclintick turned to me.

'I don't expect you are any more used to this sort of party than I am,' she said. 'As for Maclintick, he wouldn't have been here at all if it hadn't been for me. I got him into those evening trousers somehow. Of course he never wants to wear evening clothes. He couldn't find a black bow-tie at the last moment. Had to borrow a made-up one Carolo used to wear. He is tramping about in his ordinary clod-hopping black shoes too.'

147

Maclintick continued to ignore his wife, although he must have heard all this.

'What did you think of Moreland's symphony?' she continued. 'Not much of a success, Maclintick thinks. I agree with him for once.'

Maclintick caught her words. He swung round in such a rage that for a moment I thought he was going to strike her; just as I had thought she might stick a dinner knife into him when I had been to their house. There was certainly something about her manner this evening which would almost have excused physical violence even in the circumstances of Mrs Foxe's party.

'I didn't say anything of the sort, you bloody bitch,' Maclintick said, 'so keep your foul mouth shut and don't go round repeating that I did, unless you want to get hurt. It is just like your spite to misrepresent me in that manner. You are always trying to make trouble between Moreland and myself, aren't you? What I said was that the music was "not Moreland's most adventurous"—that the critics had got used to him as an *enfant terrible* and therefore might underestimate the symphony's true value. That was all. That was what I said. You know yourself that was all. You know yourself that was what I said.'

Maclintick was hoarse with fury. His hands were shaking. His anger made him quite alarming.

'Yes, Maclintick was just saying that very thing, wasn't he?' agreed Gossage, sniggering nervously at this display of uncontrolled rage. 'The words were scarcely out of his mouth, Mrs Maclintick. That is exactly what he thinks.'

'Don't ask me what he thinks,' said Mrs Maclintick calmly, not in the least put out of countenance by the force of her husband's abuse. 'He says one thing at one moment, another at another. Doesn't know his own mind in the least. I told him he was standing about as if he was in the Nag's Head. That is the pub near us where all the tarts go. I suppose that is where he thinks he is. It's the place where he is most at home. Besides, if the symphony was such a success, why wasn't Moreland better pleased? Or Matilda, for that matter? Matilda doesn't seem at all at her best tonight. I expect these grand surroundings remind her of better days.'

'I didn't say the symphony was "a great success" either,' said Maclintick, speaking now wearily, as if his outburst of anger had left him weak. 'Anyway, what do you mean? Moreland looks all right to me. What is wrong with him? Of course, it was insane of me to express any opinion in front of a woman like you.'

'Go on,' said Mrs Maclintick. 'Just go on.'

'And what reason have you for saying Matilda isn't pleased?' said Maclintick. 'I only wish I had a wife with half Matilda's sense.'

'Matilda didn't seem to be showing all that sense when I was talking to her just now,' said Mrs Maclintick, still quite undisturbed by this unpleasant interchange, indeed appearing if anything stimulated by its brutality. 'Or to be at all pleased either. Not that I care how she speaks to me. I bet she has done things in her life I wouldn't do for a million pounds. Let her speak to me how she likes. I'm not going to bring up her past. All I say is that she and Moreland were having words during the interval. Perhaps it was what they were talking about upset them, not the way the symphony was received. It is not for me to say.'

Further recrimination was terminated for the moment by the butler bringing a decanter for Maclintick with Buster's apology that no Irish whiskey was to be found in the house. Buster himself appeared a moment later, adding his own regrets for this inadequacy. I withdrew from the group, and went over to speak to Robert Tolland, who had just come into the room. Robert knew Moreland only slightly, as a notable musical figure rather than as a friend. He had probably been asked to the party at the instigation of Mrs Foxe, had perhaps dined with her to make numbers even. I had not seen him in the concert hall.

'I expected to find you and Isobel here,' he said. 'I was

asked at the last moment, I hardly know why. One of those curious afterthoughts which are such a feature of Amy Foxe's entertaining. I see Priscilla is here. Did you bring her?'

'Priscilla dined with us. You could have come to dinner too, if we had known you were on your way to this party.'

Robert gave one of his quiet smiles.

'Nice of you to suggest it,' he said, 'but there were things I had to do earlier in the evening as a matter of fact. How very attractive Mrs Moreland is. I always think so whenever I see her. What a relief that one no longer has to talk about the Abdication. Frederica is looking a lot better now that everything is settled.'

He smiled and moved away, exhaling his usual air of mild mystery. Lady Huntercombe, taking leave of Matilda with a profusion of complimentary phrases, swept after Robert. Matilda beckoned me to come and talk to her. She looked pale, seemed rather agitated, either on account of her long session with Lady Huntercombe, or perhaps because she was still feeling shaken by the strain of hearing the symphony performed.

'Give me some more champagne, Nick,' she said, clasping my arm. 'It is wonderful stuff for the nerves. Are you enjoying yourself at this smart party? I hope so.'

This manner was not at all her usual one. I thought she was probably a little drunk.

'Of course—and the symphony was a great success.'

'Did you think so?'

'Very much.'

'Are you sure?'

'Didn't you?'

'I suppose so.'

'Oh, yes.'

'You are certain, Nick?'

'Of course I am. Everything went all right. There was lots of applause. What else do you expect?'

'Yes, it was all right, I think. Somehow I hoped for more

150

real enthusiasm. It is a wonderful work, you know. It really is.'

'I am sure it is.'

'It is wonderful. But people are going to be disappointed.'

'Does Hugh himself think that?'

'I don't think it worries him,' said Matilda. 'Not in his present state of mind.'

For some reason—from the note in her voice, a sense of trouble in the air, perhaps just from natural caution—I felt safer in not enquiring what she regarded as Moreland's 'present state of mind'.

'I see your little sister-in-law, Lady Priscilla, is here,' said Matilda.

She smiled rather in Robert's manner, as if at some secret inner pleasure that was also a little bitter to contemplate.

'You've met her with us, haven't you?'

'Yes.'

'She dined with us tonight.'

'I met her once at your flat,' said Matilda, speaking slowly, as if that were an extraordinary thing to have happened. 'She is very attractive. But I don't know her as well as Hugh does.'

I suddenly felt horribly uncomfortable, as if ice-cold water were dripping very gently, very slowly down my spine, but as if, at the same time, some special circumstance prevented admission of this unaccountable fact and also forbade any attempt on my own part to suspend the process; a sensation to be recognised, I knew well, as an extension of that earlier refusal to face facts about Moreland giving Priscilla the concert ticket. That odd feeling of excitement began to stir within me always provoked by news of other people's adventures in love; accompanied as ever by a sense of sadness, of regret, almost jealousy, inward emotions that express, like nothing else in life, life's irrational dissatisfactions. On the one hand, that Moreland might have fallen in love with Priscilla (and she with him) seemed immensely interesting; on the other—to speak only callously of the Morelands' marriage and Priscilla's inexperience (if she was inexperienced)—any such situation threatened complications of a most disturbing kind on two separate fronts of one's own daily existence. As to immediate action, a necessary minimum was obviously represented by refraining from any mention to Matilda of the complimentary ticket. Silence on that point offered at least a solid foundation upon which to build; the simple principle that a friend's actions, however colourless, vis-à-vis another woman, are always better unrepeated to his wife. Contemplation of this banal maxim increased the depression that had suddenly descended on me. The proposition that Moreland was having some sort of a flirtation with Priscilla sufficiently tangible to cause Matilda—even if she had had too much champagne—to draw my attention to such goings-on appeared at once ridiculous and irritating. Probably Matilda's speculations were unco-ordinated. Quite likely Moreland and Priscilla were indeed behaving foolishly. Why draw attention to that? The matter would blow over. All three persons concerned fell in my estimation. In any case, Matilda's speculations might be wholly unfounded. Priscilla, physically speaking—socially speaking, if it came to that—was not the sort of girl Moreland usually liked. 'Nothing is more disturbing,' he used to say himself, 'than one's friends showing unexpected sexual tastes.' Priscilla, for her part, was not in general inclined towards the life Moreland lived; had never shown any sign of liking married men, a taste some girls acquire at an early age. I thought it best to change the subject.

'I see you asked Carolo,' I said.

Moreland, although always perfectly friendly—indeed, making more effort with Carolo than he usually did with gloomy, silent geniuses—never gave the impression of caring much for his company. I supposed Carolo's invitation due to some inflexion of musical politics of which I was myself ignorant, and about which, to tell the truth, I felt very little interest. However, this comment seemed to sober Matilda, or at least to change her mood.

'We had to ask him,' she said. 'No choice of mine, I can assure you. It was all on account of the Maclinticks. As Carolo lives in the same house as the Maclinticks, Hugh thought it would be awkward if he didn't get an invitation. Hugh was very anxious for Maclintick to come—in fact wouldn't hear of his not coming. Hugh and Maclintick are really great friends, you know.'

'The Maclinticks were having a full-dress row when I left them a short time ago.'

'They always are.'

'They should lay off for an hour or two on occasions like this. A short rest would renew their energies for starting again when they return home.'

'That is just married life.'

'To be married to either of the Maclinticks cannot be much fun.'

'Is it fun to be married to anyone?'

'That is rather a big question. If you admit that fun exists at all—perhaps you don't—you cannot lay it down categorically that no married people get any fun from the state of being married.'

'But I mean *married* to someone,' said Matilda, speaking quite passionately. 'Not to sleep with them, or talk to them, or go about with them. To be *married* to them. I have been married a couple of times and I sometimes begin to doubt it.'

We were now in the midst of dangerous abstractions which might once more threaten further embarrassments of the kind I hoped to avoid. Generalisations about married life could easily turn to particularisation about Moreland and Priscilla, a relationship I should prefer to investigate later, in my own way and time, rather than have handed to me on a plate by Matilda; the latter method almost certainly calling for decisions and agreements undesirable, so it seemed to me, at this stage of the story. I was also very surprised by this last piece of information: that Matilda had had a husband previous to Moreland.

'You have been married twice, Matilda?'

'Didn't you know?'

'Not the least idea.'

I wondered for a moment whether Sir Magnus Donners could possibly have married her clandestinely. If so—and that was very unlikely—an equally clandestine divorce was scarcely conceivable. That notion could be dismissed at once.

'I was married to Carolo,' she said.

'My dear Matilda.'

'That surprises you?'

'Immensely.'

She laughed shrilly.

'I thought Hugh might have told you.'

'Never a word.'

'There is no particular secret about it. The marriage lasted a very short time. It was when I was quite young. In fact pretty soon after I left home. Carolo is not a bad old thing in his way. Just not very bright. Not a bit like Hugh. We used to quarrel a good deal. Then we didn't really get on in bed. Besides, I got tired of him talking about himself all the time.'

'Understandably.'

'After I left Carolo, as you know, I was kept by Donners for a time. At least people are all aware of *that*. It is such a relief not to have to explain everything about oneself to everyone. We met just about the time when Donners was getting restive about the way Baby Wentworth was treating him. He was taking Lady Ardglass out quite often too, but she never really liked being seen with him. I think she found him terribly unsmart. So did Baby Wentworth, I believe, if it comes to that. I did not mind that drab side of him. I got tired of him for other reasons, although he can be nice in his own particular way. He is awful, of course, at times. Really

154

awful. But he can be generous—I mean morally generous
—too. I am not interested in money. One thing about
Donners, he does not know what jealousy means. When
Baby was running round with Ralph Barnby, he did not
mind at all. That did not affect me in one way, because
unlike so many women, I prefer only one man at a
time. But it is nice not to be bothered about where you
went last night, or where you are going to tomorrow afternoon. Don't you agree?'

'Certainly I do. Was Carolo like that—jealous in that
way?'

'A bit. But Carolo's chief interest is in making conquests.
He doesn't much mind who it is. I shouldn't wonder if he
doesn't run after Audrey Maclintick. Probably Maclintick
would be glad of someone to keep her quiet and take her off
his hands. What a bitch she is.'

'All the same, there is a difference between being fed up
with your wife and wanting another man to take her off
your hands.'

'There wasn't in Carolo's case. He was thankful when I
fixed myself up. That is part of his simple nature, which is
his chief charm. I had really left Donners by the time I met
Hugh. What do you think about Hugh?'

'I should guess that he was not particularly jealous as
men go.'

'Oh, I don't mean that. He isn't. I mean what do you
think of him as a man?'

'You know quite well, Matilda, that he is a great friend
of mine.'

'But his work . . . I do think he is . . . frightfully intelligent . . . a great man . . . whatever you like. Everything one says of that sort always sounds silly about someone you know—certainly someone you are married to. I had
quite enough of being told my husband was a genius when
I was Carolo's wife. But you do agree about Hugh, don't
you, Nick?'

'Yes, I do, as a matter of fact.'

'That is why I am so worried about the symphony. You see, I am sure it will not be properly appreciated. People are so stupid.'

I longed to hear more about Sir Magnus Donners; whether some of the very circumstantial, very highly coloured stories that circulated about the elaboration of his idiosyncrasies, were at all near the truth. However, the moment to acquire such information, the moment for such frivolities, if it had ever existed, was now past. The tone had become too serious. I could not imagine what the next revelation would be; certainly nothing so light-hearted as a first-hand account of a millionaire's sexual fantasies.

'Then there is this business of both of us having a career.'

'That is always difficult.'

'I don't want never to act again.'

'Of course not.'

'After all, if Hugh wanted to marry a squaw, he could easily have found a squaw. They abound in musical circles. It is the answer for lots of artists.'

'Hugh has always been against squaws. Rightly, I think. In the long run, in my opinion, a squaw is even more nuisance than her antithesis—and often cooks worse too.'

'Then why do Hugh and I find it so difficult to get on together?'

'But you always seem to get on a treat.'

'That's what you think.'

'Well, don't you—when you look at the Maclinticks, for example?'

'And then . . .'

I thought for a moment she was going to speak of the child's death, which I now saw had dislocated their marriage more seriously than anyone had supposed from the outside. Instead, she returned to her earlier theme.

'And now he has gone and fallen in love with your sister-in-law, Priscilla.'

'But——'

Matilda laughed at the way in which I failed to find any answer. There was really nothing for me to say. If it was true, it was true. From one point of view, I felt it unjust that I should be visited in this manner with Matilda's mortification; from another, well deserved, in that I had not already acquainted myself with what was going on round me.

'Of course it is all quite innocent,' said Matilda. 'That is the worst thing about it from my point of view. It would be much easier if he had fallen for some old tart like myself he could sleep with for a spell, then leave when he was bored.'

'When did all this start up?'

In asking the question, I committed myself in some degree to acceptance of her premises about Moreland and Priscilla. There seemed no alternative.

'Oh, I don't know. A month or two ago. They met at that office where she works. I knew something of the sort had happened when he came home that day.'

'But they met first at our flat.'

'They'd met before you produced her at your flat. They kept quiet about knowing each other when they met there.'

I spared a passing thought for the slyness of Priscilla; also for Matilda's all-embracing information service. Before more could be said about this uncomfortable subject, two things happened to break up our conversation. First of all the distinguished conductor—rather specially noted for his appreciation of feminine attractions—presented himself with a great deal of flourish to pay his respects to Matilda. He was known to admire her, but until that moment had been unable to escape from persons who wanted to take this opportunity of chatting with a celebrity of his calibre, finally being pinned down by Lady Huntercombe, who had descended upon him after failing to capture Robert. He had already made some opening remarks of a complimentary kind to Matilda, consciously recalling by their form of expression the elaborate courtesies of an earlier age—and I was preparing to leave Matilda to him—when my attention was diverted to something that had taken place at the far end of the room.

This was nothing less than the arrival of Stringham. At first I could hardly believe my eyes. There he was standing by the door talking to Buster. The scene was only made credible by the fact that Buster looked extremely put out. After what had been said that evening, Stringham was certainly the last person to be expected to turn up at his mother's party. He was not wearing evening clothes, being dressed, in fact, in a very old tweed suit and woollen jumper. As usual he looked rather distinguished in these ancient garments, which could not have less fitted the occasion, but somehow at the same time seemed purposely designed to make Buster appear overdressed. Stringham himself was, as formerly, perfectly at ease, laughing a lot at something he had just remarked to Buster, who, with wrinkled forehead and raised eyebrows, had for once lost all his air of lazy indifference to life, and seemed positively to be miming the part of a man who has suddenly received a disagreeable surprise. Stringham finished what he had to say, clapped Buster on the back, and turned towards his mother who came up at that moment. I was too far away to hear Mrs Foxe's words, but, as she kissed her son affectionately, she was clearly welcoming him in the manner appropriate to one returned unexpectedly from a voyage round the world. At the same time, unlike her husband, she showed no surprise or discomposure at Stringham's arrival. They spoke together for a second or two, then she returned to her conversation with Lord Huntercombe. Stringham turned away from her and strolled across the room, gazing about him with a smile. Catching sight of me suddenly, he drew back with a movement of feigned horror, then made towards the place where I was standing. I went to meet him.

'My dear Nick.'

'Charles.'

'I had no idea you had musical tastes, Nick. Why did you

keep them from me all these years? Because I never asked, I suppose. One always finds the answer to everything in one's own egotism. But how nice to meet again. I am a recluse now. I see nobody. I expect you already knew that. Everybody seems to know by now. It is just a bit like being a leper, only I don't actually have to carry a bell. They decided to let me off that. Thought I should make too much of a row, I suppose. You can't imagine what a pleasure it is to come unexpectedly upon an old friend one knew several million years ago.'

There could be no doubt that he was drunk, but, within the vast area comprised by that term, among the immensely varied states of mind and body which intoxication confers, Stringham's at this moment was that controlled exhilaration of spirit more akin to madness than carousal, which some addicts can achieve after a single glass. He looked rather ghastly when you were close to him, his skin pale and mottled, his eyes sunken and bloodshot. Even so, there was plenty of the old dash about his manner.

'I had no idea my mother would be giving a party tonight,' he said. 'Just thought I would drop in and have a word with her by the fireside as I haven't seen her for some time. What do I find but a whirl of gaiety. I really came along to tease Buster. I like doing that from time to time. It cheers me up for some reason. You know I now live in a flat at the top of a house owned by a relation of your wife's—Molly Jeavons, one of the most delightful and charming of people. I sometimes hear about you both from her or from Ted. I dote on Ted. He hasn't been very well lately, you know, and he gives wonderful descriptions of what is going on in his lower intestine—that war wound of his. One need never be bored when Ted gets on to that subject. He and I sometimes go out for the quickest of quick drinks. I am not supposed to have much in the way of drink these days. Neither is Ted. I am trying to knock off, really—but it seems such a bore to be a total abstainer, as I believe such people are called. I can have just one drink still, you know. I don't have to keep off it utterly.'

He said these words in such an appealing tone that I felt torn inwardly to think of the condition he must be in, of the circumstances in which he must live. His awareness of his own state seemed almost worse than total abandonment to the bottle. It looked very much as if he might just have come on to his mother's house that night from one of those 'very quick drinks' with Jeavons; perhaps felt unable to bring himself to return to Miss Weedon's flat and paint in gouache—if it was really with painting that he therapeutically ordered his spare time. His life with Miss Weedon was impossible to contemplate.

'Do you know this fellow Moreland?' he went on. 'I gather from Buster that the party is being given in Moreland's honour—that he is a famous musician apparently. It just shows how right it is that I should have to live as a hermit, not to know that Moreland is a famous musician— and have to be told by Buster. All the same, it cuts both ways. If you are a hermit, you can't be expected to keep up with all the latest celebrities. Buster, of course, was quite incapable of giving any real information about Moreland, the party, the guests, or anything else. He is awfully stupid, poor old Buster. An absolute ape. You know a fact that strikes one very forcibly as one grows older is that some people are intelligent and some are stupid. I don't set up as an intellectual myself—even though I am a great hand with the paintbrush, did they tell you that, Nick?—but if I were as ill-informed as Buster, I should take steps to educate myself. Go to a night-school or hire a well-read undergraduate to teach me a few things in the long vac. The person I shall have to get hold of is Norman. He will tell me all about everything. Have you met Norman yet? He is simply charming. He is—well, I don't want to labour the point, and I can see from your face you have guessed what I was going to say, and you are quite right. All the same, my mother has taken him up in a big way. You must meet Norman, Nick.'

'But I know him well. I have known him for years.'

'I am surprised at the company you must have been keeping, Nick. Known him for years, indeed. I shouldn't have thought it of you. And a married man too. But you do agree, don't you, that Norman is a delightful fellow?'

'Absolutely.'

'I knew you would. I can't tell you how good Norman has been for my mother. Brilliant ideas and helpful comment don't exactly gush from Buster, with all his manly qualities. Besides, when it comes to doing odd jobs about the house, Buster is no good with his hands. What, you say, a sailor and no good with his hands? I don't believe you. It's the perfect truth. I sometimes tease him about it. He doesn't always take that in good part. Now, at last there is someone in the house who can turn to when it comes to hanging a picture or altering the place of a piece of furniture without smashing the thing to a thousand fragments. Not only that, but Norman decides what detective stories ought to come from the Times Book Club, settles what plays must be seen, gives good advice to my mother about hats —in fact excels at all the things poor old Buster fails at so lamentably. On top of that, Norman won't be bullied. He gets his own way. He is just about the only person who deals with my mother who does get his own way.'

'Jolly good.'

'Look here, Nick, you are not being serious. I want to be serious. People are always charging me with not being sufficiently serious. There is something serious I want to ask you. You know the Abdication?'

'I heard something about it.'

'Well, I thought it was a good thing. A frightfully good thing. The only possible thing. I wish to goodness Buster would abdicate one of these days.'

'Not a hope.'

'You're right. Not a hope. I say, Nick, it is awfully nice meeting you again after all these years. Let me get you another drink. You see the extraordinary thing is that I don't feel the smallest need for drink myself. I rise above it. That shows an advance, doesn't it? Not everyone we know can make that boast with truth. I must mention to you that there are some awfully strange people at this party tonight. Not at all like the people my mother usually collects. I suppose it is them, and not me. You agree? Yes, I thought I was right. They remind me more of the days when I used to know Milly Andriadis. Poor old Milly. I wonder what has happened to her. Perhaps they have put her away too.'

While he was speaking his eyes were on Mrs Maclintick, who was now making her ways towards us.

'This lady, for example,' said Stringham. 'What could have induced her to dress like that?'

'She is coming to talk to us.'

'My God, I believe you're right.'

Mrs Maclintick arrived within range. Cold rage still possessed her. She addressed herself to me.

'That was a nice way to be spoken to by your husband,' she said. 'Did you ever hear anything like it?'

Before I could reply, Stringham caught her by the arm.

'Hullo, Little Bo-Peep,' he said. 'What have you done with your shepherdess's crook? You will never find your sheep at this rate. Don't look so cross and pout at me like that, or I shall ruffle up all those dainty little frills of yours —and then where will you be?'

The effect on Mrs Maclintick of this unconventional approach was electric. She flushed with pleasure, contorting her body into an attitude of increased provocation. I saw at once that this must be the right way to treat her; that a deficiency of horseplay on the part of her husband and his friends was probably the cause of her endemic sulkiness. No doubt something in Stringham's manner, the impression he gave that evening of having cut himself off from all normal restraints, played a part in Mrs Maclintick's submission. He was in a mood to carry all before him. Even so, she made an effort to fight back.

'What an extraordinary thing to say,' she remarked. 'And who are you, I should like to know?'

I introduced them, but neither was inclined to pay much attention to names or explanations. Stringham, for some reason, seemed set on pursuing the course he had begun. Mrs Maclintick showed no sign of discouraging him, beyond a refusal entirely to abandon her own traditional acerbity of demeanour.

'Fancy a little girl like you being allowed to come to a grown-up party like this one,' said Stringham. 'You ought to be in bed by now I'm sure.'

'If you think I don't know most of the people here,' said Mrs Maclintick, uncertain whether to be pleased or offended at this comment, 'you are quite wrong. I have met nearly all of them.'

'Then you have the advantage of me in that respect,' said Stringham, 'and so you must tell me who everyone is. For example, what is the name of the fat man wearing a dinner jacket a size too small for him—the one drinking something from a tumbler?'

If there was any doubt about the good impression Stringham had already made on Mrs Maclintick, this enquiry set him immediately at the topmost peak of her estimation.

'That's my husband,' she said, speaking at once with delight and all the hatred of which she was capable. 'He has just been vilely rude to me. He hates wearing evening clothes. The state they were in—even though he never gets into them—you wouldn't have believed. I had to tack the seam of the trousers before he could be seen in them. He isn't properly shaved either. I told him so. He said he had run out of new blades. He looks a fright, doesn't he?'

'He does indeed,' said Stringham. 'You have put the matter in a nutshell.'

'If you had heard some of the things he has been shouting

163

at me in this very room,' said Mrs Maclintick, 'you would not have credited your hearing. The man has not a spark of gratitude.'

'What do you expect with a thick neck like that?' said Stringham. 'Not gratitude, surely?'

'Language of the gutter,' said Mrs Maclintick, as if relishing her husband's phrases in retrospect. 'Filthy words.'

'Think no more of his trivial invective,' said Stringham. 'Come with me and forget the ineptitudes of married life —with which I was once myself only too familiar—in a glass of wine. Let me persuade you to drown your sorrows.

> While the Rose blows along the River Brink
> With old Stringhám the Ruby Vintage drink . . .

It isn't ruby in this case, but none the worse for that. Buster's taste in champagne is not too bad. It is one of his redeeming features.'

Mrs Maclintick was about to reply, no doubt favourably, but, before she could speak, Stringham, smiling in my direction, led her away. Why he wished to involve himself with Mrs Maclintick I could not imagine: drink; love of odd situations; even attraction to a woman he found wholly unusual; any of those might have been the reason. Mrs Maclintick was tamed, almost docile, under his treatment. I was still reflecting on the eccentricity of Stringham's behaviour when brought suddenly within the orbit of Lord Huntercombe, who was moving round the room in a leisurely way, examining the pictures and ornaments there. He had just taken up *Truth Unveiled by Time*, removed his spectacles, and closely examined the group's base. He now replaced the cast on its console table, at the same time smiling wryly in my direction and shaking his head, as if to imply that such worthless bric-à-brac should not be allowed to detain great connoisseurs like ourselves. Smethyck (a museum official, whom I had known as an undergraduate) had introduced us not long before at an exhibition of seventeeth-century pictures and furniture Smethyck himself had helped to organise, to which Lord Huntercombe had lent some of his collection.

'Have you seen your friend Smethyck lately?' asked Lord Huntercombe, still smiling.

'Not since we talked about picture-cleaning at that exhibition.'

'Before the exhibition opened,' said Lord Huntercombe, 'Smethyck showed himself anxious to point out that my *Prince Rupert Conversing with a Herald* was painted by Dobson, rather than Van Dyck. Fortunately I had long ago come to the same conclusion and had recently caused its label to be altered. I was even able to carry the war into Smethyck's country by enquiring whether he felt absolutely confident of the authenticity of that supposed portrait of Judge Jeffreys, attributed to Lely, on loan from his own gallery. What nice china there is in this house. It looks to me as if there were some Vienna porcelain mixed up with the Meissen in this cabinet. I believe Warrington knew something of china. That was why Kitchener liked him. You know, I think I shall have to inspect these a little more thoroughly.'

Lord Huntercombe tried the door of the cabinet. Although the key turned, the door refused to open. He steadied the top of the cabinet with his hand, then tried again. Still the door remained firmly closed. Lord Huntercombe shook his head. He brought out a small penknife from his pocket, opened the shorter blade, and inserted this in the crevice.

'How is Erridge?' he asked.

He spoke with that note almost of yearning in his voice, which peers are inclined to employ when speaking of other peers, especially of those younger than themselves of whom they disapprove.

'He is still in Spain.'

'I hope he will try to persuade his friends not to burn *all* the churches,' said Lord Huntercombe, without looking up, as he moved the blade of the knife gently backwards and forwards.

He had crouched on his haunches to facilitate the operation, and in this position gave the impression of an old craftsman practising a trade at which he was immensely skilled, his extreme neatness and the quick movement of his fingers adding to this illusion. However, these efforts remained ineffective. The door refused to open. I had some idea of trying to find Isobel to arrange a meeting between herself and Stringham. However, I was still watching Lord Huntercombe's exertions when Chandler now reappeared.

'Nick,' he said, 'come and talk to Amy.'

'Just hold this cabinet steady for a moment, both of you,' said Lord Huntercombe. 'There . . . it's coming . . . that's done it. Thank you very much.'

'I say, Lord Huntercombe,' said Chandler, 'I did simply worship those cut-glass candelabra you lent to that exhibition the other day. I am going to suggest to the producer of the show I'm in rehearsal for that we try and get the effect of something of that sort in the Second Act—instead of the dreary old pewter candlesticks we are now using.'

'I do not think the Victoria and Albert would mind possessing those candelabra,' said Lord Huntercombe with complacency, at the same time abstracting some of the pieces from the cabinet. 'Ah, the Marcolini Period. I thought as much. And here are some *Indianische Blumen*.'

We moved politely away from Lord Huntercombe's immediate area, leaving him in peace to pursue further researches.

'My dear,' said Chandler, speaking in a lower voice, 'Amy is rather worried about Charles turning up like this. She thought that, as an old friend of his, you might be able to persuade him to go quietly home after a time. He is a sweet boy, but in the state he is in you never know what he is going to do next.'

'It is ages since I saw Charles. We met tonight for the first time for years. I doubt if he would take the slightest notice of anything I said. As a matter of fact he has just gone off with Mrs Maclintick to whom he is paying what used to be called marked attentions.'

'That is one of the things Amy is worried about. Amy has an eye like a hawk, you know.'

I was certainly surprised to hear that Mrs Foxe had taken in the circumstances of the party so thoroughly as even to have included Mrs Maclintick in her survey. As a hostess, she gave no impression of observing the room meticulously (at least not with the implication of fear pedantic use of that term implies), nor did she seem in the smallest degree disturbed when we came up to her.

'Oh, Mr Jenkins,' she said, 'dear Charles has arrived, as you know since you have been talking to him. I thought you would not mind if I asked you to keep the smallest eye on him. His nerves are so bad nowadays. You have known him for such a long time. He is much more likely to agree to anything you suggest than to fall in with what I want him to do. He really ought not to stay up too late. It is not good for him.'

She said no more than that; gave no hint she required Stringham's immediate removal. That was just as well, because I should have had no idea how to set about any such dislodgement. I remembered suddenly that the last time a woman had appealed to me for help in managing Stringham was when, at her own party years before, Mrs Andriadis had said: 'Will you persuade him to stay?' Then it was his mistress; now, his mother. Mrs Foxe had been too discreet to say outright: 'Will you persuade him to go?' None the less, that was what she must have desired. Her discrimination in expressing this wish, her manner of putting herself into my hands, made her as successful as Mrs Andriadis in enlisting my sympathy; but no more effective as an ally. It was hard to see what could be done about Stringham. Besides, I had by then begun to learn—what I had no idea of at Mrs Andriadis's party—that to people like Stringham there is really no answer.

'Don't worry, Amy, darling,' said Chandler. 'Charles is perfectly all right for the time being. Don't feel anxious. Nick and I will keep an eye on him.'

'Will you? It would be so awful if something did go wrong. I should feel so guilty if the Morelands' party were spoiled for them.'

'It won't be.'

'I shall rely on you both.'

She gazed at Chandler with deep affection. They might have been married for years from the manner in which they talked to one another. Some people came up to say goodbye. I saw Isobel, and was about to suggest that we should look for Stringham, when Mrs Foxe turned from the couple to whom she had been talking.

'Isobel, my dear,' she said, 'I haven't seen you all the evening. Come and sit on the sofa. There are some things I want to ask you about.'

'Odd scenes in the next room,' Isobel said to me, before she joined Mrs Foxe.

I felt sure from her tone the scenes must be odd enough. I found Isobel had spoken without exaggeration. Stringham, Mrs Maclintick, Priscilla, and Moreland were sitting together in a semi-circle. The rest of the party had withdrawn from that corner of the room, so that this group was quite cut off from the other guests. They were laughing a great deal and talking about marriage, Stringham chiefly directing the flow of conversation, with frequent interruptions from Moreland and Mrs Maclintick. Stringham was resting his elbow on his knee in an attitude of burlesqued formality, from time to time inclining his head towards Mrs Maclintick, as he addressed her in the manner of a drawing-room comedy by Wilde or Pinero. These fulsome compliments and epigrammatic phrases may have been largely incomprehensible to Mrs Maclintick, but she looked thoroughly pleased with herself; indeed, seemed satisfied that she was half-teasing, half-alluring Stringham. Priscilla appeared enormously happy in spite of not knowing quite what was going on round her. Moreland was almost hysterical with laughter which he continually tried to repress by stuffing a handkerchief into his mouth. If he had fallen in love with Priscilla—the evidence for something of the sort having taken place had to be admitted—it was, I thought, just like him to prefer listening to this performance to keeping his girl to himself in some remote part of the room. This judgment was superficial, because, as I have said, Moreland could be secretive enough about his girls when he chose; while politeness and discretion called for some show of outwardly casual behaviour at this party. Even so, his behaviour that night could hardly be called discreet in general purport. It was obvious he was very taken with Priscilla from the way he was sitting beside her. He was clearly delighted by Stringham, of whose identity I felt sure he had no idea. When I approached, Mrs Maclintick was apparently describing the matrimonial troubles of some friends of hers.

'. . . and then,' she was saying, 'this first husband of hers used to come back at four o'clock in the morning and turn on the gramophone. As a regular thing. She told me herself.'

'Some women think one has nothing better to do than to lie awake listening to anecdotes about their first husband,' said Stringham. 'Milly Andriadis was like that—no doubt still is—and I must say, if one were prepared to forgo one's beauty sleep, one used to hear some remarkable things from her. Playing the gramophone is another matter. Your friend had a right to complain.'

'That was what the judge thought,' said Mrs Maclintick.

'What used he to play?' asked Priscilla.

'Military marches,' said Mrs Maclintick, 'night after night. Not surprising the poor woman had to go into a home after getting her divorce.'

'My mother would have liked that,' said Stringham. 'She adores watching troops march past. She always says going to reviews was the best part of being married to Piers Warrington.'

'Not in the middle of the night,' said Priscilla. 'He might have chosen something quieter. *Tales from Hoffman* or Handel's *Cradle Song*.'

'Nonsense,' said Moreland. '*Aut Sousa aut Nihil* has always been my motto in cases of that sort. Think if the man had played Hindemith. At least he wasn't a highbrow.'

'He was just another musical husband,' said Mrs Maclintick fiercely. 'I am not saying he was any worse than Maclintick. I am not saying he was any better. I am just telling you the way musicians treat their wives. Telling you the sort of husband I have to put up with.'

'My own complaint about marriage is a very different one,' said Stringham. 'I admit my former wife was not musical. That might have made things worse. All the same, you never know. If she had been, she could have talked all the time about music while her sister, Anne, was chattering away about Braque and Dufy. It would have formed a counter-irritant. Poor Anne. Marrying Dicky Umfraville was a dreadful judgment on her. Still, a party is no place for vain regrets—certainly not vain regrets about one's ex-sister-in-law.

'You should have seen Maclintick's sister,' said Mrs Maclintick, 'if you are going to grumble about your sister-in-law.'

'We will visit her, if necessary, dear lady, later in the evening,' said Stringham. 'The night is still young.'

'You can't,' said Mrs Maclintick. 'She's dead.'

'My condolences,' said Stringham. 'But, as I was saying, my former wife was not musical. Music did not run in the family. Mountfichet was not a house to stimulate music. You might compose a few dirges there, I suppose. Even they would have cheered the place up—the morning-room especially.'

'I was going to stay at Mountfichet once,' said Priscilla. 'Then Hugo got chicken-pox and we were all in quarantine.'

'You had a narrow escape, Lady Priscilla,' said Stringham. 'You are unaware of your good fortune. No, what I object to about marriage is not the active bad behaviour—like your musical friend playing the gramophone in the small hours. I could have stood that. I sleep abominably anyway. The gramophone would while away time in bed when one lies awake thinking about love. What broke me was the passive resistance. That was what got me down.'

Moreland began to laugh unrestrainedly again, thrusting the handkerchief in his mouth until it nearly choked him. He too had had a good deal to drink. Mrs Maclintick clenched her teeth in obvious approval of what Stringham had said. Stringham went on uninterrupted.

'It is a beautiful morning,' he said. 'For some reason you feel relatively well that day. You make some conciliatory remark. No answer. You think she hasn't heard. Still asleep perhaps. You speak again. A strangled sigh. What's wrong? You begin to go through in your mind all the awful things you might have done.'

'Maclintick never dreams of going through the awful things he has done,' said Mrs Maclintick. 'It would take far too long for one thing. Anyway, he never thinks about them at all. If you so much as mention one or two of them, he gets out of bed and sleeps on the sofa in his work-room.'

'Look here,' said Moreland, still laughing convulsively, 'I really cannot have my old friend Maclintick maligned in this manner without a word of protest. I know you are married to him, and marriage gives everyone all sorts of special rights where complaining is concerned——'

'You begin adding up your sins of commission and omission,' Stringham continued inexorably. 'Did one get tight? It seems months and months since one was tight, so it can't be that. Did one say something silly the night before? Much more likely. Not that remark about the colour of her father's face at breakfast? It couldn't have been that. She enjoyed that—even laughed a little. I don't know whether any of you ever met my former father-in-law, Major the Earl of Bridgnorth, late the Royal Horse Guards, by the way? His is a name to conjure with on the Turf. When I was married to his elder daughter, the beautiful Peggy, I was often to be seen conjuring with it on the course at Epsom, and elsewhere, but with little success, all among the bookies and Prince Monolulu and the tipster who wears an Old Harrovian tie and has never given a loser.'

'You are getting off the point, my dear sir,' said Moreland. 'We are discussing marriage, not racing. Matrimony is the point at issue.'

Stringham made a gesture to silence him. I had never before seen Moreland conversationally so completely mastered. It was hard to imagine what the two of them would have made of each other in more sober circumstances. They were very different. Stringham had none of Moreland's passionate self-identification with the arts; Moreland was without Stringham's bitter grasp of social circumstance. At the same time they had something in common. There was also much potential antipathy. Each would probably have found the other unsympathetic over a long period.

'And then,' said Stringham, lowering his voice and raising his eyebrows slightly, 'one wonders about making love . . . counts up on one's fingers . . . No . . . It can't be that . . .'

Mrs Maclintick gave a raucous laugh.

'I know!' Stringham now almost shouted, as if in sudden enlightenment. 'I've got it. It was going on about what a charming girl Rosie Manasch is. That was a bloody silly thing to do, when I know Peggy hates Rosie like poison. But I'm wandering . . . talking of years ago . . . of the days before Rosie married Jock Udall . . .'

'Heavens,' said Moreland. 'Do you know the Manasches? I once conducted at a charity concert in their house.'

Stringham ignored him.

'But then, on the other hand,' he went on, in a slower, much quieter voice, 'Rosie may have nothing whatever to do with it. One's wife may be ill. Sickening for some terrible disease. Something to which one has never given a thought. She is sinking. Wasting away under one's eyes. It is just one's own callousness about her state. That is all that's wrong. You begin to get really worried. Should you get up and summon a doctor right away?'

'The doctor always tells Maclintick to drink less,' said Mrs Maclintick. 'Always the same story. "Put a drop more water in it," he says, "then you will feel better." You might just as well talk to a brick wall. Maclintick is not going to drink less because a doctor tells him to. If he won't stop after what I've said to him, is it likely he will knock off for a doctor? Why should he?'

'Why, indeed, you little rogue?' said Stringham, tapping Mrs Maclintick's knee with a folded copy of the concert programme, which had somehow found its way into his hand. 'Well, of course, in the end you discover that all this ill humour is nothing to do with yourself at all. In fact your wife is hardly aware that she is living in the same house with you. It was something that somebody said about her to someone who gossiped to somebody she knew when that somebody was having her hair done. Neither less nor more than that. All the same, it is you, her husband, who has to bear the brunt of those ill-chosen remarks by somebody about something. I've talked it all over with Ted Jeavons and he quite agrees.'

'I adore Uncle Ted,' said Priscilla, anxious to show that she herself had perfectly followed this dissertation.

'And you, Black-eyed Susan,' said Stringham, turning again in the direction of Mrs Maclintick, at the same time raising the programme interrogatively, 'do you too suffer in your domestic life—of which you speak with such a wealth of disillusionment—from the particular malaise I describe: the judgment of terrible silences?'

That was a subject upon which Mrs Maclintick felt herself in a position to speak authoritatively; the discussion, if uninterrupted, might have proceeded for a long time. Moreland was showing some signs of restlessness, although he and the others sitting there seemed to be finding some release from themselves, and their individual lives, in what was being said. The remainder of Mrs Foxe's guests, although in fact just round the corner, appeared for some reason infinitely far away. Then, all at once, I became aware that a new personality, an additional force, had been added to our group. This was a woman. She was standing beside me. How long she had been there, where she came from, I did not know.

It was Miss Weedon. She had probably avoided having herself announced in order to make quietly for the place where Stringham was to be found. In any case, her long association with the house as one of its inmates made such a formality almost inappropriate. As usual, she managed to look both businesslike and rather elegant, her large sharp nose and severe expression adding to her air of efficiency, suggesting on the whole a successful, fairly chic career woman. Enclosed in black, her dress committed her neither to night nor day; suitable for Mrs Foxe's party, it would have done equally well for some lesser occasion. She did not look at all like the former governess of Stringham's sister, Flavia, although there remained something dominating and controlling about Miss Weedon, hinting that she was used to exercising some form of professional authority. Undoubtedly her intention was to take Stringham home. No other objective could have brought her out at this hour of the night. Priscilla, who had probably met Miss Weedon more than once at the Jeavonses'—where Miss Weedon was a frequent guest before moving in as an occupant of the house itself—was the first to notice her.

'Hullo, Miss Weedon,' she said blushing.

Priscilla moved, probably involuntarily, further from Moreland, who was sitting rather close to her on the sofa. Miss Weedon smiled coldly. She advanced a little deeper into the room, her mysterious, equivocal presence casting a long, dark shadow over the scene.

'Why, hullo, Tuffy,' said Stringham, suddenly seeing Miss Weedon too. 'I am so glad you have turned up. I wondered if I should see you. I just dropped in to say good evening to Mamma, whom I hadn't set eyes on for ages, only to find the gayest of gay parties in progress. Let me introduce everyone. Lady Priscilla Tolland—you know Tuffy, of course. How silly of me. Now this is Mrs Maclintick, who has been telling me some really hair-raising stories about musical people. I shall never listen to an orchestra again without the most painful speculations about the home life of the players. Nick, of course, you've often met. I'm afraid I don't know your name, Mr——?'

'Moreland,' said Moreland, absolutely enchanted by Stringham's complete ignorance of his identity.

'Moreland!' said Stringham. 'This is Mr Moreland, Tuffy. Mr Moreland for whom the whole party is being given. What a superb *faux pas* on my part. A really exquisite blunder. How right it is that I should emerge but rarely. Well, there we are—and this, I nearly forgot to add, Mr Moreland, is Miss Weedon.'

He was still perfectly at ease. There was not the smallest sign to inform a casual observer that Stringham was now looked upon by his own family, by most of his friends, as a person scarcely responsible for his own actions; that he was about to be removed from his mother's house by a former secretary who had taken upon herself to look after him, because—I suppose—she loved him. All the same, although nothing outward indicated that something dramatic was taking place, Stringham himself, after he had performed these introductions, had risen from his chair with one of his random, easy movements, so that to me it was clear he knew the game was up. He knew that he must be borne away by Miss Weedon within the next few minutes to whatever prison-house now enclosed him. Moreland and Priscilla glanced at each other, recognising a break in the rhythm of the party, probably wanting to make a move themselves, but unaware quite what was happening. Mrs Maclintick, on the other hand, showed herself not at all willing to have the group disposed of in so arbitrary a manner. She turned a most unfriendly stare on Miss Weedon, which seemed by its contemptuous expression to recognise in her, by some unaccountable feminine intuition, a figure formerly subordinate in Mrs Foxe's household.

'We have been talking about marriage,' said Mrs Maclintick aggressively.

She addressed herself to Miss Weedon, who in return gave her a smile that cut like a knife.

'Indeed?' she said.

'This gentleman and I have been comparing notes,' said Mrs Maclintick, indicating Stringham.

'We have, indeed,' said Stringham laughing. 'And found a lot to agree about.'

He had dropped his former air of burlesque, now appeared completely sober.

'It sounds a very interesting discussion,' said Miss Weedon.

She spoke in a tone damaging to Mrs Maclintick's self-esteem. Miss Weedon was undoubtedly prepared to take anybody on; Mrs Maclintick; anybody. I admired her for that.

'Why don't you tell us what you think about marriage yourself?' asked Mrs Maclintick, who had drunk more champagne than I had at first supposed. 'They say the onlooker sees most of the game.'

'Not now,' said Miss Weedon, in the cosmically terminating voice of one who holds authority to decide when the toys must be returned to the toy-cupboard. 'I have my little car outside, Charles. I thought you might like a lift home.'

'But he is going to take me to a night-club,' said Mrs Maclintick, her voice rising in rage. 'He said that after we had settled a few points about marriage we would go to a very amusing place he knew of.'

Miss Weedon looked at Stringham without a trace of surprise or disapproval; just a request for confirmation.

'That was the suggestion, Tuffy.'

He laughed again. He must have known by experience that in the end Miss Weedon would turn out to hold all the cards, but he showed no sign yet of capitulation.

'The doctor begged you not to stay up too late, Charles,' said Miss Weedon, also smiling.

She was in no degree behind Stringham where keeping one's head was concerned.

'My medical adviser did indeed prescribe early hours,' said Stringham. 'You are right there, Tuffy. I distinctly recollect his words. But I was turning over in my mind the possibility of disregarding such advice. Ted Jeavons was speaking recently of some night haunt he once visited where he had all kind of unusual adventures. A place run by one, Dicky Umfraville, a bad character whom I used to see in my Kenya days and have probably spoken of. Something about the sound of the joint attracted me. I offered to take Mrs Maclintick there. I can hardly go back on my promise. Of course, the club has no doubt closed down by now. Nothing Dicky Umfraville puts his hand to lasts very long. Besides, Ted was a little vague about the year his adventure happened—it might have been during the war, when he was a gallant soldier on leave from the trenches. That all came in when he told the story. However, if defunct, we could always visit the Bag of Nails.'

Mrs Maclintick snatched facetiously at him.

'You know perfectly well I shall hate any of those places,' she said gaily, 'and I believe you are only trying to get me there to make me feel uncomfortable.'

Miss Weedon remained unruffled.

'I had no idea you were planning anything like that, Charles.'

'It wasn't exactly planned,' said Stringham. 'Just one of those brilliant improvisations that come to me of a sudden. My career has been built up on them. One of them brought me here tonight.'

'But I haven't agreed to come with you yet,' said Mrs Maclintick, with some archness. 'Don't be too sure of that.'

'I recognise, Madam, I can have no guarantee of such an honour,' said Stringham, momentarily returning to his former tone. 'I was not so presumptuous as to take your company for granted. It may even be that I shall venture forth into the night—by no means for the first time in my chequered career—on a lonely search for pleasure.'

'Wouldn't it really be easier to accept my offer of a lift?' said Miss Weedon.

She spoke so lightly, so indifferently, that no one could possibly have guessed that in uttering those words she was issuing an order. There was no display of power. Even Stringham must have been aware that Miss Weedon was showing a respect for his own situation that was impeccable.

'Much, much easier, Tuffy,' he said. 'But who am I to be given a life of ease?

> Not for ever by still waters
> Would we idly rest and stay . . .

I feel just like the hymn. Tonight I must take the hard road that leads to pleasure.'

'We could give this lady a lift home too, if she liked,' said Miss Weedon.

She glanced at Mrs Maclintick as if prepared to accept the conveyance of her body at whatever the cost. It was a handsome offer on Miss Weedon's part, a very handsome offer. No person could have denied that.

'But I am not much in the mood for going home, Tuffy,' said Stringham, 'and I am not sure that Mrs Maclintick is either, in spite of her protests to the contrary. We are young. We want to see life. We feel we ought not to limit our experience to musical parties, however edifying.'

There was a short pause.

'If only I had known this, Charles,' said Miss Weedon.

She spoke sadly, almost as if she were deprecating her own powers of dominion, trying to minimise them because their very hugeness embarrassed her; like the dictator of some absolutist state who assures journalists that his most imperative decrees have to take an outwardly parliamentary form.

'If only I had known,' she said, 'I could have brought your notecase. It was lying on the table in your room.'

Stringham laughed outright.

'Correct, as usual, Tuffy,' he said.

'I happened to notice it.'

'Money,' said Stringham. 'It is always the answer.'

'But even if I had brought it, you would have been much wiser not to stay up late.'

'Even if you had brought it, Tuffy,' said Stringham, 'the situation would remain unaltered, because there is no money in it.'

He turned to Mrs Maclintick.

'Little Bo-Peep,' he said, 'I fear our jaunt is off. We shall have to visit Dicky Umfraville's club, or the Bag of Nails, some other night.'

He made a movement to show he was ready to follow Miss Weedon.

'I didn't want to drag you away,' she said, 'but I thought it might save trouble as I happen to have the car with me.'

'Certainly it would,' said Stringham. 'Save a lot of trouble. Limitless trouble. Untold trouble. I will bid you all good night.'

After that, Miss Weedon had him out of the house in a matter of seconds. There was the faintest suspicion of a reel as he followed her through the door. Apart from that scarcely perceptible lurch, Stringham's physical removal was in general accomplished by her with such speed and efficiency that probably no one but myself recognised this trifling display of unsteadiness on his feet. The moral tactics were concealed almost equally successfully until the following day, when they became plain to me. The fact was, of course, that Stringham was kept without money; or at least on that particular evening Miss Weedon had seen to it that he had no more money on him than enabled buying the number of drinks that had brought him to his mother's house. He must have lost his nerve as to the efficacy of his powers of cashing a cheque; perhaps no longer possessed a cheque-book. Otherwise, he would undoubtedly have proceeded with the enterprise set on foot. Possibly fatigue, too, stimulated by the sight of Miss Weedon, had played a part in evaporating desire to paint the town red in the company of Mrs Maclintick; perhaps in the end Stringham was inwardly willing to 'go quietly'. That was the most likely of all. While these things had been happening, Moreland and Priscilla slipped away. I found myself alone with Mrs Maclintick.

'Who was she, I should like to know,' said Mrs Maclintick. 'Not that I wanted all that to go wherever it was he wanted to take me. Not in the least. It was just that he was so pressing. But what a funny sort of fellow he is. I didn't see why that old girl should butt in. Is she one of his aunts?'

I was absolved from need to explain about Miss Weedon to Mrs Maclintick, no easy matter to embark upon, by seeing Carolo drifting towards us. A dinner jacket made him look more melancholy than ever.

'Coming?' he enquired.

'Where's Maclintick?'

'Gone home.'

'Full of whiskey, I bet.'

'You bet.'

'All right.'

Stringham had made no great impression on her. She must have seen him as one of those eccentric figures naturally to be encountered in rich houses of this kind. That was probably the most judicious view of Stringham for her to take. Certainly there was no way for Mrs Maclintick to guess that a small, violent drama had been played out in front of her; nor would she have been greatly interested if some explanation of the circumstances could have been revealed. Now—in her tone to Carolo—she re-entered, body and soul, the world in which she normally lived. The two of them went off together. I began to look once more for Isobel. By the door Commander Foxe was saying goodbye to Max Pilgrim.

'Well,' said Commander Foxe, when he saw me, 'that was neatly arranged, wasn't it?'

'What was?'

'Persuading Charles to go home.'

'Lucky Miss Weedon happened to look in, you mean?'

'There was a good reason for that.'

'Oh?'

'I rang her up and told her to come along,' said Commander Foxe briefly.

That answer was such a simple one that I could not imagine why I had not guessed it without having to be told. Those very obvious tactical victories are always the victories least foreseen by the onlooker, still less the opponent. Mrs Foxe herself might feel lack of dignity in summoning Miss Weedon to remove her own son from the house; for Buster, no such delicacy obstructed the way. Indeed, this action could be seen as a beautiful revenge for much owed to Stringham in the past; the occasion, for example, when Buster and I had first met in the room next door, and Stringham, still a boy, had seemed to order Buster from the house. No doubt other old sores were to be paid off. The relationship between Commander Foxe and Miss Weedon herself was also to be considered. Like two rival powers

—something about Miss Weedon lent itself to political metaphor—who temporarily abandon their covert belligerency to combine against a third, there was a brief alliance; but also, for Miss Weedon, diplomatically speaking, an element of face-losing. She had been forced to allow her rival to invoke the treaty which demanded that in certain circumstances she should invest with troops her own supposedly pacific protectorate or mandated territory. In fact there had been a victory for Commander Foxe all round. He was not disposed to minimise his triumph.

'Pity about poor old Charles,' he said.

'I'll have to say good night.'

'Come again soon.'

'That would be nice.'

A general movement to leave was taking place among the guests. Mrs Maclintick and Carolo had already disappeared. Gossage still remained deep in conversation with Lady Huntercombe. There was no sign of the Morelands, or of Priscilla. Isobel was talking to Chandler. We went to find our hostess and say goodbye. Mrs Foxe was listening to the famous conductor, like Gossage, unable to tear himself away from the party.

'I do hope the Morelands enjoyed themselves,' said Mrs Foxe. 'It was so sad Matilda should have had a headache and had to go home. I am sure she was right to slip away. She is such a wonderful wife for someone like him. As soon as he heard she had gone, he said he must go too. Such a strain for a musician to have a new work performed. Like a first night—and Norman tells me first nights are agony.'

Mrs Foxe spoke the last word with all the feeling Chandler had put into it when he told her that. Robert joined us in taking leave.

'It was rather sweet of Charles to look in, wasn't it?' said Mrs Foxe. 'I would have asked him, of course, if I hadn't known parties were bad for him. I saw you talking to him. How did you think he was?'

'I hadn't seen him for ages. He seemed just the same. We had a long talk.'

'And you were glad to see him again?'

'Yes, of course.'

'I think he was right to go back with Tuffy. He can be rather difficult sometimes, you know.'

'Well, yes.'

'I do hope everyone enjoyed themselves,' said Mrs Foxe. 'There was a Mr Maclintick who had had rather a lot to drink by the time he left. I think he is a music critic. He was so sweet when he came to say goodbye to me. He said: "Thank you very much for asking me, Mrs Foxe. I don't like grand parties like this one and I am not coming to another, but I appreciate your kindness in supporting Moreland as a composer." I said I so much agreed with him about grand parties—which I *simply* hate—but I couldn't imagine why he should think this was one. All the same, I said, I should arrange it quite differently if I ever gave another, and I hoped he would change his mind and come. "Well, I shan't come," he said. I told him I knew he would because I should ask him so nicely. He said: "I suppose you are right, and I shall." Then he slipped down two or three steps. I do hope he gets home all right. Such a relief when people speak their minds.'

'What's happened to Priscilla?' Isobel asked Robert.

'Somebody gave her a lift.'

At that moment Lord Huntercombe broke in between us. Carrying a piece of chain in his hand, he was delighted by some discovery he had just made. Mrs Foxe turned towards him.

'Amy,' he said, 'are you aware that this quatrefoil cup is a forgery?'

FOUR

If so tortuous a comparison of mediocre talent could ever
be resolved, St John Clarke was probably to be judged a
'better' writer than Isbister was painter. However, when
St John Clarke died in the early spring, he was less well
served than his contemporary in respect of obituaries. Only
a few years before, Isbister had managed to capture, perhaps helped finally to expend, what was left on an older,
more sententious tradition of newspaper panegyric. There
were more reasons for this than the inevitably changing
taste in mediocrity. The world was moving into a harassed
era. At the time of St John Clarke's last illness, the National
Socialist Party of Danzig was in the headlines; foreign
news more and more often causing domestic events to
be passed over almost unnoticed. St John Clarke was one of
these casualties. If Mark Members was to be believed, St
John Clarke himself would have seen this unfair distribu-
tion of success, even posthumous success, as something
in the nature of things. In what Members called 'one of
St J.'s breakfast table agonies of self-pity', the novelist had
quite openly expressed the mortification he felt in contrasting his old friend's lot with his own.

'Isbister was beloved of the gods, Mark,' he had cried
aloud, looking up with a haggard face from *The Times* of
New Year's Day and its list of awards, 'R.A. before he was
forty-five—Gold Medallist of the Paris Salon—Diploma of
Honour at the International Exhibition at Amsterdam—
Commander of the Papal Order of Pius IX—refused a
knighthood. Think of it, Mark, a man the King would
have delighted to honour. What recognition have I had
compared with these?'

'Why did Isbister refuse a knighthood?' Members had
asked.

'To spite his wife.'

'That was it, was it?'

'Those photographs the Press resurrected of Morwenna standing beside him looking out to sea,' said St John Clarke, 'they were antediluvian—diluvian possibly. It was the Flood they were looking at, I expect. They'd been living apart for years when he died. Of course Isbister himself said he had decided worldly honours were unbefitting an artist. That didn't prevent him from telling everyone of the offer. Absolutely everyone. He had it both ways.'

In those days Members was still anxious to soothe his employer.

'Well, you've had a lot of enjoyable parties and country house visits to look back on, St J.,' he said. 'Rather a different life from Isbister's, but a richer one in my eyes.'

'One week-end at Dogdene twenty years ago,' St John Clarke had answered bitterly. 'Forced to play croquet with Lord Lonsdale . . . Two dinners at the Huntercombes', both times asked the same night as Sir Horrocks Rusby . . .'

This was certainly inadequate assessment of St John Clarke's social triumphs, which, for a man of letters, had been less fruitless than at that moment his despair presented them. Members, knowing what was expected of him, brushed away with a smile such melancholy reminiscences.

'But it will come . . .' he said.

'It will come, Mark. As I sit here, the Nobel Prize will come.'

'Alas,' said Members, concluding the story, 'it never does.'

As things fell out, the two most alert articles to deal with St John Clarke were written, ironically enough, by Members and Quiggin respectively, both of whom spared a few crumbs of praise for their former master, treating him at no great length as a 'personality' rather than a writer: Members, in the weekly of which he was assistant literary editor, referring to 'an ephemeral, if almost painfully sincere, digression into what was for him the wonderland of

185

fauviste painting'; Quiggin, in a similar, rather less eminent publication to which he contributed when hard up, guardedly emphasising the deceased's 'underlying, even when patently bewildered, sympathy with the Workers' Cause'. No other journal took sufficient interest in the later stages of St John Clarke's career to keep up to date about these conflicting aspects of his final decade. They spoke only of his deep love for the Peter Pan statue in Kensington Gardens and his contributions to Queen Mary's Gift Book. Appraisal of his work unhesitatingly placed *Fields of Amaranth* as the peak of his achievement, with *E'en the Longest River* or *The Heart is Highland*—opinion varied —as a poor second. *The Times Literary Supplement* found 'the romances of Renaissance Italy and the French Revolution smacked of Wardour Street, the scenes from fashionable life in the other novels tempered with artificiality, the delineations of poverty less realistic than Gissing's.'

I was surprised by an odd feeling of regret that St John Clarke was gone. Even if an indifferent writer, his removal from the literary scene was like the final crumbling of a well-known landmark; unpleasing perhaps, at the same time possessed of a deserved renown for having withstood demolition for so long. The anecdotes Members and Quiggin put round about him had given St John Clarke a certain solidity in my mind; more, in a way, than his own momentary emergence at Lady Warminster's. This glimpse of him, then total physical removal, brought home, too, the blunt postscript of death. St John Clarke had merely looked ill at Hyde Park Gardens; now, like John Peel, he had gone far, far away, with his pen and his press-cuttings in the morning; become one of those names to which the date of birth and death may be added in parentheses, as their owners speed to oblivion from out of reference books and 'literary pages' of the newspapers.

As an indirect result of Mrs Foxe's party, relations with the Morelands were complicated by uncertainty and a little embarrassment. No one really knew what was happening between Moreland and Priscilla. They were never seen together, but it was very generally supposed some sort of a love affair was in progress between them. Rather more than usual Priscilla conveyed the impression that she did not want to be bothered with her relations; while an air of discomfort, faint but decided, pervaded the Moreland flat, indicating something was amiss there. Moreland himself had plunged into a flood of work. He took the line now that his symphony had fallen flat—to some extent, he said, deservedly—and he must repair the situation by producing something better. For the first time since the early days when I had known him, he seemed interested only in professionally musical affairs. We heard at second-hand that Matilda was to be tried out for the part of Zenocrate in Marlowe's *Tamburlaine*. This was confirmed by Moreland himself when I met him by chance somewhere. The extent of the gossip about Moreland and Priscilla was revealed to me one day by running into Chips Lovell travelling by Underground. Lovell had by now achieved his former ambition of getting a job on a newspaper, where he helped to write the gossip column, one of a relatively respectable order. He was in the best of form, dressed with the greatest care, retaining that boyish, innocent look that made him in different ways a success with both sexes.

'How is Priscilla?' he asked.

'All right, so far as I knew.'

'I heard something about her and Hugh Moreland.'

'What sort of thing?'

'That they were having a walk-out together.'

'Who said so?'

'I can't remember.'

'I didn't know you knew Moreland.'

'I don't. Only by name.'

'It doesn't sound very probable, does it?'

'I have no idea. People do these things.'

Although I liked Lovell, I saw no reason to offer help so far as his investigation of the situation of Moreland and

Priscilla. As a matter of fact I had not much help to offer. In any case, Lovell, inhabiting by vocation a world of garbled rumour, was to be treated with discretion where the passing of information was concerned. I was surprised at the outspokenness with which he had mentioned the matter. His enquiry seemed stimulated by personal interest, rather than love of gossip for its own sake. I supposed he still felt faint dissatisfaction at having failed to make the mark to which he felt his good looks entitled him.

'I always liked Priscilla,' he said, using a rather consciously abstracted manner. 'I must see her again one of these days.'

'What has been happening to you, Chips?'

'Do you remember that fellow Widmerpool you used to tell me about when we were at the film studio? His name always stuck in my mind because he managed to stay at Dogdene. I took my hat off to him for getting there. Uncle Geoffrey is by no means keen on handing out invitations. You told me there was some talk of Widmerpool marrying somebody. A Vowchurch, was it? Anyway, I ran into Widmerpool the other day and he talked about you.'

'What did he say?'

'Just mentioned that he knew you. Said it was sensible of you to get married. Thought it a pity you couldn't find a regular job.'

'But I've got a regular job.'

'Not in his eyes, you haven't. He said he feared you were a bit of a drifter with the stream.'

'How was he otherwise?'

'I never saw a man so put out by the Abdication,' said Lovell. 'It might have been Widmerpool himself who'd had to abdicate. My goodness, he had taken it to heart.'

'What specially upset him?'

'So far as I could gather, he had cast himself for a brilliant social career if things had worked out differently.'

'The Beau Brummell of the new reign?'

'Not far short of that.'

'Where did you run across him?'

'Widmerpool came to see me in my office. He wanted me to slip in a paragraph about certain semi-business activities of his. One of those quiet little puffs, you know, which don't cost the advertising department anything, but warm the heart of the sales manager.'

'Did you oblige?'

'Not me,' said Lovell.

By no means without a healthy touch of malice, Lovell had also a fine appreciation of the power-wielding side of his job.

'I hear your brother-in-law, Erry Warminster, is on his way home from Spain,' he said.

'First I've heard of it.'

'Erry's own family are always the last to hear about his goings-on.'

'What's your source?'

'The office, as usual.'

'Is he bored with the Spanish war?'

'He is ill—also had some sort of row with his own side.'

'What is wrong with him?'

'Touch of dysentery, someone said.'

'Serious?'

'I don't think so.'

We parted company after arranging that Lovell should come and have a drink with us at the flat in the near future. The following day, I met Quiggin in Members's office. He was in a sulky mood. I told him I had enjoyed his piece about St John Clarke. Praise was usually as acceptable to Quiggin as to most people. That day the remark seemed to increase his ill humour. However, he confirmed the news about Erridge.

'Yes, yes,' he said impatiently. 'Of course it is true that Alfred is coming back. Don't his family take any interest in him? They might at least have discovered that.'

'Is he bad?'

'It is a disagreeable complaint to have.'

'But a whole skin otherwise. That is always something if there is a war on.'

'Alfred is too simple a man to embroil himself in practical affairs like fighting an ideological war,' said Quiggin severely. 'A typical aristocratic idealist, I'm afraid. Perhaps it is just as well his health has broken down. He has never been strong, of course. He is the first to admit it. In fact he is too fond of talking about his health. As I have said before, Alf is rather like Prince Myshkin in *The Idiot*.'

I was surprised at Quiggin's attitude towards Erridge's illness. I tried to work out who Quiggin himself would be in Dostoevsky's novel if Erridge was Prince Myshkin and Mona—presumably—Natasya Filippovna. It was all too complicated. I could not remember the story with sufficient clarity. Quiggin spoke again.

'I have been hearing something of Alf's difficulties from one of our own agents just back from Barcelona,' he said. 'Alf seems to have shown a good deal of political obtuseness —perhaps I should say childlike innocence. He appears to have treated POUM, FAI, CNT, and UGT, as if they were all the same left-wing extension of the Labour Party. I was not surprised to hear that he was going to be arrested at the time he decided to leave Spain. If you can't tell the difference between a Trotskyite-Communist, an Anarcho-Syndicalist, and a properly paid-up Party Member, you had better keep away from the barricades.'

'You had, indeed.'

'It is not fair on the workers.'

'Certainly not.'

'Alfred's place was to organise in England.'

'Why doesn't he go back to his idea of starting a magazine?'

'I don't know,' said Quiggin, in a voice that closed the subject.

Erridge was in Quiggin's bad books; a friend who had disappointed Quiggin to a degree impossible to conceal; a man who had failed to rise to an historic occasion. I supposed that Quiggin regarded Erridge's imminent return, however involuntary, from the Spanish war in the light of a betrayal. This seemed unreasonable on Quiggin's part, since Erridge's breakdown in health was, after all, occasioned by an attempt to further the cause Quiggin himself had so energetically propagated by word of mouth. Even if Erridge had not fought in the field (where Howard Cragg's nephew had already been killed), he had taken other risks in putting his principles into practice. If it was true that he was marked down for arrest, he might have been executed behind the lines. Quiggin had staked less on his enthusiasms. However, as things turned out there was probably a different reason that afternoon for Quiggin's displeasure on Erridge's account.

Erridge himself arrived in London a day or two later. He was not at all well, and went straight into a nursing home; the nursing home, at it happened, in the passages of which I had encountered Moreland, Brandreth, and Widmerpool. This accommodation was found for her brother by Frederica, ideologically perhaps the furthest removed from Erridge, in certain other respects the closest of the Tollands to him, both from nearness in age and a shared rigidity of individual opinion. The two of them might disagree; they understood each other's obstinacies. When Erridge had settled down at the nursing home, his brothers and sisters visited him there. They were given a lukewarm welcome. Erridge was one of those egotists unable effectively to organise to good effect his own egotism, to make a public profit out of it. He had no doubt enjoyed unusual experiences. These he was unable, or unwilling, to share with others. Isobel brought back a description of a ragged beard protruding over the edge of sheets entirely covered by what appeared to be a patchwork quilt of Boggis & Stone publications dealing with different aspects of the Spanish predicament. Norah, who shared to some extent Erridge's political standpoint, was openly contemptuous.

'Erry always regards himself as the only person in the

world who has ever been ill,' she said. 'His time in Spain seems to have been a total flop. He didn't get up to the front and he never met Hemingway.'

Erridge, as Norah—and Quiggin before her—had remarked, was keenly interested in his own health; in general not good. Now that he was ill enough for his condition to be recognised as more than troublesome, this physical state was not unsympathetic to him. The sickness gave his existence an increased reality, a deeper seriousness, elements Erridge felt denied him by his family. Certainly he could now claim to have returned from an area of action. Although he might prefer to receive his relations coldly, he was at least assured of being the centre of Tolland attention. However, as it turned out, he enjoyed this position only for a short time, when his status was all at once prejudiced by his brother Hugo's motor accident.

Hugo Tolland had 'come down' from the university not long before this period, where, in face of continual pressure of a threatening kind from the authorities, he had contrived to stay the course for three years; even managing, to everyone's surprise, to scrape some sort of degree The youngest of the male Tollands, Hugo was showing signs of becoming from the family's point of view the least satisfactory. Erridge, it was true, even before his father died, had been written off as incurably odd; but Erridge was an 'eldest son'. Even persons of an older generation—like his uncle, Alfred Tolland—who preferred the conventions to be strictly observed, would display their own disciplined acceptance of convention by recognising the fact that Erridge's behaviour, however regrettable, was his own affair. An eldest son, by no means beyond the reach of criticism, was at the same time excluded from the utter and absolute public disapproval which might encompass younger sons. Besides, no one could tell how an eldest son might turn out after he 'succeeded'. This was a favourite theme of Chips Lovell's, who used to talk of 'the classic case of Henry V and Faʼstaff'. Erridge might be peculiar; the fact remained he would be—now was—head of the family. Hugo was quite another matter. Hugo would inherit between three and four hundred a year when twenty-one and have to make his own way in the world.

While still at the university, Hugo showed no sign of wishing to prepare himself for that fate. Outwardly, he was a fairly intelligent, not very good-looking, unhappy, rather amusing young man, who kept himself going by wearing unusual clothes and doing perverse things. Because his own generation of undergraduates tended to be interested in politics and economics, both approached from a 'leftish' angle, Hugo liked to 'pose'—his own word—as an 'aesthete'. He used to burn joss-sticks in his rooms. He had bought a half-bottle of Green Chartreuse, a liqueur he 'sipped' from time to time, which, like the Widow's cruse, seemed to last for ever; for only during outbreaks of consciously bad behaviour was Hugo much of a drinker. At first Sillery had taken him up, no doubt hoping Hugo might prove an asset in the field where Sillery struggled for power with others dons. Hugo had turned out altogether intractable. Even Sillery, past master at dealing with undergraduates of all complexions and turning their fallibilities to his own advantage, had been embarrassed by Hugo's arrival at one of his tea parties laden with a stack of pro-Franco pamphlets, which he had distributed among the assembled guests. The company had included a Labour M.P.—a Catholic, as it happened—upon whom Sillery, for his own purposes, was particularly anxious to make a good impression. The story had been greatly enjoyed by Sillery's old enemy, Brightman, who used to repeat it night after night—*ad nauseam*, his colleagues complained, so Short told me—at High Table.

'Hugo will never find a place for himself in the contemporary world,' his sister Norah had declared.

Norah's conclusion, reached after an argument with Hugo about Spain, was not much at variance with the opinion of the rest of the family. However, this judgment turned out to be a mistaken one. Unlike many outwardly more promising young men, Hugo found a job without apparent difficulty. He placed himself with Baldwyn Hodges Ltd., antique dealers, a business which undertook a certain amount of interior decorating as a sideline. Although far from being the sort of firm Molly Jeavons would—or, financially speaking, could—employ for renovating her own house, its managing director, Mrs Baldwyn Hodges herself, like so many other unlikely people, had fetched up at the Jeavonses' one evening when Hugo was there. Very expert at handling rich people, Mrs Baldwyn Hodges was a middle-aged, capable, leathery woman, of a type Mr Deacon would particularly have loathed had he lived to see the rise of her shop, which had had small beginnings, to fashionable success. Hugo and Mrs Baldwyn Hodges got on well together at the Jeavonses'. They met again at the Surrealist Exhibition. Whatever the reason— probably, in fact, Hugo's own basic, though not then generally recognised, toughness—Mrs Baldwyn Hodges showed her liking for Hugo in a practical manner by taking him into her business as a learner. He did not earn much money at first; he may even have paid some sort of fee at the start; but he made something on commission from time to time and the job suited him. In fact Hugo had shown signs of becoming rather good at selling people furniture and advising them about their drawing-room walls. Chips Lovell (who had recently been told about Freud) explained that Hugo was 'looking for a mother'. Perhaps he was right. Mrs Baldwyn Hodges certainly taught Hugo a great deal.

All the same, Hugo's employment did not prevent him from frequenting the society of what Mr Deacon used to call 'naughty young men'. When out on an excursion with companions of this sort, a car was overturned and Hugo's leg was broken. As a result of this accident, Hugo was confined to bed for some weeks at Hyde Park Gardens, where he set up what he himself designated 'a rival *salon*' to Erridge's room at the nursing home. This situation, absurd as the reason may sound, had, I think, a substantial effect upon the speed of Erridge's recovery. Hugo even attempted to present his own indisposition as a kind of travesty of Erridge's case, pretending that the accident to the car had been the result of political sabotage organised by his sister Norah and Eleanor Walpole-Wilson. It was all very silly, typical of Hugo. At the same time, visiting Hugo in these circumstances was agreed to be more amusing than visiting Erridge. However, even if Erridge made no show of enjoying visitors, and was unwilling to reveal much of his Spanish experiences, he tolerated the interest of other people in what had happened to him in Spain. It was another matter if his relations came to his bedside only to retail the antics of his youngest brother, who represented to Erridge the manner of life of which he most disapproved. The consequence was that Erridge returned to Thrubworth sooner than expected. There he met with a lot of worry on arrival, because his butler, Smith, immediately went down with bronchitis.

At about the same time Erridge left London, Moreland rang me up. Without anything being said on either side, our meetings had somehow lapsed. We had spoken together only at parties or on such occasions when other people had been around us. It was ages since we had had one of those long talks about life, or the arts, which had been such a predominant aspect of knowing Moreland in the past. On the telephone his voice sounded restrained, practical, colourless; as he himself would have said 'the sane Englishman with his pipe'.

'How is Matilda?'

'Spending a good deal of time out on her own with rehearsals and so on. She is going out with some of her theatre people tonight as a matter of fact.'

'Come and dine.'

'I can't. I'm involved in musical business until about ten. I said I would drop in on Maclintick then. I thought you might feel like coming too.'

'Why?'

'The suggestion was made to help myself out really. I agree it isn't a very inviting prospect.'

'Less inviting than usual? Do you remember our last visit?'

'Well, you know what has happened?'

'No.'

'Maclintick's wife has walked out on him.'

'I hadn't heard.'

'With Carolo.'

'How rash.'

'On top of that Maclintick has lost his job.'

'I never thought of him as having a job.'

'He did, all the same. Now he hasn't.'

'Did a paper sack him?'

'Yes. I thought we might meet at a pub, then go on to see Maclintick at his house. He just sits there working all the time. I have been talking to Gossage about Maclintick. We are a bit worried. A visit might cheer him up.'

'I am sure he would much rather see you alone.'

'That is just what I want to avoid.'

'Why not take Gossage?'

'Gossage is busy tonight. Anyway, he is too old a friend. He gets on Maclintick's nerves.'

'But so do I.'

'In a different way. Besides, you don't know anything about music. It is musical people Maclintick can't stand.'

'I only see Maclintick once every two years. We never hit it off particularly well even spaced out at those intervals.'

'It is because Maclintick never sees you that I want you to come. I don't want an embarrassing time with him *tête-à-tête*. I am not up to it these days. I have troubles of my own.'

'All right. Where shall we meet?'

Moreland, from his extensive knowledge of London drinking places, named a pub in the Maclintick neighbourhood. I told Isobel what had been arranged.

'Try and find out what is happening about Priscilla,' she said. 'For all we know, they may be planning to run away together too. One must look ahead.'

The Nag's Head, the pub named by Moreland, was a place of no great attraction. I recalled it as the establishment brought to Mrs Maclintick's mind by her husband's uncouth behaviour at Mrs Foxe's party. Moreland looked tired when he arrived. He said he had been trudging round London all day. I asked for further details about the Maclintick situation.

'There are none to speak of,' Moreland said. 'Audrey and Carolo left together one afternoon last week. Maclintick had gone round to have a talk with his doctor about some trouble he was having with his kidneys. Not flushing out properly or something. He found a note when he returned home saying she had gone for good.'

'And then he lost his job on top of it?'

'He had written rather an astringent article about a concert he was covering. The paper didn't put it in. Maclintick made a fuss. The editor suggested Maclintick might be happier writing for a periodical aiming at a narrower public. Maclintick agreed that he himself had been feeling that for some time. So they parted company.'

'He is absolutely broke?'

'Probably a few minor irons in the fire. I don't know. Maclintick is not a chap who manages his business affairs very well.'

'Is he looking for another job?'

'He has either been working at his book or knocking them back pretty hard since all this happened—and who shall blame him?'

We set off for Maclintick's house.

'When is Matilda's play coming on?'

'They don't seem to know exactly.'

Moreland showed no sign of wishing to pursue the subject of Matilda's stage career. I did not press the question. I wondered whether he knew that Matilda had told me of her former marriage to Carolo. We passed once more through those shadowy, desolate squares from which darkness had driven even that small remnant of life that haunted them by day. Moreland was depressed and hardly spoke at all. The evening before us offered no prospect to stimulate cheerfulness. At last we reached Maclintick's horrible little dwelling. There was a light upstairs. I felt at low ebb. However, when Maclintick opened the front door he appeared in better condition than I had been led to expect. He wore no collar and had not shaved for several days, but these omissions seemed deliberate badges of emancipation from the servitudes of marriage and journalism, rather than neglect provoked by grief or despair. On the contrary, the nervous tensions to which he had been subjected during the previous few days had to some extent galvanised his normally crabbed manner into a show of geniality.

'Come in,' he said. 'You'll need a drink.'

There was a really colossal reek of whiskey as we crossed the threshold.

'How are things?' said Moreland, sounding not very sure of himself.

'Getting the sack keeps you young,' said Maclintick. 'You ought to try it, both of you. I have been able to settle down to some real work at last, now that I am quit of that bloody rag—and freer in other respects too, I might add.'

In spite of this rather aggressive equanimity displayed by Maclintick himself, an awful air of gloom hung over the house. The sitting-room was unspeakably filthy, dirty tea cups along the top of the glass-fronted bookcase, tumblers stained with beer dregs among the hideous ornaments of the mantelpiece. In the background, an atmosphere of unmade beds and unwashed dishes was dominated by an abominable, indefinable smell. As people do when landed in a position of that sort, Maclintick began at once to discuss his own predicament; quite objectively, as if the experience was remote from himself, as if—which in a sense was true—there was no earthly point in our talking of anything else but Maclintick's personal affairs.

'When I realised she had gone,' he said, 'I heaved a great sigh of relief. That was my first reaction. Later, I grasped the fact that I had to get my own supper. Found something I liked for a change—sardines and plenty of red pepper—and a stiff drink with them. Then I started turning things over in my mind. I began to think of Carolo.'

Moreland laughed uneasily. He was a person not well equipped to deal with human troubles. His temperament was without that easy, unthinking sympathy which reacts in a simple manner, indicating instinctively the right thing to say to someone desperately unhappy. He also lacked that subjective, ruthless love of presiding over other people's affairs which often makes basically heartless people adept at offering effective consolation. 'I never know the right moment to squeeze the bereaved's arm at a funeral,' he had once said. 'Some people can judge it to a nicety.' In short, nothing but true compassion for Maclintick's circumstances could have brought Moreland to the house that night. It was an act of friendship of some magnitude.

'Is Carolo in a job?' Moreland asked.

'Carolo taking a job seems to have touched off matters,' said Maclintick, 'or perhaps *vice versa*. He has at last decided that his genius will allow him to teach. Somewhere in the North-Midlands, I was told, his own part of the world. I can't remember now. He spoke about it a short time before they went off together. Left without paying his rent, need I say? I wonder how he and Audrey will hit it off. I spent yesterday with a solicitor.'

'You are getting a divorce?'

Maclintick nodded.

'Why not,' he said, 'when you've got the chance? She might change her mind. Let me fill your glasses.'

All this talk was decidedly uncomfortable. I did not think Moreland, any more than myself, knew whether Maclintick was in fact glad to have ridded himself of his wife, or, on the contrary, was shattered by her leaving him. Either state was credible. To presume that, because they were always quarrelling, Maclintick necessarily wished to be parted from her, could be wholly mistaken. In the same way, it was equally difficult to know whether Maclintick was genuinely relieved at ceasing to work for the paper that had employed him until the previous week, or was, on the contrary, desperately worried at the prospect of having to look for another job. So far as the job was concerned, both states of mind probably existed simultaneously; perhaps so far as the wife was concerned too. Moreland clearly felt uncertain what line to take in his replies to Maclintick, who himself appeared to enjoy keeping secret his true feelings while he discussed the implications of his own position.

'Did I ever tell you how I met Audrey?' he asked suddenly.

We had been talking for a time about jobs on papers. Moreland had been pronouncing on the subject of musical journalism in particular; but sooner or later Maclintick abandoned the subject in hand, always returning to the matter of his wife. The question did not make Moreland look any happier.

'Never,' he said.

'It was through Gossage,' Maclintick said.

'How very unexpected.'

'There was a clerk in Gossage's bank who was keen on Sibelius,' said Maclintick. 'They used to talk about music together whenever Gossage went to the bank to cash a cheque or have a word about his overdraft—if Gossage ever has anything so irregular as an overdraft, which I doubt.'

'When Gossage went there to bank the bribes given him

by corrupt musicians who wanted good notices,' suggested Moreland.

'Possibly,' said Maclintick. 'I wish some of them offered an occasional bribe to me. Well, Gossage invited this young man, Stanley by name, to come with him to a private performance of some chamber music.'

Moreland laughed loudly at this, much louder than the story demanded at this stage. That was from nerves. I found myself laughing a lot too.

'Stanley asked if he might bring his sister along,' said Maclintick. 'I too had to go to the chamber music for my sins. The sister turned out to be Audrey.'

Moreland seemed as much surprised by this narration as I was myself. To produce such autobiographical details was altogether unlike Maclintick. The upheaval in his life had changed his whole demeanour.

'I took a fancy to her as soon as I set eyes on her,' Maclintick said. 'Funny that, because she hasn't much in the way of looks. That was a bad day for me—a bad day for both of us, I suppose.'

'What happened?' asked Moreland.

His curiosity had been aroused. Even Moreland, who knew Maclintick so much better than myself, found these revelations surprising.

'Do you know,' said Maclintick, speaking slowly as if still marvelling at his own ineptitude in such matters, 'do you know I did not exchange a word with her the whole evening. We were just introduced. I couldn't think of anything to say. She drifted off somewhere. I went home early.'

'What did you do next?'

'I had to make Gossage arrange another meeting. It took the hell of a lot of doing. Gossage didn't care for the idea at all. He liked Stanley, but he didn't want to get mixed up with his sister.'

'And then?'

'I didn't know anything about the machinery for taking

women out, even when Gossage brought us together again.'

'How did you manage to get married then?'

'God knows,' said Maclintick. 'I often wonder.'

'There must have been a moment when some agreement was reached.'

'There was never much agreement about it,' said Maclintick. 'We started having rows straight away. But one thing is interesting. Gossage told me afterwards that on the night of the chamber music Audrey only opened her lips once—that was to ask him to tell her my name again and enquire what I did for a living.'

'No use fighting against fate,' said Moreland laughing. 'I've always said it.'

'Gossage told her I was a musician,' said Maclintick. 'Her comment was "Oh, God".'

'I find that a very natural one to make,' said Moreland.

'She isn't absolutely tone-deaf,' said Maclintick, speaking as if he had given the matter deep thought. 'She has her likes and dislikes. Quite good at remembering facts and contradicting you about them later. She'd been dragged by her brother to the chamber music. I never quite know why.'

'Brought her as a chaperone,' said Moreland.

'All the music in the family went into Stanley,' said Maclintick. 'I shall miss seeing Stanley once in a while. We used to have beer evenings together twice a year. Stanley can't drink Irish whiskey. But you know, it's astonishing what technical jargon women will pick up. Audrey would argue about music with me—with anyone. I've heard her make Gossage contradict himself about his views on *Les Six*. Odd the way music comes out in a family. I get it through my mother who was half Jewish. My father and grandfather were in the linen trade. They may have gone to a concert occasionally. That was about the extent of it.'

Moreland took this opportunity to guide conversation back into general channels.

'You can't tell what families are going to throw up,' he

said. 'Look at Lortzing whose family were hereditary hangmen in Thuringia for two hundred years. Then suddenly the Lortzings cease to be hangmen and produce a composer.'

'You could be a musical hangman, I suppose,' said Maclintick. 'Hum tunes while you worked.'

'I could well imagine some of the musicians one knows becoming hangmen,' said Moreland.

'Surprising Lortzing didn't become a critic with an ancestry like that,' said Maclintick. 'Had it in his blood to execute people when need be—would also know the right knot to tie when it came to his own turn to shuffle off this mortal coil. Lortzing wrote an opera about your friend Casanova, didn't he? Do you remember that night at Casanova's Chinese Restaurant years ago? We talked about seducers and Don Juan and that sort of thing. That painter, Barnby, was there. I believe you were with us too, weren't you, Jenkins? For some reason I have often thought of that evening. I was thinking of it again last night, wondering if Carolo was one of the types.'

Moreland winced slightly. I did not know whether or not Maclintick was aware that Carolo had once been married to Matilda. Probably did not know that, I decided. Maclintick was a man who normally took little interest in the past history of other people. It was even surprising to find him showing such comparative interest in his own past history.

'Carolo doesn't come into the Casanova-Don Juan category,' said Moreland. 'He hasn't the vitality. Too passive. Passivity is not a bad method, all the same. Carolo just sits about until some woman either marries him, or runs away with him, from sheer desperation at finding nothing whatever to talk about.'

Maclintick nodded his head several times, showing ponderous enjoyment at this view of Carolo's technique in seduction. He filled the glasses.

'I suppose one of the tests of a man is the sort of woman

he wants to marry,' he said. 'You showed some sense, Moreland, and guessed right. I should have stayed out of the marriage market altogether.'

'Marriage is quite a problem for a lot of people,' Moreland said.

'You know Audrey was my ideal in a sort of way,' said Maclintick, who after drinking all day—probably several days—was becoming thick in his speech and not always absolutely coherent. 'I've no doubt that was a mistake to start off with. There is probably something wrong about thinking you've realised your ideal—in art or anywhere else. It is a conception that should remain in the mind.'

'It wasn't for nothing that Petrarch's Laura was one of the de Sade family,' said Moreland.

'My God, I bet it wasn't,' said Maclintick. 'She'd have put him through it if they'd married. I shall always think of her being a de Sade whenever I see that picture of them again. You know the one. It is always to be found on the walls of boarding houses.'

'The picture you are thinking of, Maclintick, represents Dante and Beatrice,' Moreland said, 'not Petrarch and Laura. But I know the one you mean—and I expect the scene in question was no less unlike what actually happened than if depicting the other couple.'

'You are absolutely right, Moreland,' said Maclintick, now shaking with laughter. 'Dante and Beatrice—and a bloody bad picture, as you say. As a matter of fact, it's the sort of picture I rather like. Pictures play no part in my life. Music fulfils my needs, with perhaps a little poetry, a little German philosophy. You can keep the pictures, whether they tell a story or not.'

'Nowadays you can have both,' said Moreland, cheered by the drink and at last recovering his spirits. 'The literary content of some Piccassos makes *The Long Engagement* or *A Hopeless Dawn* seem dry, pedantic studies in pure abstraction.'

'You might as well argue that *Ulysses* has more "story"

than *Uncle Tom's Cabin* or *The Rosary*,' said Maclintick. 'I suppose it has in a way. I find all novels lacking in probability.'

'Probability is the bane of the age,' said Moreland, now warming up. 'Every Tom, Dick, and Harry thinks he knows what is probable. The fact is most people have not the smallest idea what is going on round them. Their conclusions about life are based on utterly irrelevant—and usually inaccurate—premises.'

'That is certainly true about women,' said Maclintick. 'But anyway it takes a bit of time to realise that all the odds and ends milling about round one are the process of living. I used to feel with Audrey: "this can't be marriage" —and now it isn't.'

Suddenly upstairs the telephone bell began to ring. The noise came from the room where Maclintick worked. The sound was shrill, alarming, like a deliberate warning. Maclintick did not move immediately. He looked greatly disturbed. Then, without saying anything, he took a gulp from his glass and went off up the stairs. Moreland looked at me. He made a face.

'Audrey coming back?' he said.

'We ought to go soon.'

'We will.'

We could faintly hear Maclintick's voice; the words inaudible. It sounded as if Maclintick were unable to understand what he was being asked. That was likely enough considering the amount he had drunk. A minute later he returned to the sitting-room.

'Someone for you, Moreland,' he said.

Moreland looked very disturbed.

'It can't be for me,' he said. 'No one knows I'm here.'

'Some woman,' said Maclintick.

'Who on earth can it be?'

'She kept on telling me I knew her,' said Maclintick, 'but I couldn't get hold of the name. It was a bloody awful line. My head is buzzing about too.'

Moreland went to the stairs. Maclintick heaved himself on to the sofa. Closing his eyes, he began to breathe heavily. I felt I had had a lot to drink without much to show for it. We remained in silence. Moreland seemed to be away for centuries. When he returned to the room he was laughing.

'It was Matilda,' he said.

'Didn't sound a bit like Matilda,' said Maclintick, without opening his eyes.

'She said she didn't know it was you. You sounded quite different.'

'I'm never much good at getting a name on the bloody telephone,' said Maclintick. 'She said something about her being your wife now I come to think of it.'

'Matilda forgot her key. I shall have to go back at once. She is on the doorstep.'

'Just like a woman, that,' said Maclintick. 'There was always trouble about Carolo's key.'

'We'll have to go.'

'You don't expect me to see you out, do you? Kind of you to come.'

'You had better go to bed, Maclintick,' said Moreland. 'You don't want to spend the night on the sofa.'

'Why not?'

'Too cold. The fire will be out soon.'

'I'll be all right.'

'Do move, Maclintick,' said Moreland.

He stood looking down with hesitation at Maclintick. Moreland could be assertive about his own views, was said to be good at controlling an orchestra; he was entirely without the power of assuming authority over a friend who needed 'managing' after too much to drink. I remembered the scene when Widmerpool and I had put Stringham to bed after the Old Boy Dinner, and wondered whether an even odder version of that operation was to be re-enacted here. However, Maclintick rolled himself over into a sitting

206

position, removed his spectacles, and began to rub his eyes just in the manner of my former housemaster, Le Bas, when he could not make up his mind whether or not one of his pupils was telling the truth.

'Perhaps you are right, Moreland,' Maclintick said.

'Certainly I am right.'

'I will move if you insist.'

'I do insist.'

Then Maclintick made that harrowing remark that established throughout all eternity his relationship with Moreland.

'I obey you, Moreland,' he said, 'with the proper respect of the poor interpretative hack for the true creative artist.'

Moreland and I both laughed a lot, but it was a horrible moment. Maclintick had spoken with that strange, unearthly dignity that a drunk man can suddenly assume. We left him making his way unsteadily upstairs. By a miracle there was a taxi at the other end of the street.

'I hope Maclintick will be all right,' said Moreland, as we drove away.

'He is in rather a mess.'

'I am in a mess myself,' Moreland said. 'You probably know about that. I won't bore you with the complications of my own life. I hope Matty will not be in too much of a fret when I get there. What can she be thinking of, forgetting her key? Something Freudian, I suppose. I am glad we went to see Maclintick. What did you think about him?'

'I thought he was in a bad way.'

'You did?'

'Yes.'

'Maclintick is in a bad way,' said Moreland. 'It is no good pretending he isn't. I don't know where it will end, I don't know where anything will end. It was strange Maclintick bringing up Casanova's Chinese Restaurant.'

'Dragging up your past.'

'Barnby went straight to the point,' said Moreland. 'I was struck by that. One ought to make decisions where women are concerned.'

'What are your plans—roughly?'

'I have none, as usual. You are already familiar with my doctrine that every man should have three wives. I accept the verdict that under the existing social order such an arrangement is not viable. That is why so many men are in such a quandary.'

We drove on to where I lived. Moreland continued in the taxi on his way to find Matilda. Isobel was asleep. She woke up at one moment and asked: 'Did you hear anything interesting?' I told her, 'No'. She went to sleep again. I went to sleep for an hour or two, then woke up with a start, and lay there thinking how grim the visit to Maclintick had been; not only grim, but cautiously out of focus; a pocket in time; an evening that pertained in character to life some years before. Marriage reduced in number interludes of that kind. They belonged by their nature to an earlier period: the days of the Mortimer and Casanova's Chinese Restaurant. Maclintick's situation was infinitely depressing; yet people found their way out of depressing situations. Nothing was more surprising than man's capacity for survival. Before one could look round, Maclintick would be in a better job, married to a more tolerable wife. All the same, I felt doubtful about that happening. Thinking uneasy thoughts, I fell once more in a restless, disenchanted sleep.

The atmosphere of doom that hung over Maclintick's house, indeed over the whole quarter in which he lived—or so it seemed the night Moreland and I had called on him—proved categorical enough. Two or three days later a paragraph appeared in the evening paper stating that Maclintick's body had been found 'in a gas-filled room': no doubt the room in which he worked designated by his wife as the 'only one where you can keep warm in the house'. The escape of gas had been noticed; the police broke in. The paper described Maclintick as a 'writer on musical subjects'. As with the passing of St John Clarke, new disturbing developments of the European situation prevented Maclintick's case from gaining the attention that a music critic's suicide might attract in more peaceful times. The news was horrifying, yet there was no shock about it. It was cold, slow-motion horror, the shaping of a story recognisably unfinished. I tried to get in touch with Moreland. There was no reply to the telephone. The Morelands' flat seemed always empty. Then one day when I tried again, Matilda answered. She began talking about Moreland at once.

'The poor boy has been having an awful time about Maclintick,' she said. 'You know how he hates even the mildest business talks. Now he is landed with inquests and goodness knows what.'

Matilda had always got on well with Maclintick. He was one of those uncomfortably poised men whom she handled to perfection. There was every reason to suppose that Maclintick's death would distress her. At the same time, I was immediately aware from the sound of her voice on the line that she was pleased about something; the fact of Maclintick's suicide had eased her life for one reason or another. We talked for a time about Maclintick and his affairs.

'Poor old Carolo,' she said.

'You think he is in for it?'

'He has caught something this time.'

'And your play?'

'Coming on soon. I think it will be a success.'

I arranged to see Moreland. The meeting took place a day or two later. He looked as if he had been having a disagreeable time. I asked about Maclintick.

'Gossage and I had to do all the clearing up,' Moreland said. 'It was pretty good hell.'

'Why you two?'

'There did not seem to be anyone else. I can't tell you what we were let in for. It was an awful thing to happen. Of course, one saw it coming. Nothing more certain. That didn't make it any better. Maclintick was a great friend of mine in a way. He could be tiresome. He had some very good points too. It was nice of him not to have done himself in, for example, the night we left him there. That would have been even more awkward.'

'It certainly would.'

'I've no reason to suppose he didn't feel just as much like taking the jump then as three days later.'

'Do you remember when he talked of suicide in Casanova's?'

'Suicide was always one of Maclintick's favourite subjects.'

'It was?'

'Of course.'

'He said then that he gave himself five years.'

'He lasted about eight or nine. Gossage has been very good about sorting the musical stuff. There is a mass of it to deal with.'

'Any good?'

Moreland shook his head.

'The smell in the house was appalling,' he said. 'Absolutely frightful. Gossage had to go and stand in the street for a time to recover.'

'Anything been heard of Mrs Maclintick?'

'I had a line from her asking me to deal with certain things. I think Carolo wants to keep out of it as much as possible for professional reasons—rather naturally.'

'Do you think Maclintick just could not get on without that woman?'

'Maclintick always had his fair share of melancholia, quite apart from anything brought on by marriage or the lack of it.'

'But his wife clearing out brought matters to a head?'

'Possibly. It must be appalling to commit suicide, even though one sometimes feel a trifle like it. Anyway, the whole Maclintick business has made certain things clearer to me.'

'As for example?'

'Do you remember when we used to talk about the Ghost Railway and say how like everyday life it was—or at least one's own everyday life?'

'You mean rushing downhill in total darkness and crashing through closed doors?'

'Yes—and the body lying across the line. The Maclintick affair has reminded me of the disagreeable possibilities of the world one inhabits; the fact that the fewer persons one involves in it the better.'

'How do you mean? However you live there are always elements of that sort.'

'I know, but you get familiar with the material you yourself have to cope with. You may have heard that I have been somewhat entangled with a person not far removed from your own family circle.'

'Rumours percolate.'

'So I supposed.'

'But you would be surprised to learn my own ignorance of detail.'

'Glad to hear it. Need I say more? You must surely appreciate the contrast between the sort of thing I have been engaged upon in connexion with poor old Maclintick's mortal remains during the last few days, and the kind of atmosphere one prefers when attempting to conduct an idyllic love affair.'

'I can see that.'

'I do not suggest my daily routine comes within several million light-years of an idyll—but it normally rises a few degrees above what life has been recently.'

I began to understand the reason why Matilda had sounded relieved when we had spoken on the telephone a day or two before.

'The fact is,' said Moreland, 'very few people can deal with more than a limited number of emotional problems at any given moment. At least I can't. Up to a point, I can walk a tightrope held at one end by Matilda, and at the other by the person of whom you tell me you are already apprised. But I can't carry Maclintick on my back. Maclintick gassing himself was just a bit too much.'

'But what are you explaining to me?'

'That any rumours you hear in future can be given an unqualified denial.'

'I see.'

'Forgive my bluntness.'

'It suits you.'

'I hope I have made myself clear.'

'You haven't, really. There is still a lot I should like to know. For example, did you really contemplate terminating your present marriage?'

'It looked like that at one moment.'

'With the agreement of the third party?'

'Yes.'

'And now she knows you think differently?'

'She sees what I mean.'

'And thinks the same?'

'Yes.'

I too could see what he meant. At least I thought I could. Moreland meant that Maclintick, in doing away with himself, had drawn attention, indeed heavily underlined, the conditions of life to which Moreland himself was inexorably committed; a world to which Priscilla did not yet belong, even if she were on her way to belonging there. I do not think Moreland intended this juxtaposition of lot to be taken in its crudest aspect; that is to say in the sense that Priscilla was too young, too delicate a flower by birth and upbringing to be associated with poverty, unfaithfulness, despair, and death. If he supposed that—which I doubt —Moreland made a big mistake. Priscilla, like the rest of her family, had a great deal of resilience. I think Moreland's realisation was in the fact of Maclintick's desperate condition; Maclintick's inability to regulate his own emotional life; Maclintick's lack of success as a musician; in short the mess of things Maclintick had made, or perhaps had had visited upon him. Moreland was probably the only human being Maclintick had whole-heartedly liked. In return, Moreland had liked Maclintick; liked his intelligence; liked talking and drinking with him. By taking his own life, Maclintick had brought about a crisis in Moreland's life too. He had ended the triangular relationship between Moreland, Priscilla, and Matilda. Precisely in what that relationship consisted remained unrevealed. What Matilda thought, what Priscilla thought, remained a mystery. All sides of such a situation are seldom shown at once, even if they are shown at all. Only one thing was certain. Love had received one of those shattering jolts to which it is peculiarily vulnerable from extraneous circumstance.

'This Maclintick business must have held up all work.'

'As you can imagine, I have not done a stroke. I think Matilda and I may try and go away for a week or two, if I can raise the money.'

'Where will you go?'

'France, I suppose.'

The Morelands went abroad the following week. That Sunday, Isobel's eldest sister, Frederica, rang up and asked if she could come to tea. This suggestion, on the whole a little outside the ordinary routine of things with Frederica, who was inclined to make plans some way ahead, suggested she had something special to say. As it happened, Robert, too, had announced he would look in that afternoon,' so the day took on a distinctly family aspect. Frederica and Robert could be received at close quarters, be relied upon to be reasonably cordial to one another. That would not have been true of Frederica and Norah. Hugo was another dangerous element, preferably to be entertained without the presence of his other brothers and sisters. With Frederica and Robert there was nothing to worry about.

As soon as Frederica arrived, it was evident she had recently learnt something that had surprised her a great deal. She was a person of controlled, some—Chips Lovell, for example—thought even rather forbidding exterior; a widow who showed no sign of wanting to remarry and found her interests, her work and entertainment, in her tours of duty as Lady-in-Waiting. However, that afternoon she was freely allowing herself to indulge in the comparatively undisciplined relaxation of arousing her relations' curiosity.

'I expect you have heard of a writer called St John Clarke,' she said, almost as soon as she had sat down.

This supposition, expressed by some of my friends, would have been a method of introducing St John Clarke's name within a form of words intended to indicate that in their eyes, no doubt equally in my own, St John Clarke did not grade as a sufficiently eminent literary figure for serious persons like ourselves ever to have heard of him. The phrase would convey no sense of enquiry; merely a scarcely perceptible compliment, a very minor demonstration of mutual self-esteem. With Frederica, however, one could not be sure. She had received a perfectly adequate education, indeed rather a good one, to fit her for her position in life, but she did not pretend to 'know' about writing. Indeed, she was inclined to pride herself on rising above the need to discuss the ways and means of art in which some of her relations and friends interminably indulged.

'I like reading books and going to plays,' she had once remarked, 'but I do not want to talk about them all the time.'

If Frederica had, in practice, wholly avoided an uninstructed predisposition to lay down the law on aesthetic matters, there would have been much to be said for this preference. Unhappily, you could never be certain of her adherence to such a rule of conduct. She seemed often to hold just as strong views on such matters as those who felt themselves most keenly engaged. Besides, her disinclination to discuss these subjects in general, left an area of uncertainty as to how far her taste, for example, in books and plays, had taken her; her self-esteem could be easily, disastrously, impaired by interpreting too literally her disavowal of all intellectual interests. In the same way, Frederica lumped together in one incongruous, not particularly acceptable agglomeration, all persons connected with painting, writing and music! I think she suspected them, in that time-honoured, rather engaging habit of thought, of possessing morals somehow worse than other people's. Her mention of St John Clarke's name was for these reasons unexpected.

'Certainly I have heard of St John Clarke,' I said. 'He has just died. Isobel and I met him lunching at Hyde Park Gardens not long before he was taken ill.'

'Not me,' said Isobel, 'I was being ill myself.'

'St John Clarke used to lunch at Hyde Park Gardens?' said Frederica. 'I did not know that. Was he often there?'

'He used to turn up at Aunt Molly's too,' said Isobel. 'You must remember the story of Hugo and the raspberries——'

'Yes, yes,' said Frederica, showing no sign of wishing to hear that anecdote again, 'I had forgotten it was St John Clarke. But what about him?'

'Surely you read *Fields of Amaranth* secretly when you were growing up?' said Isobel. 'There was a copy without the binding in that cupboard in the schoolroom at Thrubworth.'

'Oh, yes,' said Frederica, brushing off this literary approach as equally irrelevant. 'But what sort of a man was St John Clarke?'

That was a subject upon which I felt myself something of an expert. I began to give an exhaustive, perhaps too exhaustive, account of St John Clarke's life and character. No doubt this searching analysis of the novelist was less interesting to others—certainly less interesting to Frederica—than to myself, because she broke in almost immediately with a request that I should stop.

'It really does not matter about all that,' she said. 'Just tell me what he was like.'

'That was what I was trying to tell you.'

I felt annoyed at being found so inadequate at describing St John Clarke. No doubt it would have been better to have contained him in one single brief, brilliant epigram; I could not think of one at that moment. Besides, that was not the kind of conversational technique Frederica approved. I was attempting to approach St John Clarke from another angle, when Robert arrived. Whatever Frederica had been leading up to was for the moment abandoned. Robert, in his curiously muted manner, showed signs of animation.

'I have got a piece of news,' he said.

'What?' said Frederica. 'Have you heard too, Robert?'

'I don't know what you mean,' said Robert. 'So far as I am aware. I am the sole possessor of this particular item.'

'What is it?'

'You will all know pretty soon anyway,' said Robert, in a leisurely way, 'but one likes to get in first. We are going to have a new brother-in-law.'

'Do you mean Priscilla is engaged?'

'Yes,' said Robert. 'Priscilla—not Blanche.'

'Who to?'

'Who do you think?'

A few names were put forward.

'Come on,' said Isobel. 'Tell us.'

'Chips Lovell.'

'When did this happen?'

'This afternoon.'

'How did you find out?'

'Chips had just been accepted when I arrived back at the house.'

'He was almost a relation before,' said Frederica.

On the whole she sounded well disposed, at least looking on the bright side; because there must have been much about Chips Lovell which did not recommend itself to Frederica. She may have feared worse. Moreland's name was unlikely to have reached her, but she could have heard vague, unsubstantiated gossip stemming ultimately from the same source.

'I guessed something must be in the air when Priscilla told me she was leaving that opera job of hers,' said Robert. 'At one moment she thought of nothing else.'

We talked about Chips Lovell for a time.

'Now,' said Frederica, 'after that bit of news, I shall get back to my own story.'

'What is your story?' asked Robert. 'I arrived in the middle.'

'I was talking about St John Clarke.'

'What about him?'

'Whom do you think St John Clarke would leave his money to?' said Frederica.

'That is a big question, Frederica,' I said.

Revelation coming from Frederica on the subject of St John Clarke's last will and testament would be utterly unexpected. I had certainly wondered, at the time of St John Clarke's death, who would get his money. Then the matter had gone out of my head. The beneficiary was unlikely to be anyone I knew. Now, at Frederica's words, I began to speculate again about what surprising bequest, or bequests, might have been made. St John Clarke was known to possess no close relations. Members and Quiggin had often remarked on that fact after they left his employment, when it was clear that neither of them could hope for anything but a small legacy for old times' sake; and even that was to the greatest degree improbable. There was the German secretary, Guggenbühl. He had moved on from St John Clarke without a quarrel, although with some encouragement, so Quiggin said, because of St John Clarke's growing nervousness about the orthodoxy of Guggenbühl's Marxism. The choice was on this account unlikely to have fallen on Guggenbühl. There remained the possibility of some forgotten soul from that earlier dynasty of secretaries—back before the days of Members and Quiggin—who might have been remembered in St John Clarke's last months; a line whose names, like those of prehistoric kings, had not survived, or at best were to be met with only in the garbled forms of popular legend, in this case emanating from the accumulated conflux of St John Clarke myth propagated by Members and Quiggin. Again, the Communist Party was a possible legatee; St John Clarke seeking amends for his days of bourgeois licence, like a robber baron endowing the Church with his lands.

Even if St John Clarke had left his worldly goods to 'the Party', Frederica would scarcely bother about that, though such a bequest might finally confirm her distrust for men of letters. I was at a loss to know what had happened. Frederica saw she had said enough to command attention. To hold the key to information belonging by its essential nature to a sphere quite other than one's own gives peculiar satisfaction. Frederica was well aware of that. She paused for a second or two. The ransoming of our curiosity was gratifying to her.

'Who?' I asked.

'Whom do you think?'

'We can't spend the afternoon guessing things,' said Isobel. 'Our invention has been exhausted by Priscilla's possible fiancés.'

Robert, who probably saw no reason to concern himself with St John Clarke's affairs, and was no doubt more interested in speculating on the prospect of Chips Lovell as a brother-in-law, began to show loss of interest. He strolled across the room to examine a picture. Frederica saw that to hold her audience, she must come to the point.

'Erridge,' she said.

That was certainly an eye-opener.

'How did you discover this?'

'Erry told me himself.'

'When?'

'I stayed a night at Thrubworth. There were some legal papers of mine Erry had to sign. Taking them there seemed the only way of running him to earth. He just let out this piece of information quite casually as he put his pen down.'

'How much is it?' asked Robert, brought to heel by the nature of this disclosure.

'That wasn't so easy to find out.'

'Roughly?'

'St John Clarke seems to have bought an annuity of some sort that no one knew about,' said Frederica. 'So far as I can gather, there is about sixteen or seventeen thousand above that. It will be in the papers, of course, when the will is proved.'

'Which Erry will get?'

'Yes.'

'He will hand it over to his Spanish friends,' said Robert tranquilly.

'Oh, no, he won't,' said Frederica, with some show of bravado.

'Don't be too sure.'

'One can't be sure,' said Frederica, speaking this time more soberly. 'But it sounded as if Erry were not going to do that.'

'Why not?'

'He didn't leave Spain on very good terms with anyone.'

'The money would pay off the overdraft on the estate account,' said Isobel.

'Exactly.'

'And the woods would not have to be sold.'

'In fact,' said Robert, 'this windfall might turn out to be most opportune.'

'I don't want to speak too soon,' said Frederica, 'especially where Erry is concerned. All the same, so far as I could see, there seemed hope of his showing some sense for once.'

'But will his conscience allow him to show sense?' said Robert.

I understood now why Quiggin had been so irritable when we had last met. He must already have known of St John Clarke's legacy to Erridge. By that time Quiggin could scarcely have hoped himself for anything from St John Clarke, but that this golden apple should have fallen at Erridge's feet was another matter. To feel complete unconcern towards the fact of an already rich friend unexpectedly inheriting so comparatively large a capital sum would require an indifference to money that Quiggin never claimed to possess. Apart from that was the patron-protégé relationship existing between Erridge and Quiggin, complicated by the memory of Mona's elopement. Quiggin's ill humour was not surprising in the circumstances. It was, indeed, pretty reasonable. If St John Clarke had been often provoked by Members and Quiggin during his life, the last laugh had to some extent fallen to St John Clarke after death. At the same time, it was not easy to see what motives had led St John Clarke to appoint Erridge his heir. He may have felt that Erridge was the most likely among the people he knew to use the money in some manner sympathetic to his own final fancies. On the other hand, he may have reverted on his death-bed to a simpler, more old-world snobbery of his early years, or to that deep-rooted, time honoured tradition that money should go to money. It was impossible to say. These, and many other theories, were laid open to speculation by this piece of news, absurd in its way; if anything to do with money can, in truth, be said to be absurd.

Did Chips mention when he and Priscilla are going to be married?' asked Isobel.

The question reminded me that Moreland, at least in a negative manner, had taken another decisive step. I thought of his recent remark about the Ghost Railway. He loved these almost as much as he loved mechanical pianos. Once, at least, we had been on a Ghost Railway together at some fun fair or on a seaside pier; slowly climbing sheer gradients, sweeping with frenzied speed into inky depths, turning blind corners from which black, gibbering bogeys leapt to attack, rushing headlong towards iron-studded doors, threatened by imminent collision, fingered by spectral hands, moving at last with dreadful, ever increasing momentum towards a shape that lay across the line.

Tim Parks

Loving Roger

'A tight, disturbing novel . . . mordantly illuminating on the way love contains the seeds of vindictiveness and hatred.'
Observer

'Extremely compelling . . . the human observation is witty, acute and sensitive . . . absolute authenticity.'
Sunday Telegraph

'With his chillingly elegant prose and frighteningly deadpan narrative, Tim Parks has written, not a whodunnit, but a brilliant whydunnit.'
Today

'A tale that is cruel, upsetting and compellingly credible.'
London Standard

Flamingo

Tim Parks

Loving Roger

'A tight, disturbing novel . . . mordantly illuminating on the way love contains the seeds of vindictiveness and hatred.'
Observer

'Extremely compelling . . . the human observation is witty, acute and sensitive . . . absolute authenticity.'
Sunday Telegraph

'With his chillingly elegant prose and frighteningly deadpan narrative, Tim Parks has written, not a whodunnit, but a brilliant whydunnit.'
Today

'A tale that is cruel, upsetting and compellingly credible.'
London Standard

Flamingo

Flamingo

Flamingo is a quality imprint publishing both fiction and non-fiction. Below are some recent titles.

Fiction
- ☐ The House on Moon Lake *Francesca Durante* £3.50
- ☐ The Blacksmith's Daughter *Shaun Herron* £3.50
- ☐ The Red Men *Patrick McGinley* £3.95
- ☐ The Pale Sergeant *James Murray* £3.50
- ☐ Liberation of Margaret McCabe *Catherine Brophy* £3.50
- ☐ Mating Birds *Lewis Nkosi* £3.50
- ☐ Lady's Time *Alan Hewat* £3.95
- ☐ The Mind and Body Shop *Frank Parkin* £3.50
- ☐ Perfect English *Paul Pickering* £3.50

Non-fiction
- ☐ Rain or Shine *Cyra McFadden* £3.50
- ☐ Love is Blue *Joan Wyndham* £3.50
- ☐ Love Lessons *Joan Wyndham* £2.95

You can buy Flamingo paperbacks at your local bookshop or newsagent. Or you can order them from Fontana Paperbacks, Cash Sales Department, Box 29, Douglas, Isle of Man. Please send a cheque, postal or money order (not currency) worth the purchase price plus 22p per book (or plus 22p per book if outside the UK).

NAME (Block letters) _____

ADDRESS_____

_____

_____